# Sometimes
## I *Lie*

# Sometimes
## I *Lie*

### Alice
### Feeney

FLATIRON
BOOKS
NEW YORK

SOMETIMES I LIE. Copyright © 2018 by Alice Feeney. All rights reserved. Printed in the United States of America. For information, address Flatiron Books, 175 Fifth Avenue, New York, N.Y. 10010.

www.flatironbooks.com

Designed by Donna Sinisgalli Noetzel

Library of Congress Cataloging-in-Publication Data

Names: Feeney, Alice, author.
Title: Sometimes I lie / Alice Feeney.
Description: First edition. | New York : Flatiron Books, 2018.
Identifiers: LCCN 2017045151 | ISBN 9781250144843 (hardcover) | ISBN 9781250191892 (international) | ISBN 9781250144836 (ebook)
Subjects: LCSH: Coma—Patients—Fiction. | Married women—Fiction. | Psychological fiction.
Classification: LCC PR6106.E34427 S66 2018 | DDC 813/.6—dc23
LC record available at https://lccn.loc.gov/2017045151

Our books may be purchased in bulk for promotional, educational, or business use. Please contact your local bookseller or the Macmillan Corporate and Premium Sales Department at 1-800-221-7945, extension 5442, or by email at MacmillanSpecialMarkets@macmillan.com.

First Edition: March 2018

10  9  8  7  6  5  4  3  2  1

For my Daniel. And for her.

# Sometimes
## I *Lie*

My name is Amber Reynolds. There are three things you should know about me:

*1. I'm in a coma.*
*2. My husband doesn't love me anymore.*
*3. Sometimes I lie.*

# Now

*Boxing Day, December 2016*

I've always delighted in the free fall between sleep and wakefulness. Those precious few semiconscious seconds before you open your eyes, when you catch yourself believing that your dreams might just be your reality. A moment of intense pleasure or pain, before your senses reboot and inform you who and where and what you are. For now, for just a second longer, I'm enjoying the self-medicated delusion that permits me to imagine that I could be anyone, I could be anywhere, I could be loved.

I sense the light behind my eyelids and my attention is drawn to the platinum band on my finger. It feels heavier than it used to, as though it is weighing me down. A sheet is pulled over my body. It smells unfamiliar and I consider the possibility that I'm in a hotel. Any memory of what I dreamt evaporates. I try to hold on, try to be someone and stay somewhere I am not, but I can't. I am only ever me and I am here, where I already know I do not wish to be. My limbs ache and I'm so very tired; I don't want to open my eyes, until I remember that I can't.

Panic spreads through me like a blast of icy cold air. I can't recall where this is or how I got here, but I know who I am. *My name is Amber Reynolds. I am thirty-five years old. I'm married to Paul.* I repeat these three things in my head, holding on to them tightly, as though they might save me, but I'm mindful that some part of the story is lost, the last few pages ripped out. When the memories are as complete as I can manage, I bury them until they are quiet enough inside my head to allow me to think, to feel, to try to make sense of it all. One memory refuses to comply, fighting its way to the surface, but I don't want to believe it.

The sound of a machine breaks into my consciousness, stealing my last few fragments of hope and leaving me with nothing except the unwanted knowledge that I am in a hospital. The sterilized stench of the place makes me want to gag. I hate hospitals. They are the home of death and regrets that missed their slots, not somewhere I would ever choose to visit, let alone stay.

There were people here before, strangers, I remember that now. They used a word I chose not to hear. I recall lots of fuss, raised voices, and fear, not just my own. I struggle to unearth more, but my mind fails me. Something very bad has happened, but I cannot remember what or when.

*Why isn't he here?*

It can be dangerous to ask a question when you already know the answer.

*He does not love me.*

I bookmark that thought.

I hear a door open. Footsteps, then the silence returns but it's spoiled, no longer pure. I can smell stale cigarette smoke, the sound of pen scratching paper to my right. Someone coughs to my left and I realize there are two of them. Strangers in the dark. I feel colder than before and so terribly small. I have never known a terror like the one that takes hold of me now.

I wish someone would say something.

"Who is she?" asks a woman's voice.

"No idea. Poor love, what a mess," replies another woman.

I wish they'd said nothing at all. I start to scream.

*My name is Amber Reynolds! I'm a radio presenter! Why don't you know who I am?*

I shout the same sentences over and over, but they ignore me, because on the outside I am silent. On the outside, I am nobody and I have no name.

I want to see the me they have seen. I want to sit up, reach out and touch them. I want to feel something again. Anything. Anyone. I want to ask a thousand questions. I think I want to know the answers. They used the word from before too, the one I don't want to hear.

The women leave, closing the door behind them, but the word stays behind, so that we are alone together and I am no longer able to ignore it. I can't open my eyes. I can't move. I can't speak. The word bubbles to the surface, popping on impact, and I know it to be true.

*Coma.*

# Then

*One week earlier—*
*Monday, December 19, 2016*

I tiptoe downstairs in the early-morning darkness, careful not to wake him. Everything is where it ought to be and yet I'm sure something is missing. I pull on my heavy winter coat to combat the cold and walk through to the kitchen to begin my routine. I start with the back door and repeatedly turn the handle until I'm sure it is locked:

Up, down. Up, down. Up, down.

Next, I stand in front of the large range oven with my arms bent at the elbows, as though I am about to conduct the impressive orchestra of gas hobs. My fingers form the familiar shape: the index and middle finger finding the thumb on each hand. I whisper quietly to myself, while visually checking that all of the knobs and dials are switched off. I do a complete sweep three times, my fingernails clicking together to create a Morse code that only I can decipher. Once satisfied that every-thing is safe and secure, I go to leave the kitchen, lingering briefly in the doorway, wondering if today is a day when I might need to turn back and begin the whole routine again. It isn't.

I creep across creaking floorboards into the hall, pick up my bag, and check the contents. Phone. Wallet. Keys. I close it, open it, then check again. Phone. Wallet. Keys. I check a third time on my way to the front door. I stop for a moment and am shocked to see the woman inside the mirror staring back at me. I have the face of someone who might have been pretty once—I barely recognize her now. A mixed palette of light and dark. Long black lashes frame my large green eyes. Sad shadows have settled beneath them, thick brown eyebrows above. My skin is a pale canvas stretched over my cheekbones. My hair is so brown it's almost black, and lazy straight strands rest on my shoulders for lack of a better idea. I brush it roughly with my fingers before scraping it back into a ponytail, securing the hair off my face with a band from my wrist. My lips part as though I am going to say something, but only air escapes my mouth. A face for radio stares back.

I remember the time and remind myself that the train won't wait for me. I haven't said good-bye, but I don't suppose it matters. I switch off the light and leave the house, checking three times that the front door is locked before marching down the moonlit garden path.

It's early, but I'm already late. Madeline will be in the office by now, the newspapers will have been read, raped of any good stories. The producers will have picked through the paper carcasses, before being barked at and bullied into getting her the best interviews for this morning's show. Taxis will be on their way to pick up and spit out overly excited and underprepared guests. Every morning is different and yet has become completely routine. It's been six months since I joined the *Coffee Morning* team and things are not going according to plan. A lot of people would think I have a dream job, but nightmares are dreams too.

I briefly stop to buy coffee for myself and a colleague in the foyer, then climb the stone steps to the fifth floor. I don't like lifts. I fix a smile on my face before stepping into the office and reminding myself that this is what I do best: change to suit the people around me. I can do "Amber the friend" or "Amber the wife," but right now it's time for "Amber from *Coffee Morning*." I can play all the parts life has cast me in, I know all my lines; I've been rehearsing for a very long time.

The sun has barely risen but as predicted, the small, predominately female team has already assembled. Three fresh-faced producers, powered by caffeine and ambition, sit hunched over their desks. Surrounded by piles of books, old scripts, and empty mugs, they tap away on their keyboards as though their cats' lives depend on it. In the far corner, I can see the glow of Madeline's lamp in her own private office. I sit down at my desk and switch on the computer, returning the warm smiles and greetings from the others. People are not mirrors—they don't see you how you see yourself.

Madeline has gone through three personal assistants this year.

Nobody lasts very long before she discards them. I don't want my own office and I don't need a PA, I like sitting out here with everyone else. The seat next to mine is empty. It's unusual for Jo not to be here by now and I worry that something might be wrong. I look down at the spare coffee getting cold, then talk myself into taking it to Madeline's office. Call it a peace offering.

I stop in the open doorway like a vampire waiting to be invited in. Her office is laughably small, literally a converted store cupboard, because she refuses to sit with the rest of the team. There are framed photos of Madeline with celebrities squeezed onto every inch of the fake walls, and a small shelf of awards behind her desk. She doesn't look up. I observe the ugly short hair, gray roots making themselves known beneath the black spikes. Her chins rest on top of each other, while the rest of her rolled flesh is thankfully hidden beneath the baggy black clothes. The desk lamp shines on the keyboard, over which Madeline's ring-adorned fingers hover. I know she can see me.

"I thought you might need this," I say, disappointed with the simplicity of the words given how long it took me to find them.

"Put it on the desk," she replies, her eyes not leaving the screen.

*You're welcome.*

A small fan heater splutters away in the corner and the burnt-scented warmth snakes up around my legs, holding me in place. I find myself staring at the mole on her cheek. My eyes do that sometimes: focus on a person's imperfections, momentarily forgetting that they can see me seeing the things they'd rather I didn't.

"Did you have a nice weekend?" I venture.

"I'm not ready to talk to people yet," she says. I leave her to it.

Back at my desk, I scan through the pile of post that has gathered since Friday: a couple of ghastly-looking novels that I will never read, some fan mail, and an invite to a charity gala that catches my eye. I sip my coffee and daydream about what I might wear and whom I would take along if I went. I should do more charity work, really, I just never seem to have the time. Madeline is the face of Crisis Child as well as the voice of *Coffee Morning*. I've always found her close relationship with the country's biggest children's charity slightly strange, given that she hates children and never had any of her own. She never even married. She's completely alone in life but never lonely.

Once I've sorted the post, I read through the briefing notes for this morning's program. It's always useful to have a bit of background knowledge before the show. I can't find my red pen, so I head for the stationery cupboard.

It's been restocked.

I glance over my shoulder and then back at the neatly piled shelves of supplies. I grab a handful of Post-it notes, then I take a few red pens, pushing them into my pockets. I keep taking them until they are all gone and the box is empty. I leave the other colors behind. Nobody looks up as I walk back to my desk. They don't see me empty everything into my drawer and lock it.

Just as I'm starting to worry that my only friend here isn't making an appearance today, Jo walks in and smiles at me. She's dressed the same as always, in blue denim jeans and a white top, like she can't move on from the nineties. The boots she says she hates are worn down at the heel and her blond hair is damp from the rain. She sits at the desk next to mine, opposite the rest of the producers.

"Sorry I'm late," she whispers. Nobody apart from me notices.

The last to arrive is Matthew, the editor of the program. This is not unusual. His skinny chinos are straining at the seams, worn low to accommodate the bulge around his middle. They're slightly too short for his long legs, revealing colorful socks above his brown, shiny shoes. He heads straight to his tidy desk by the window without saying hello. Why a team of women who produce a show for women is managed by a man is beyond my comprehension. But then Matthew took a chance and gave me this job when my predecessor abruptly left, so I suppose I should be grateful.

"Matthew, can you step into my office now that you're here?" says Madeline from across the room.

"And he thought his morning couldn't get any worse," Jo whispers. "Are we still on for drinks after work?"

I nod, relieved that she isn't going to disappear straight after the show again.

We watch Matthew grab his briefing notes and hurry into Madeline's office, his flamboyant coat still flapping at his sides as though it wishes it could fly. Moments later he storms back out, looking red-faced and flustered.

"We better go through to the studio," says Jo, interrupting my thoughts. It seems like a good plan given we're on in ten minutes.

"I'll see if Her Majesty is ready," I reply, pleased to see that I've made Jo smile. I catch Matthew's eye as he raises a neatly arched eyebrow in my direction. I should not have said that out loud.

As the clock counts down to the top of the hour, everyone moves into place. Madeline and I make our way to the studio to resume our familiar positions on a darkened center stage. We are observed through an enormous glass window from the safety of the gallery, like two very different animals mistakenly placed in the same enclosure. Jo and the rest of the producers sit in the gallery. It is bright and loud, with a million different-colored buttons that look terribly complicated given the simplicity of what we actually do: talk to people and pretend to enjoy it. In contrast, the studio is dimly lit and uncomfortably silent. There is just a table, some chairs, and a couple of microphones. Madeline and I sit in the gloom, quietly ignoring each other, waiting for the on-air light to go red and the first act to begin.

"Good morning, and welcome to Monday's edition of *Coffee Morning*. I'm Madeline Frost. A little later on today's show, we'll be joined by best-selling author E. B. Knight, but before that, we'll be discussing the rising number of female breadwinners, and for today's phone-in, we're inviting you to get in touch on the subject of imaginary friends. Did you have one as a child? Perhaps you still do. . . ."

The familiar sound of her on-air voice calms me and I switch to autopilot, waiting for my turn to say something. I wonder if Paul is awake yet. He hasn't been himself lately—staying up late in his writing shed, coming to bed just before I get up, or not at all. He likes to call the shed a cabin. I like to call things what they are.

We spent an evening with E. B. Knight once, when Paul's first novel took off. That was over five years ago now, not long after we first met. I was a TV reporter at the time. Local news, nothing fancy. But seeing yourself on-screen does force you to make an effort with your appearance, unlike radio. I was slim then, I didn't know how to cook—I didn't have anyone to cook for before Paul and rarely made an effort just for myself. Besides, I was too busy working. I mostly did pieces about potholes or the theft of lead from church roofs, but one day, serendipity decided to intervene. Our showbiz reporter got sick and I was sent to interview some hotshot new author instead of her. I hadn't even read his book. I was hungover and resented having to do someone else's job for them, but that all changed when he walked in the room.

Paul's publisher had hired a suite at the Ritz for the interview. It felt like a stage and I felt like an actress who hadn't learned her lines. I remember feeling out of my depth, but when he sat down in the chair opposite me, I realized he was more nervous than I was. It was his first television interview and I somehow managed to put him at ease. When he asked for my card afterwards I didn't really think anything of it, but my cameraman took great pleasure in commenting on our "chemistry" all the way back to the car. I felt like a schoolgirl when he called that night. We talked and it was easy, as though we already knew each other. He said he had to go to a book awards ceremony the week after and didn't have a date. He wondered if I might be free. I was. We sat at the same table as E. B. Knight for the ceremony. It was like having dinner with a legend and a very memorable first date. She was charming, clever, and witty. I've been looking forward to seeing her again ever since I knew they had booked her as a guest.

"Good to see you," I say, as the producer brings her into the studio.

"Nice to meet you too," she replies, taking her seat. Not a flicker of recognition; how easy I am to forget.

Her trademark white bob frames her petite eighty-year-old face. She's immaculate. Even her wrinkles are neatly arranged. She looks soft around the edges, but her mind is sharp and fast. Her cheeks are pink with blusher and her blue eyes are wise and watchful, darting around the studio before fixing on their target. She smiles warmly at Madeline as though she is meeting a hero. Guests do that sometimes. It doesn't bother me, not really.

After the show, we all shuffle into the meeting room for the debrief. We sit, waiting for Madeline, the room falling silent when she finally arrives. Matthew begins talking through the stories, what worked well, what didn't. Madeline's face isn't happy. Her mouth contorts so that it looks like she's unwrapping toffees with her arse. The rest of us keep quiet and I allow my mind to wander once more.

*Twinkle twinkle little star.*

Madeline interjects with a frown.

*How I wonder what you are.*

She tuts, rolls her eyes.

*Up above the world so high.*

When Madeline has run out of unspoken criticisms, the team stands and begins to file out.

*Like a diamond in the sky.*

"Amber, can I have a word?" says Matthew, dragging me from my daydream. Judging by his tone, I don't have a choice. He closes the meeting room door and I sit back down, searching his face for clues. As usual, he is impossible to read, void of emotion; his mother could have just died and you'd never know. He takes a biscuit from the plate we leave out for the guests and gestures for me to do the same. I shake my head. When Matthew wants to make a point he always seems to take the scenic route. He tries to smile at me but soon tires from the effort and takes a bite of his biscuit instead. A couple of crumbs make themselves at home on his thin lips, which frequently part and snap shut, making him look like a goldfish, as he struggles to find the right words.

"So, I could make small talk, ask how you are, pretend that I care, that sort of thing, or I can come straight to the point," he says. A knot of dread ties itself in my stomach.

"Go on," I say, wishing that he wouldn't.

"How are things now with you and Madeline?" he asks, taking another bite.

"Same as always, she hates me," I reply too soon. My turn to wear the fake smile now, the label still attached so I can return it when I'm done.

"Yes, she does, and that's a problem," says Matthew. I shouldn't be surprised by this and yet I am. "I know she didn't make your life easy when you first joined the team, but it's been hard for her too, adjusting to having you around. This tension between the two of you, it doesn't seem to be improving. You might think people don't pick up on it, but they do. The two of you having good chemistry is really important for the show and the rest of the team." He stares at me, waiting for a response I don't know how to give. "Do you think you might be able to work on your relationship with her?"

"Well, I suppose I can try. . . ."

"Good. I didn't realize quite how unhappy the situation was making her until today. She's delivered a bit of an ultimatum." He pauses, then clears his throat before carrying on. "She wants me to replace you."

I wait for him to say more but he doesn't. His words hang in the space between us while I try to make sense of them.

"Are you firing me?"

"No!" he protests, but his face gives a different response while he considers what to say next. His hands come to meet each other in front of his chest, palms facing, just the fingertips touching, like a skin-colored steeple or a halfhearted prayer. "Well, not yet. I'm giving you until the New Year to turn this around. I'm sorry that all this has come about just before Christmas, Amber." He uncrosses his long legs, as though it's an effort, before his body retreats as far back from me as his chair will allow. His mouth reacts by twisting itself out of shape, as though he's just tasted something deeply unpleasant while he waits for my response. I don't know what to say to him. Sometimes I think it's best to say nothing at all—silence cannot be misquoted. "You're great, we love you, but you have to understand that Madeline *is Coffee Morning,* she's been presenting it for twenty years. I'm sorry, but if I have to choose between the two of you, my hands are tied."

# Now

*Boxing Day, December 2016*

I try to picture my surroundings. I'm not on a ward, it's too quiet for that. I'm not in a mortuary; I can feel myself breathing, a slight pain in my chest each time my lungs inflate with oxygen and effort. The only thing I can hear is the muffled sound of a machine beeping dispassionately close by. It's oddly comforting—my only company in an invisible universe. I start to count the beeps, collecting them inside my head, fearful they might end and unsure what that would mean.

I conclude that I am in a private room. I picture myself confined within my clinical cell, time slowly dripping down the four walls, forming puddles of dirty sludge that will slowly rise up to drown me. Until then, I am existing in an infinite space where delusion is married to reality. That is all I am doing right now, existing and waiting. For what, I do not know. I've been returned to my factory settings as a human being, rather than a human doing. Beyond the invisible walls, life goes on, but I am still, silent, and contained.

The physical pain is real and demanding to be felt. I wonder how badly I am injured. A viselike grip tightens around my skull, throbbing in time with my heartbeat. I begin to assess my body from top to bottom, searching in vain for an explanatory self-diagnosis. My mouth is being held open, I can feel a foreign object sandwiched between my lips, my teeth, pushing past my tongue and sliding down my throat. My body seems strangely unfamiliar, as though it might belong to someone else, but everything is accounted for, all the way down to my feet and toes. I can feel all ten of them and it brings such a sense of relief. I am all here in body and mind, I just need someone to switch me back on.

I wonder what I look like, whether someone has brushed my hair or cleaned my face. I'm not a vain person. I would rather be heard but not seen, preferably not noticed at all. I'm nothing special, I'm not like *her*. I'm more of a shadow, really. A dirty little smudge.

Although I am frightened, some primal instinct tells me that I will get through this. I will be okay, because I have to be. And because I always am.

I hear a door open and the sound of footsteps coming toward the bed. I can see the shadows of movement shuffling behind my veiled vision. There are two of them. I smell their cheap perfume and hairspray. They are talking, but I can't quite make out the words, not yet. For now it is just noise, like a foreign film with no subtitles. One of them takes my left arm from beneath the sheet. It is a curious sensation, like when you pretend your limbs are floppy as a child. I flinch internally at the feel of her fingertips on my skin. I do not like to be touched by strangers. I do not like to be touched by anyone, not even *him*, not anymore.

She wraps something around my upper left arm and I conclude it is a tourniquet as it tightens on my flesh. She gently puts my arm back down and walks around to the other side. The second nurse—I presume that's who they are—stands at the end of my bed. I hear the sound of paper being manipulated by inquisitive fingers and I imagine that she is either reading a novel or my hospital file down there. The sounds sharpen themselves.

"Last one to hand over, then you can skedaddle. What happened to this one?" asks the woman closest to me.

"Came in late last night. Some sort of accident," replies the other. She is moving as she speaks. "Let's get some daylight in here, shall we, see if we can't cheer things up a bit?" I hear the scratchy sound of curtains being reluctantly drawn back and find myself enveloped in a brighter shade of gloom. Then, without warning, something sharp stabs my arm. It is an alien sensation and the pain pulls me inside of myself. I feel something cool swim beneath my skin, snaking into my body until it becomes a part of me. Their voices bring me back.

"Have they called the next of kin?" asks the older-sounding one.

"There's a husband. Tried several times, straight to voicemail," replies the other. "You'd think he'd have noticed his wife was missing on Christmas Day."

*Christmas Day.*

I scan my library of memories, but too many of the shelves are empty. I don't remember anything about Christmas. We normally spend it with my family.

*Why is nobody with me?*

I notice that my mouth feels terribly dry and I can taste stale blood. I'd give anything for some water and wonder how I can get their attention. I focus all of myself on my mouth, on forming a shape and making a dent, however tiny, in the deafening silence, but nothing comes. I am a ghost trapped inside myself.

"Right, well, I'm off home, if you're happy?"

"See you later, say hi to Jeff."

The door swings open and I can hear a radio in the distance. The sound of a familiar voice reaches my ears.

"She works on *Coffee Morning,* by the way, they found her work pass in her bag when they brought her in," says the nurse who is leaving.

"Does she now? Never heard of her."

*I can hear you!*

The door swings shut, the silence returns, and then I am gone, I am not there anymore, I am silently screaming in the darkness that has swallowed me.

*What has happened to me?*

Despite my internal cries, on the outside I am voiceless and perfectly still. In real life I'm paid to talk on the radio but now I am silenced, now I am nothing. The darkness churns my thoughts until the sound of the door opening again makes everything stop. I presume that the second nurse is leaving me too and I want to shout out, to beg her to stay, to explain I'm just a little lost down the rabbit hole and need some help finding my way back. But she is not leaving. Someone else has entered the room. I can smell him, I can hear him crying, and I sense his overwhelming terror at the sight of me.

"I'm so sorry, Amber. I'm here now."

He holds my hand a little too tightly. I am the one who has lost myself; he lost me years ago and now I will not be found. The remaining nurse departs, to give us space or privacy or perhaps just because she can sense the situation is too uncomfortable, that something is not as it should be. I don't want her to go, I don't want her to leave me alone with him, but I don't know why.

"Can you hear me? Please wake up," he says, over and over.

My mind recoils from the sound of his voice. The vise tightens around my skull once more, as though a thousand fingers are pushing at my temples. I can't remember what happened to me, but I know, with unwavering certainty, that this man, my husband, had something to do with it.

# Then

*Monday, December 19, 2016—*
*Afternoon*

I was grateful at first, when Matthew said I could take the rest of the day off. The team had already scattered for lunch, which meant I could avoid any questions or fake concern. It's only now, as I make my way along Oxford Street, like a salmon swimming against a tide of tourists and shoppers, that I realize he did it for himself; no man wants to sit and stare at a woman's tear-stained face, knowing that he's responsible.

Despite being a December afternoon, the sky is bright blue, the sun pushing its way through the scattered unborn clouds to create the illusion of a nice day against a backdrop of haze and doubt. I just need to stop and think, so I do. Right in the middle of the crowded street, to the annoyance of everyone else.

"Amber?"

I look up at the smiling face of a tall man standing right in front of me. At first, nothing comes, but then a flicker of recognition, followed by a flood of memories. Edward.

"Hi, how are you?" I manage.

"I'm great. It's so good to see you."

He kisses me on the cheek. I shouldn't care what I look like, but I wrap my arms around myself as though I'm trying to hide. I notice he looks almost exactly the same. He's hardly aged at all, despite the ten years it must have been since I last saw him. He's tanned, as though he's just come back from somewhere hot, flecks of blond in his brown hair, no hint of gray. He looks so healthy, clean, still uncommonly comfortable in his own bronzed skin. His clothes look new, expensive, and I suspect the suit beneath the long woolen coat is handmade. The world was always too small for him.

"Are you okay?" he asks. I remember that I've been crying. I must look awful.

"Yes. Well, no. Just had a bit of bad news, that's all."

"I'm sorry to hear that."

I nod while he waits for a conversation I don't know how to have. All I can seem to remember is how badly I hurt him. I never really explained why I couldn't see him anymore. I just left his flat one morning, ignored his calls, and completely cut him off. He was studying in London, we both were. I still lived at home, so I stayed at his flat as often as I could, until it was over, then I never went back.

A woman texting as she walks collides into me. She shakes her head as though it is my fault she wasn't looking where she was going. The jolt shakes some words from their hiding place.

"Are you in London for Christmas?" I ask.

"Yes. I've just moved down here actually, with my girlfriend, new job in the Big Smoke." My sense of relief is soon replaced by something else. But of course he's moved on. I tell myself I'm happy for him and force my face to reply with a less than enthusiastic smile accompanied by a lackluster nod.

"I can see this isn't a good time," he says. "But look, here's my card. It would be lovely to catch up at some point. I'm meeting someone and I'm late, but it's great to see you, Amber." I take the card and have another attempt at smiling. He touches me on the shoulder and disappears back into the crowd. He couldn't wait to get away.

I gather all the little pieces of myself together and switch to autopilot. My legs carry me to a small bar just off Oxford Street. I used to come here with Paul when we started dating. We don't come here anymore—I can't remember the last time we went out. I thought the familiarity of the place would make me feel safe, but it doesn't. I order a large glass of red wine and maneuver my way to the only free table near the open fire. There's no guard. I move my chair a little farther away from it, despite wanting to get warm. I stare at my glass of Malbec, successfully blocking out the seasonal chaos rushing around. I need to persuade a woman who doesn't like anyone to like me, and if

I stare at my drink for long enough, I'm hoping I'll think of a solution. At the moment, I've got nothing.

I take a sip of the wine, just a small one. It's good. I close my eyes, swallow it down, and enjoy the sensation as it coats my throat. I've been so foolish. Everything was going well and now I've risked it all. I should have tried harder with Madeline, should have stuck to the plan. I can't lose this job, not yet. There will be a solution, I'm just not convinced that I can come up with it on my own. I need *her*. I regret the thought and decide I need another drink instead.

When my glass is empty I order another and pull my phone out of my bag while I wait. I dial Paul's number. I should have called him straight away, don't know why I didn't. He doesn't answer, so I try again. Nothing, just his voicemail. I don't leave a message. My second glass of wine arrives and I take a sip. I need it to numb myself but I know I should slow down. I have to maintain a coherent state of mind if I'm going to get things back on track, which I will, because I must. I should be able to deal with this on my own, but I can't.

"I see you've started without me," says Jo, unwrapping a ridiculously long scarf from around her neck and sliding into the chair opposite. Her smile vanishes when she takes a proper look at my face. "What's wrong? You look like shit."

"You don't know, then?"

"Know what?"

"I had a chat with Matthew."

"That explains your depressive state," she says, glancing down at the wine list.

"I think I'm going to lose my job."

Jo stares at my face as though looking for something.

"What the fuck are you talking about?"

"Madeline has given him an ultimatum. Either I go or she will."

"And he's told you you're out? Just like that?"

"Not quite. I have until the New Year to change her mind."

"So change her mind."

"How?"

"I don't know, but they can't do this to you."

"My contract ends in January, so they can just not renew it without there being any mess, I wouldn't have a leg to stand on. Plus, I suppose it gives them time to find a suitable replacement over the Christmas break." I watch Jo process everything I've said and I can see she's reached the same conclusion I had a couple of hours ago.

"Drama really follows you like a shadow, doesn't it?"

"I'm fucked, aren't I?"

"Not yet. We'll think of something, but first we're going to need more wine," she says.

"Can I get another glass of this, please?" I ask a passing waiter. I turn back to Jo. "I can't lose this job."

"You won't."

"I haven't had time to do everything I needed to do." The waiter is still hovering nearby and gives me a look of concern. I smile. He nods politely and goes to get the wine. I glance around the bar and a straw poll of eyes confirms that I'm being too loud. It happens sometimes when I'm tired or drunk. I remind myself to be quiet.

As soon as the wine arrives, Jo tells me to take a notepad and pen out of my bag. She instructs me to write PROJECT MADELINE in big red letters across the top of a blank page, so I do, underlining the words for good measure. Jo is the kind of girl who likes to write everything down. Being like that can get you into trouble if you aren't careful. She stares at the notepad and I drink some more of the wine, enjoying the feel of its warmth surging down through my body. I smile and Jo grins back; we've had the same idea at the same time, like we so often do. She tells me what to write and I furiously scribble every word on the pad, struggling to keep up with what I'm hearing. It's a good idea.

"She thinks they'll never get rid of her. Madeline Frost *is Coffee Morning,*" says Jo. I notice that she hasn't touched her glass.

"That's exactly what Matthew said. Perhaps it could be a new jingle," I say, expecting her to smile. She doesn't.

"But she doesn't know how your chat with Matthew went. So, maybe what we need to do is get Madeline to think they've had enough of her temper tantrums and that they are going to get rid of *her,*" she says.

"But they'd never do that."

"She doesn't know that for sure. Nobody is irreplaceable anymore, and I'm starting to think if we plant enough seeds, the idea will start to grow. If she didn't have that job, she'd be nothing. It's her life, it's all she has."

"Agreed. But how? There isn't enough time, not now." I start to cry again. I can't help it.

"It's okay. Cry if you need to, get it out of your system. Luckily you're a pretty crier."

"I'm not a pretty anything."

"Why do you do that? You're beautiful. Admittedly, you could make more of an effort. . . ."

"Thanks."

"Sorry, but it's true. Not wearing makeup doesn't make you look pale and interesting, it just makes you look pale. You've got a nice figure but it's like you're always trying to hide beneath the same old clothes."

"I am trying to hide."

"Well, stop it."

She's right, I'm a mess. My mind rewinds to Edward. He must have thought he'd had a lucky escape not ending up with me.

"I just bumped into an ex on Oxford Street," I say, studying her face for a reaction.

"Which one?"

"There's no need to say it like that, there weren't that many."

"More than me. Who was it?"

"It doesn't matter. I just felt like such a frump, such a loser. I wish he hadn't seen me looking like that, that's all."

"Who cares? Right now you just need to focus on what matters. Go and buy yourself a new wardrobe—a few new dresses, some new shoes, something with a heel, and get some makeup while you're at it. You need to look really happy and confident tomorrow, just stick it all on a credit card. Madeline knew he would tell you today, so she'll be expecting you to be upset, probably doesn't think you'll come in at all, but you will. We'll start some rumors on social media. We'll take control of the situation. You know what you have to do."

"Yes, I do."

"So go shopping, then go home. Get an early night and come in tomorrow looking fabulous, as though you don't have a care in the world."

I do as I'm told, drain my glass and pay the bill. I've always stayed within the lines when coloring in my life, but now I'm prepared to let things get a bit messy. Before leaving the bar, I rip the Project Madeline page from my notebook, screw it up, and throw it on the open fire, watching the white paper brown and burn.

# Now

*Boxing Day, December 2016—*
*Evening*

When I first start to fall, I forget to be afraid, too busy noticing that the hand that pushed me looked so much like my own. But as I plummet into the darkness below, my worst fears follow me down. I want to scream, but I can't. That familiar hand is now tightly clasped over my mouth. I can't make a sound, I can barely breathe. When the terror shakes me from the recurring nightmare, I awake into another. I still don't recall what happened to me, no matter how hard I try, no matter how badly I need to know.

People seem to come and go, a cacophony of murmurs, strange sounds and smells. Ill-defined shapes linger over and around me, as though I am underwater, drowning in my own mistakes. Sometimes it feels like I am lying at the bottom of a murky pond, the weight of the dirty liquid pushing down on me, filling me up with secrets and filth. There are moments when I think it would be a relief to drown, for it all to be over. Nobody can see me down here, but then I was always rather invisible. The new world around me turns in slow motion just out of reach, while I remain perfectly still, down in the darkness.

Occasionally I manage to resurface just long enough to focus on the sounds, to speed them up so that they become recognizable to me again, like right now. I can hear the sound of a paper page being turned, no doubt one of the silly crime novels he is so fond of. The others come and go but he is always here, I am no longer alone. I wonder why he hasn't put the book down and rushed to my side now that I'm awake and then remember that for him I am not awake, for him nothing has changed. All sense of time has left me. It could be day or night. I am a silent, living corpse. I hear a door open and someone enters the room.

"Hello, Mr. Reynolds. You shouldn't really be here this late but I suppose we can make an exception just this once. I was here when they brought your wife in last night."

*Last night?*

It feels like I've been here for days.

The doctor's voice sounds familiar, but then I suppose it would if he's been treating me. I imagine what he looks like. I picture a serious man with tired eyes, a furrowed brow eroded into a series of lines by all the sadness he must have seen. I imagine him wearing a white coat, then I remember that they don't do that anymore, they just look like everyone else, and so the man I imagined fades away.

I hear Paul drop his book and fumble around like a fool; he's always been intimidated by medical professionals. I bet he stands to shake his hand, in fact I know he will. I don't need to see him to know exactly how he'll behave. I can predict his every move.

"Do you need someone to take a look at your hand?" asks the doctor.

*What's wrong with his hand?*

"No, it's fine," says Paul.

"You've bruised it quite badly, are you sure? It's no trouble."

"It looks worse than it is, but thank you. Do you know how long she'll be like this? Nobody will give me an answer." Paul's voice sounds strange to me, small and strangled.

"It's very difficult to say at this stage. Your wife sustained quite serious injuries in the crash. . . ." And then I zone out for a while as his words repeat themselves in my head. I try so hard, but still nothing, no memory of any accident. I don't even have a car.

"You said you were here when she arrived. Was there anyone else? I mean, was anyone else hurt?" asks Paul.

"Not that I'm aware of."

"So she was alone?"

"No other vehicles were involved. It's a difficult question for me to ask, but there are some marks on your wife's body. Do you know how she got them?"

*What marks?*

"I presumed from the accident," says Paul. "I didn't see them before. . . ."

"I see. Has your wife ever tried to harm herself?"

"Of course not! She's not that sort of person."

*What sort of person am I, Paul?*

Perhaps if he'd paid me a little more attention he might know.

"You mentioned she was upset when she left home yesterday, do you know what about?" asks the doctor.

"Just stuff. Things have been difficult at work."

"And everything was all right at home?"

All three of us share an uncomfortable silence until Paul's voice smashes it.

"When she wakes up, will she still be herself? Will she remember everything?" I am so focused on wondering what it is that he doesn't want me to remember, I almost miss the answer.

"It's too early to tell if she will make a full recovery. Her injuries are very serious. She wasn't wearing a seat belt . . ."

*I always wear a seat belt.*

". . . she would have been traveling at some speed to have gone through the windshield like that, and she sustained a serious blow to the head on impact. She's lucky to be here at all."

*Lucky.*

"All we can do is take things one day at a time," says the doctor.

"But she will wake up, won't she?"

"I'm sorry. Is there anyone we can call to be with you? A relative? A friend?"

"No. She's all I've got," says Paul.

I soften when I hear him say those words about me. They didn't used to be true. When we met, he was so popular, everyone wanted a piece of him. His first novel was an overnight success. He hates it when I say that, always describes it as the overnight success that took him ten years. It didn't last, though. Things got even better, then they got a lot worse. He couldn't write after that, the words wouldn't come. His success broke him and his failure broke us.

I hear the door close and wonder if I am alone again, then I hear a faint clicking sound and picture Paul sending a text message. The image jars a little and I realize I can't remember him texting anyone before. The only other people in his life now are his mother, who refuses to communicate other than the occasional phone call when she wants something, and his agent, who tends to e-mail now that they don't have much to talk about anymore. Paul and I text each other but I guess I'm not there when he does that. My thoughts are so loud he hears them.

"I've told them where you are." He sighs and comes a little closer to the bed. He must mean my family. I don't have many friends. An inexplicable chill makes its way down my spine as the silence settles over us once more.

I feel a stab of hurt about my parents. I don't doubt that he's tried to contact them, but they travel a lot and can be tricky to get hold of these days. We often go weeks without speaking at all, although that isn't always to do with their foreign trips. I wonder when they will come, then I rearrange the thought and wonder if they'll come at all. I am not their favorite child, I am the daughter they always had.

"Bitch," says Paul, in a voice I barely recognize as his. I hear the legs of his chair scrape against the floor. The shadows over my eyelids darken and I know that he is standing right over me. Once more I feel the urge to scream and so I do. But nothing happens.

His face is so close to mine now that I can feel his hot breath on my neck as he whispers in my ear. "Hold on."

I don't know what the words mean, but the door opens and I am saved.

"Oh my God, Amber." My sister, Claire, has arrived.

"You shouldn't be here," says Paul.

"Of course I should. You should have called me sooner."

"I wish I hadn't called you at all."

I don't understand the conflict between the two dark shadows looming over me. Claire and Paul have always got on.

"Well, I'm here now. What happened?" she asks, coming closer.

"They found her a few miles from the house. The car is a wreck."

"Nobody cares about your bloody car."

*I never drive Paul's car. I never drive.*

"Everything will be okay, Amber," says Claire, taking my hand.

"I'm here now." Her cold fingers wrap themselves around my own and it takes me back to when we were young. She always liked holding hands. I didn't.

"She can't hear you, she's in a coma," says Paul, sounding strangely pleased.

"A coma?"

"Proud of yourself?"

"I know you're upset, but this isn't my fault."

"Isn't it? I thought you had a right to know, but you're not welcome here."

My mind is racing and I don't understand anything that is being said. I feel like I'm in a parallel universe where nobody around me makes sense anymore.

"What happened to your hand?" Claire asks.

*What's wrong with his hand?*

"Nothing."

"You should get a doctor to look at that."

"It's fine."

The room I can't see starts to spin. I struggle to stay on the surface, but the water swirls around and inside me, swallowing me back down into the darkness.

"Paul, please. She's my sister."

"She warned me not to trust you."

"You're being ridiculous."

"Am I?" Everything is so much quieter than before. "Get out."

"Paul!"

"I said get out!"

There's no hesitation this time. I hear my sister's heeled feet retreat from the room. The door opens and closes and I am alone again with a man who sounds like my husband, but behaves like a stranger.

# Then

I get off the train and make my way along the quiet, suburban streets toward home and Paul. I'm still not convinced anything can be done to save my job, but maybe this will at least buy me enough time to do what I need to do. I won't tell him. Not yet. I might never need to.

It wouldn't be the first job that I've lost since we've been together. My career as a TV reporter came to an abrupt end two years ago when my editor got a bit too friendly once too often. He had a rather hands-on approach. One evening his hand slipped right up under my skirt and the next day someone keyed his BMW in the staff parking lot. He thought it was me and I never got on air again after that. I never got groped again either. I quit before he found an excuse to fire me and it was a relief, to be honest; I hated being on TV. But Paul was devastated. He liked that version of me. He loved her. I got under his feet at home all the time. I wasn't the woman he married. I was unemployed, I didn't dress the same, and I no longer had any stories to tell. Last year at a wedding, the couple sitting next to us asked what I did. Paul answered before I had a chance to. "Nothing." The somebody he loved became a nobody he loathed.

He said it made it hard for him to write, me being at home all the time. He had a fancy shed built at the bottom of the garden, so he could pretend that I wasn't. Claire spotted the advert for the *Coffee Morning* job six months ago. She sent me the link and suggested I apply. I didn't think I'd get it, but I did.

I stumble up the garden path and feel inside my handbag for my key. I'm puzzled by the sound of music and laughter inside the house.

Paul is not alone. I remember that I tried calling him this afternoon but he never answered and didn't bother to call me back. My hands shake a little as I open the front door.

They are sitting on the sofa, laughing, Paul in his usual seat, Claire in mine. An almost empty bottle of wine and two glasses pose for a tedious still life on the table in front of them.

She doesn't even like red.

They look a little shocked to see me and I feel like an intruder in my own home.

"Hello, Sis. How are you?" says Claire, getting up to kiss me on both cheeks. Her designer skinny jeans look as though they've been sprayed on, petite pedicured feet protruding beneath them. Her tight white top reveals a little more than it should as she stands up. I don't remember seeing it before, must be new. She dresses as though we are still young, as though men still look at us that way. If they do, I don't see them. Her long blond hair has been straightened within an inch of its life and is tucked behind her ears as though she is wearing an invisible headband. Everything about her appearance is neat, tidy, controlled. We couldn't look more different. She stands too close, waiting for me to say something. Her perfume infiltrates my nostrils, my throat, I can taste it on my tongue. Familiar but dangerous. Sickly sweet.

"I thought you were going out after work tonight?" says Paul from his seat.

His eyes narrow slightly at the sight of my shopping bags, some new outfits folded neatly in a cradle of tissue paper inside. I silently dare him to say something. It's my money, I earned it. I'll spend it on what I like. I put the bags down, noticing the deep red grooves the plastic handles have carved into my fingers.

"Something came up," I say in Paul's direction before turning to Claire. "I didn't know you were coming round, is everything all right?" I know what's going on here.

"Everything's fine. David is working late, again. I came over to see you for a girly chat, but I forgot that unlike me you have a social life."

She's trying too hard; her smile looks like it's hurting her face.

"Where are the children?" I ask. Her smile fades.

"With a neighbor, they're fine. I wouldn't leave them with anyone unreliable." She turns to Paul, but he just stares at the floor. Her lips are stained from the wine and her cheeks a little flushed. She has never been able to handle her drink. I see it then, the look in her eyes—that flash of danger that I've seen before. She knows I've spotted it and that I haven't forgotten what it means. "I should go, it's later than I thought," she says.

"I'd invite you to stay, but I need to talk to my husband." I meant to say Paul, but my subconscious deemed it necessary to change the script.

"Of course. Well, I'll see you both soon. Hope everything is okay at work," she says, picking up her coat and bag, leaving her half-drunk glass of wine on the table. As soon as the door closes I am overwhelmed with regret. I know I should go after her, apologize so she knows I still love her, that we're okay. But I don't.

"Well, that was awkward," says Paul.

I don't respond, don't even look at him. Instead I double lock the front door without thinking and pick up Claire's glass, walking out to the kitchen. He follows me and stands in the doorway as I tip the crimson liquid into the sink. Dark red splashes stain the white porcelain and I turn on the tap to wash them away.

"Yes, it was a little strange coming home to find my husband and sister enjoying a cozy night in together." The memory of the wine I drank myself earlier slurs my words a little. I can see from Paul's expression that he thinks I'm being ridiculous, or jealous, or both. It isn't that. I'm scared of what this means, finding them like this. I'm pretty sure she knew I wouldn't be here, and she'd offloaded the kids, so she'd planned it. I can't explain it to him. He wouldn't believe me; he doesn't know her like I do or understand what she's capable of.

"Don't be ridiculous. I meant you, just telling her to leave like that. She came round here to see you, she's feeling really down."

"Well, maybe she should phone first if she really wants to see me."

"She said she did, several times. You didn't return any of her calls." I remember that Claire did call today, twice. The first time during my chat with Matthew, as though she had known something was wrong. I turn to face Paul but the words won't come. Everything about him in this moment seems to irritate me. He's still an attractive man but elements of the life he has chosen have left him worn and used, like a shiny piece of silver that becomes dull and tarnished over time. He's too thin, his skin looks like it has forgotten the sun, and his hair is too long for a man his age, but then he never did grow up. I can see from the set of his jaw that he's angry with me, and for some reason that turns me on. We haven't had sex for months, not since our anniversary. Maybe that's how it will be from now on, an annual treat.

I turn to face the oven, my fingers forming the familiar shapes. I didn't used to do this in front of him, but I don't care anymore.

"Did something happen at work today?" he asks.

I don't reply.

"I don't know why you stay there."

"Because I need to."

"Why? We don't need the money. You could try and get a job in TV again."

A layer of silence spreads itself over the conversation, smothering the words we always think but never say. Radio killed his TV star. I continue to stare at the oven and start to count under my breath.

"Will you stop doing that? It's nuts," he says.

I ignore him and carry on with my routine. I can feel him staring at me.

*The wheels on the bus go round and round.*

All we seem to do lately is argue.

*Round and round.*

The harder I try to hold us together, the faster we fall apart.

*Round and round.*

I'm not someone who cries; I have other ways of expressing my sadness.

*The wheels on the bus go round and round.*

I wish I could tell him the truth.

*All day long.*

A memory from my childhood switches itself on inside my head. I wish it wouldn't.

"Are you okay?" Paul asks, finally leaving the doorway.

"No," I whisper, and let him hold me.

It's the truth, but not the whole of it.

# Before

Dear Diary,

Today was an interesting day—I started at a new school. That is not very interesting, it happens quite often, but today it felt different, as though maybe things will work out this time. My new form teacher seems nice. When Mum meets her, I bet she'll say, "Mrs. MacDonald likes her food, doesn't she?" Mum says that sort of thing a lot, it's her way of saying someone is overweight. Mum says it is important to look your best, because even if people shouldn't judge a book by its cover, they still do. Mrs. MacDonald is older than Mum but younger than Nana was. She introduced me to the class without making a song and dance of it like teachers normally do, then told me to take a seat. There was only one empty desk at the back of the room, so I sat there. As first days at school go, today was okay. Mum says we'll definitely stick around this time, but she's said that before.

The class is reading the diary of a girl called Anne Frank, but they've only just started, so I haven't missed too much. The girl at the desk next to mine let me share her copy. She said I should call her Taylor, which is actually her surname, not her first name, but whatever. I noticed the dusting of chalk on her blazer and I already know she's one of those kids, the sort the others don't like.

For our homework, we have to write a diary entry every day for a week, a bit like Anne Frank, but she did it for much longer. The best part of this is that we don't even have to hand it in, because Mrs. MacDonald says diaries should always be private. I thought about not doing it at all, nobody would know, but Mum and Dad are arguing again downstairs so I thought I may as well give it a go.

I don't think my diary is going to be as interesting as Anne Frank's. I'm not a very interesting person. Mrs. MacDonald says if we get stuck with what to write, we should just think of three honest things to say about ourselves. She says that everyone can think of three things and that being honest with yourself is more important than being honest with others. So, here are my first three things to share with you. They are all true.

1. I'm almost ten.
2. I don't have any friends.
3. My parents don't love me.

The thing about the truth is that it sucks.

My nana died of cancer. We moved in with her when she got sick, but it didn't make her better. She was sixty-two, which sounds old, but Mum said it was actually quite young to die. I used to spend a lot of time with Nana, she always took me to cool places and listened to me. She never had a lot of money, but she gave me this diary last Christmas. She thought writing down how I felt might help me deal with things. Nearly a whole year has gone by and I didn't listen, but now I wish I had. I wish I had written down all the things she used to say, because I've already started to forget them.

I think my parents used to love me, but I disappointed them so often that the love got rubbed out. They don't even love each other, they argue and shout at each other all the time. They argue about lots of things, but mostly about all the money that we don't have. They also argue about me. They were so loud once that one of our old neighbors called the police. Mum said it was all very embarrassing and when the police left, they argued even more because of that. We don't live there now, so Mum says it doesn't matter anymore and that people should mind their own business. She said it would be a "fresh start" when we moved here and "wouldn't it be nice to make some new friends?" She hadn't noticed that I didn't have any old ones.

I used to make friends whenever we moved to a new place, but I always felt really sad when I had to say good-bye. I don't bother now. I don't need friends anyway. When people ask if I'd like to come to their birthday parties, I just say no thank you and that I'm not allowed, even though I would be. I don't even show Mum the invites, I just put them in the bin. The problem with going to other people's houses is that then they want to visit yours. Nana always said that books made better friends than people anyway. Books will take you anywhere if you let them, she used to say, and I think she was right.

After Nana died, Mum said we would redecorate but we haven't. I sleep in Nana's room in the bed where she went to sleep one day and never woke up. Mum said I could get a new bed, but I don't want to, not yet. Sometimes I think I can still smell her, which is silly because the sheets have been washed loads and they're not even the same ones. There are two beds in my room. The other one was Granddad's, but he didn't die there, he died in a home that wasn't his.

I can't hear anything, which means they've stopped arguing, for now. What happens next is that Dad will open a bottle of red wine and pour himself a large glass. Meanwhile, Mum will take something out of the freezer for dinner and make herself a drink that looks like water but isn't. I'm never going to drink alcohol when I grow up, I don't like what it does to people. We'll eat our microwaved lasagna in silence for a while, before one of them remembers to ask about my first day. I'll tell them it was fine, talk a little bit about the teachers and my classes, and they'll pretend to listen. As soon as Dad has finished eating, he'll take what's left of the wine and go to his study. It used to be Nana's sewing room. Dad renamed it but he doesn't do any studying in there, he watches the little TV. Mum will wash up and I'll sit in the lounge by myself watching the big TV until it's time for bed. Then, at nine o'clock Mum will tell me to go upstairs. She sets an alarm to remind herself to do this. Once I'm in bed and they think I'm asleep, they'll start arguing again. Nana used to sing me a song to help me go to sleep when I was little. *The wheels on the bus go round and round.* I didn't used to like it, but now I sometimes hum it to myself to drown out the sound of Dad shouting and Mum crying. That's pretty much my life. I told you it wasn't as interesting as Anne Frank's.

# Now

*Tuesday, December 27, 2016*

I can hear heavy rain, like a relentless army of tiny fingernails tapping on the window, trying to wake me from this bottomless sleep. When each angry drop fails to break the spell, I picture it turning into a tear and crying its way down the glass. I think it must be night; it's quieter than before. I imagine being able to stand up, walk to the window, and reach my hand into the outside, to feel the rain on my skin and look up at the night sky. I long for that and I wonder if I will ever see the stars again. We are all made of flesh and stars, but we all become dust in the end. Best to shine while you can.

I am alone, but I keep hearing Paul's voice in my head. *Hold on.* I'm trying to, but things keep slipping from my grasp. I don't understand why he and Claire were arguing, they've always got on so well. My sister is younger than me but has always been one step ahead. I'm told we do look alike, but she is blond and beautiful and I'm more of a dark-haired disappointing cover artist. She was the new and improved daughter my parents always wanted; they thought she was perfect. So did I at first, but as soon as she arrived into our family, I was forgotten. They never knew her the way I did, they didn't see what I saw.

I feel myself start to drift away. I fight it for as long as I am able, then, just as I'm about to surrender, the door opens.

I know it's her.

Claire has always worn the same perfume as our mother; she is a creature of habit. And she always wears too much. I can also smell a subtle waft of her fabric-conditioned clothes as she slowly walks around the room. I expect she's wearing something fitted and feminine, something far too small for me to squeeze into. I hear her kitten heels tap the floor and wonder what she is looking at. She takes her time. She is alone.

She pulls up a chair and sits down close to the bed, her turn to read to me in mute now. I hear pages being turned sporadically—she came prepared. I can imagine her manicured hands holding the book on her lap. I start to picture my room as a sterile library, and myself as a ghostly librarian who imposes a sentence of silence on all who enter. *Shhh.* Claire reads fast in real life, so when I don't hear the pages turn too often, I know she's just pretending. She's good at that.

"I wish our parents were here," she says.

*I'm glad they're not.*

She wishes they were here for her, not for me. They'd probably think it was my fault, like always. I hear her put the book she's been pretending to read down and come to stand a little closer. My thoughts get louder until I am forced to listen, but they rush around my head and collide with each other, so I can never stay on one thought long enough to make any sense of it. Claire's face is so close to mine now that I can taste the coffee on her breath.

"You still have glass in your hair," she whispers.

As soon as her words land in my ears, I feel myself being pulled back quickly. It's like going through a very long dark tunnel, backwards. I find myself sitting on a high branch of a dead tree. I look down and notice I'm still wearing my hospital gown. I recognize the street beneath my feet. I live near here, I'm almost home. There's a rumble of a storm in the distance and I can smell burning, but I'm not afraid. I reach out to touch the rain that has started falling, but my hand remains perfectly dry. Everything I see is the darkest shade of black, apart from a tiny light in the distance. I'm so happy to see it, until I realize that it isn't a star, it's a headlight. It's joined by a twin. The wind picks up and I see a car coming down the road toward me, too fast. I look down at the street below and see a little girl wearing a pink, fluffy dressing gown in the middle of the road. She's singing.

*Twinkle twinkle little star.*

She turns her head up toward me.

*How I wonder who you are.*

She's got the words wrong.

*Up above the world so sad.*

The car is close now. I scream at her to get off the road.

*It's not the drugs. You're going mad.*

It's only then that I notice she doesn't have a face.

I watch as the car swerves to avoid her, skids, then smashes into the tree I am sitting in. The force of the impact almost knocks me from the branch, but someone in the distance tells me to *hold on.* Below me, time has slowed. The little girl laughs uncontrollably and I watch in horror as a woman's body smashes out of the windshield. She flies through the air in slow motion, wearing a cape of a thousand shards of glass. Her body lands hard on the street directly below. I look back at the little girl. She's stopped laughing. She raises her index finger to where her lips should be. *Shhh.* I look back over at the body of the woman. I know that it's me down there, but I don't want to see any more. I close my eyes. Everything is silent, except the car radio, which is still playing Christmas songs from within the twisted metal shell. The music stops abruptly and I hear Madeline's voice on the crackly airwaves. I sit on my branch and put my hands over my ears, but I can still hear her repeating the same words over and over.

*Hello and welcome to* Coffee Morning.

*Nothing happens by accident.*

I start to scream but Madeline's voice just gets louder. I hear a door open and I fall straight from the tree, back into my hospital bed.

"I'm back," says Paul.

"I can see that," says Claire.

"Which means you can go now. When I'm here, you're not. That's what we agreed."

"That's what you agreed," she says. "I'm not leaving."

Claire picks up her discarded book from the end of the bed and sits back down in her chair. Everything is silent for a while, then I hear Paul sit down on the other side of the room. It feels like we stay like this for a very long time. I'm not sure if I'm awake or asleep for all of it. I don't know if there are moments that I missed. The hours are being stolen from me, episodes I wanted to see, deleted before I've had a chance to watch.

I hear more voices, new ones. Everyone seems to be talking over each other at first, so that the words get tangled on their way to my ears. I have to concentrate very hard to straighten them out.

"Mr. Reynolds? I'm DCI Jim Handley and this is PC Healey. Could we speak with you outside?" says a man's voice from the doorway.

"Of course," says Paul. "Is it to do with the accident?"

"It might be best if we spoke alone," says the detective.

"It's fine, I'll go," says Claire.

The knot in the pit of my stomach tightens as she exits the room. I hear the door click shut before someone clears their throat.

"It was your car that your wife was driving night before last, is that right?" the detective asks.

"Yes," Paul answers.

"Do you know where she was going?"

"No."

"But you saw her leave?"

"Yes."

I hear a long, drawn-out intake of breath. "Shortly after your wife was brought to hospital by ambulance, two of our colleagues went to your home. You weren't there."

"I was out looking for her."

"On foot?"

"That's right. I was at home the next morning when they came back."

"So you knew that police officers had been to your property the night before?"

"Well, not at the time, no, but you just said they—"

"The officers who came to your house yesterday morning were sent to inform you that your wife was at the hospital. The first set of police officers were sent the night before because someone had reported you and your wife arguing loudly in the street." Paul doesn't say anything. "If you didn't know where your wife was going, then where did you go to look for her?"

"I was drunk; it was Christmas, after all. I wasn't thinking logically, I just wandered around for a while. . . ."

"I see that your hand is bandaged up, how did that happen?"

"I don't remember."

*He's lying, I can tell, but I don't know why.*

"We've spoken to some of the staff who were here when your wife was first brought in. They say that some of her injuries are older than those she sustained in the crash. Do you have any idea how she might have got them?"

*What injuries?*

"No," says Paul.

"You didn't notice the marks on her neck or the bruising on her face?" asks the female police officer.

"No," he says again.

"I do think it's best we speak to you somewhere more private, Mr. Reynolds," says the detective. "We'd like to invite you to come to the station with us."

The room is silent.

# Then

Managed to get you a table at the Langham, pulled some strings," I say.

"Marvelous. What for?" says Matthew, without looking up from his computer screen. We're on air in just under ten minutes and almost everyone, including Madeline, has already gone through to the studio.

"Brunch," I say.

"With who?" He looks up at me, giving me his half-full attention. Then I see his expression change as he notices my new dress, my makeup, my hair, bullied into shape by brushes and hot air. He sits up a little straighter and his left eyebrow exerts itself into an appreciative arch. I find myself wondering whether he is actually gay or whether I had just presumed that he was.

"Today's panel. The 'women in their fifties' guests. We talked about it last week," I say.

"Did we?"

"Yes. You said you'd take them out after the show, talk through some future ideas."

"What future ideas?"

"You said we needed to be more innovative, shake things up a bit."

"That does sound like me."

It doesn't. When he hesitates, I bombard him with more well-rehearsed words. "They're expecting to meet you straight after the show, but I can cancel it if you want me to, make up some excuse?"

"No, no. I think I do remember now. Is Madeline joining us?"

"No, it's just you and the guests." He frowns. "So they can talk freely about what they think works and what doesn't." I didn't rehearse that part, but the words form themselves and do the trick.

"Okay, I suppose that makes sense. I've got a physio appointment at three, so I'll need to head home straight after."

"Sure thing, boss."

"And joining us now on *Coffee Morning* are Jane Williams, the editor of *Savoir-Faire,* the UK's biggest-selling women's monthly magazine, and the writer and broadcaster Louise Ford, to talk about women working in the media in their fifties," says Madeline, before taking a sip of water. For once, she looks as uncomfortable as I feel in the studio. I dig my fingernails into my knees beneath the desk as hard as I can, and the pain calms me enough to stop me from running out of the tiny, dark room.

I set up a fake Twitter account last night—took me five minutes when Paul was having a shower before we went to bed. I posted a few pictures of cats I found on the Internet and had over a hundred followers by the time I woke up. I hate cats. I can't pretend to understand social media either. I mean, I get it, I just don't understand why so many people spend so much time engaging with it. It's not real. It's just noise. Still, I'm glad that they do. *Is Madeline Frost leaving Coffee Morning?* has been retweeted eighty-seven times since I posted it twenty minutes ago and the #FrostBitesTheDust hashtag is proving very popular. That bit was Jo's idea.

The makeup I don't normally wear feels heavy on my skin. My red lipstick matches my new dress and the carefully selected armor makes me feel safe. The protective mask hides my scars and soothes my conscience; I'm only doing what I must to survive. I catch myself slipping out of character and stare down at my red fingers. At first I think I'm bleeding, but then realize I've been picking the skin off my red-stained lips.

I sit on my hands for a moment, to hide them from myself. I have to stay calm or I'll never get through this. I realize I'm chewing on my lower lip now, my teeth picking up where my fingers left off. I stop and focus all of my attention on Madeline's half-empty glass. The hiss and fizz of the sparkling water it holds seems to get louder as my eyes translate the sound to my ears. I retune them to the noise of her voice instead and try to steer myself back to center.

I smile at each of the studio guests sitting around the table with us. So good of them to come in at such short notice. I study their faces as they continue to talk over one another, all of them present and incorrect for the same reason: self-promotion. Each one of us is sitting here with a motive today. If you were to strip us all down to our purest intentions, the lowest common denominator would always be wanting to be listened to, needing to be heard above the noise of modern life. For once I don't want to be the one asking the questions. I wish someone would listen to my answers and tell me whether my version of the truth is still correct. Sometimes the right thing to do is wrong, but that's just life.

The smile stretched on my face starts to ache. My attempt to portray a happy persona has been effective but exhausting and I find myself repeatedly checking the clock on the studio wall. Time is running out for me and yet, here in this room, it has slowed down, trapping me in locked minutes. Each time my eyes bore of looking down at the script, they look up at the clock until I become transfixed, following the large hand as it plots its clockwise rotation to oblivion. A sound of ticking that I have never noticed before today gets louder and louder until I can barely hear what the guests are saying. I see the faces of the team in the gallery, and it feels like they're all staring at me. I look for Jo, but she isn't there. I'm picking the skin off my lip again. I stop, irritated by my lack of self-control, and rub my lipstick-stained fingers on the cloth of my dress. Red on red. I must try harder not to be myself.

When the show finally reaches its conclusion, I take pleasure in watching Madeleine retreat to her office, knowing exactly what she'll find there. I thank the guests, someone has to, and leave them with Matthew, who has his coat on, ready to take them out. I pop to the toilets to check that my mask is still in place. Madeline's current PA is there, staring at herself in the mirror. She looks tired and there is a sadness behind her eyes that makes me want to save her. I smile and she gives me a halfhearted smile in return. One of her many jobs each morning is to go through Madeline's mail—she's too busy and important to read it herself. There's always a tidy pile to tackle: press releases, invites, free stuff, the usual. She gets more post than the rest of the team put together, including me. Then there's the fan mail. That gets left on her desk after the show. She likes to read anything that looks like a personal letter herself once we're off air and then she marks the ones that she deems worthy of a reply with a small red sticker. She doesn't keep the letters. She inhales the admiration and breathes out arrogance, her own bespoke photosynthesis. The letters with red stickers get sent a signed photo of Madeline. She doesn't write the replies, she doesn't even sign the photos, that's another job for her PA. I watch her reapply her makeup and wonder how she feels pretending to be someone that she's not every day.

I head for the meeting room and wait with the others for the debrief. Jo gives me a nod as I take a seat: Project Madeline is so far going according to plan. A low rumble of chatter has sparked over the online rumors of Madeline's departure, and I'm pleased to hear word is spreading. Lies can seem true when told often enough. The hot gossip is extinguished as soon as she enters the room. Madeline slams the glass door behind her and sits down at the table. I'm guessing she's seen Twitter too. She can't figure out how to print her own scripts, but she can tweet. I know she checks her account after each show to make sure her fifty thousand "followers" still adore her, and discovering that she's trending for all the wrong reasons will not have gone down well.

"Where's my coffee?" she barks at nobody in particular. Her PA's face burns bright red.

"It's . . . right there, Madeleine," she says, pointing at the steaming cup on the desk.

"That's not my mug. How many times do I have to tell you?"

"It's in the dishwasher."

"Then wash it. By hand. Where's Matthew?"

I stare at her, this successful, formidable woman, and wonder where all her anger comes from. I know things about Madeline, things that I shouldn't and that she'd rather I didn't, but it still doesn't explain all the hate. I clear my throat and ball my hands into fists beneath the table. Time to deliver my lines.

"Matthew has taken Jane and Louise out for a meeting and some food," I say.

"What? Why?" asks Madeline.

"I'm not sure. He said he'll be out of the office for the rest of the day."

Madeline is quiet for a moment. Everyone waits while she looks down at the table, a small frown folding itself onto her already heavily lined face.

"Right, well, maybe someone else can explain to me where this 'Women at Fifty' idea came from. This morning was the first I heard about it."

I let the others do the talking while I sit back and study my enemy. Her dark-rimmed glasses perch on the end of her upturned nose and behind them her dead eyes dart around the room.

*Baa baa, black sheep, have you any wool?*

Her long, witchlike nails drum an impatient beat on her notebook and I spot something poking out from between its white pages—the crisp edge of a red envelope. She's read it, then. I smile to myself.

Step one is complete.

# Before

Dear Diary,

So Taylor, the girl I sit next to in class, wants to be friends. She didn't say that, but I can just tell. It's a problem. She's a nice girl, doesn't seem to be very popular, but that isn't what's bothering me. Being popular isn't all it's cracked up to be, people expect too much from you. Far better to blend in with the crowd, that way when you do shine, people notice.

One of the popular kids was mean to Taylor in the changing rooms before hockey today. Kelly O'Neil, who always has a tan because her family goes on lots of holidays, is not a nice person. She called Taylor flat-chested, which is stupid, we're all flat-chested—we're ten. Everyone laughed, not because it was funny, but because they're scared of Kelly, which is also stupid. She's just a spoilt moron. Taylor's cheeks went all red but she did a good job of blinking away the tears in her eyes. Nana used to say that if you didn't let the tears out of you they can turn to poison. Mum says only babies cry and that it is a sign of weakness. I think it must depend on the type of tears because I catch her crying all the time.

There are three things I've cried about recently, when nobody could see:

1. Nana being dead.
2. My fountain pen leaking all over *Little Women*.
3. Going to bed with no dinner and my tummy hurting so badly I couldn't sleep.

Hockey was cold and boring. It started to rain halfway through but we carried on playing. The PE teacher said that a little rain never hurt anyone.

She looked like she could do with some exercise herself. She said the grass on the hockey pitch was bare in places from overuse and undercare, so I tried not to run on the bald patches, hoping that would help. I was running for the ball on the wet grass when I slid. I stretched my hands out in front of me to break my fall, and let go of my stick. It was only when I stood up afterwards that I saw what had happened. My stick had flown through the air and hit Kelly O'Neil in the face. Her nose was bleeding and everything. It was an accident, so I didn't feel too bad about it. Nana used to say that there was no such thing as accidents and that everything happens for a reason. I don't know what I think about that. Sometimes stuff happens when you don't mean it and just because no one believes you, it doesn't mean that you did it on purpose.

I just heard a plate smash downstairs. I listened on the landing for a while. Dad was yelling that it nearly hit his head. Plates don't tend to fly through the air by themselves, so I'm guessing Mum threw it at him. They smash plates for fun in a country called Greece. I heard Kelly O'Neil telling people about that in the changing rooms before hockey. She's been to Greece on holiday. Twice. I've never been abroad, but I have been to Brighton. We went there for the weekend once, me, Mum, and Dad. I think they were happy then. They're definitely not happy now. I can't remember what Dad looks like when he smiles. Mum looks sad all the time and is bigger than she used to be. She's started wearing leggings with stretchy waistbands instead of her jeans. Maybe that's why Dad is so angry all the time. I did hear him say that she had let herself go, which means not looking as good as you used to and being unattractive.

I've closed my bedroom door but I can still hear them. I've got Nana's doorstop on the bed with me now for company, seeing as it no longer has a job to do. I like the feel of it, heavy brown metal, shaped like a robin. It was one of Nana's favorite things and now it is one of mine. The best thing about being a bird is that you can always fly away. This one can't though, he has to stay here, with me, in our room. He can't fly, or sing, or build a nest of his own somewhere far from here. I bet he would if he could though.

I'm going to have a big think about whether to be friends with Taylor or not. Nana always said it was good to sleep on things, which means if you think about the thing you're worried about when you go to sleep, then you'll dream about it and hopefully wake up with the right answer in your head. I tend to forget my dreams as soon as I've woken up—they've never shown me the answer to anything.

# Then

I get home early, hoping to talk to Paul, but he isn't here. I expect he's gone for a walk. He does that a lot, says it helps with the writing when the words won't come. The words often don't come lately and I think his world must get awfully quiet. The house is quiet too and I'm not sure what to do. I open the fridge and stare at its contents for far longer than is necessary; there's barely anything inside. I grab a cold soft drink and sit down at the kitchen table, facing out at the garden. The cloudless sky is bright blue, the grass is green, only the leafless trees and chill in the air give away the fact that this isn't a summer's day. It's a very different scene from the one I stared at last week, home alone one night while Paul was on one of his research trips, convinced that somebody was out there in the darkness, trying to get in. I swear I heard footsteps and the sound of someone attempting to open the back door. Paul thinks I dreamt it. I shake the thought.

The can makes a *psst* noise when I open it with my fingernail, as though it wants to tell me a secret. I take a sip. It's so cold it hurts my teeth, but I enjoy the tingling sensation and drink it down. I look back out at the garden and see a robin perched on a fencepost. I stare at him while he appears to stare back. It all happens so fast. A mess of feathers in full flight hurtle straight at me with such speed and determination until the glass doors get in the way. The thud of the impact makes me jump and I accidently knock my drink over. The robin's tiny body falls backwards, almost in slow motion, and lands on the grass. I rush to the patio doors but don't open them. Instead I stand and stare at the tiny bird lying on its back, flapping its wings in mock flight, its eyes already closed. I'm not sure how long we are frozen like that, the creature fighting for breath as I involuntarily hold my own, but time eventually catches up with what has happened.

The robin stops moving; its wings lay down by its side.

Its red chest sinks until it is still.

Two tiny legs lower themselves down onto the damp grass.

I feel somehow responsible but I can't open the door or go outside. I need the safety of the glass barrier between us for now. I crouch down on my knees, lowering my face to get a better look, as though I might see the life leave the bird's body through its beak. I remember a friend telling me once that robins were the dead revisiting you with a message. I wonder what kind of message this is supposed to be, and notice the hairs on my arms standing on end.

The knock on the glass startles me. I look up to see Claire's face at the window. She doesn't notice the bird, even though she is only a few steps away from it. I stand to open the door and she steps inside without waiting to be invited, as though she owns the place. She helped us find this house, spotted it online and arranged an early viewing with the estate agent. I went along with it, it's a nice house, but choosing something and owning it are not the same thing.

"What are you doing?" she asks, taking off her coat. She's perfectly groomed as usual, her clothes crisp and clean despite having two young children, not a hair out of place. I hate the way she always comes round the back of the house to see if I'm at home. Anyone else would ring the doorbell at the front and take a hint if nobody answered, but not Claire. She's asked for a key a few times now. I always say I'll get one cut but never do.

"Nothing, I thought I saw something."

"You're home early."

"It's a bit quieter than normal because of Christmas."

"Paul not here?" she asks, putting her jacket on the back of a kitchen chair, making herself at home.

"Doesn't look like it." I regret my choice of words as soon as they are spoken. My tone doesn't go unnoticed, it never does.

"Well, I'm glad I caught you on your own," she says. I nod. I do feel caught.

"Do you want a drink of something?"

"No, I'm okay, can't stay long, have to pick up the twins," she says, sitting down at the table. I take a paper towel and mop up the spilt drink before sitting down opposite her, my seat still warm from before. I can't help staring over her shoulder at the dead bird just outside the door.

"So?" I ask, without meaning to sound abrupt. My exchanges with Claire aren't the same as the conversations I have with other people. It's like when you turn on the radio and they're playing the song that you were already humming inside your head. You can't possibly have known what was coming, but somehow you did. That's what it's like with Claire.

"So . . . I'm worried about you. I thought maybe we should talk," she says.

"I'm fine."

"Are you? You don't look fine. You've been ignoring my calls."

"I've been busy. I have a full-time job." I study her face for a moment, stalling for time as my mouth rejects each form of words my mind suggests. She looks so much younger than I do, as though her face has forgotten to age over the last few years. "I'm just tired, that's all." I wish I could tell her the truth, share the sort of secrets that normal sisters share, but I wouldn't know where to begin. We have everything and nothing in common and our mother tongue doesn't contain that kind of vocabulary.

"Do you remember the boy I dated in my last year at university?" I ask. She shakes her head. She's lying and I already regret bringing it up.

"What was his name?"

"Edward. You didn't like him. Not that that will jog your memory, you never liked any of them."

"I liked Paul," she says. I ignore the past tense.

"I bumped into him on Oxford Street yesterday, one of those crazy coincidences, I suppose."

"I think I do remember. Tall, quite good-looking, very sure of himself."

"I don't think you ever met him."

"Is there a point to this story? You're not going to have an affair, are you?"

"No, I'm not going to have an affair. I was just making conversation."

I stare at the table for a while, wishing she would just leave, but she doesn't.

"How are things with Paul?"

"You tell me, you've spent more time with him than I have lately." I'm surprised at my choice of words, which are far braver than I'm feeling. We're sailing into unfamiliar territory here. I'm aware that I've started speaking in a language she doesn't understand and for the first time we might need an interpreter. She stands to go, removing her coat from the back of the chair. I don't try to stop her.

"I've obviously caught you at a bad time, I'll leave you to it." She opens the back door before turning back. "Remember I'm only around the corner," she adds before leaving.

Her final words feel like more of a threat than a comfort. I listen as she walks down the side of the house, the sound of crunching gravel getting fainter until I hear the gate slam shut.

My thoughts return to the robin. For a moment I believe it must have come back to life and flown away, but as I get closer to the glass, my eyes find its brown body lying motionless on a carpet of green. I can't leave it there, broken and alone. I open the back door and wait a second or two before stepping outside, cautious not to disturb the disturbing. It takes me a while to summon enough courage to reach down and pick up the bird. It's lighter than I imagined, as though it is made of nothing but feathers and air. The thud as its tiny corpse lands at the bottom of the bin echoes the sound of it hitting the glass and I can't shake the feeling of guilt that's come over me. I step back inside and wash my hands, soaping and scrubbing my skin beneath the scalding water three times. When I have dried them, I turn the tap back on and do it all again and again until there is no soap left. I push my hands, still wet this time, into my pockets, and try to stop thinking about them. I feel strange about dispensing with a life as though it is rubbish. There one minute, gone the next, all because of one wrong decision, one wrong turn.

# Now

It's becoming harder to separate the dreams from my reality and I'm scared of both. Even when I do remember where, I don't know when I am anymore. Morning has broken and there's no afternoon or evening anymore either. I have escaped time and I wish it would find me again. It has a smell of its own, time. Like a familiar room. When it's no longer your own you crave it, you salivate and you hunger for it, you realize you'd do anything to have it back. Until it is yours again, you steal stolen seconds and gobble up misused minutes, sticking them all together to make a delicate chain of borrowed time, hoping it will stretch. Hoping it will be long enough to reach the next page. If there is a next page.

I can smell my lost time. And something else. I have been alone for a while now. Paul has not returned and nobody has been in my room since I started counting the seconds. I stopped at seven thousand, which means I have been lying in my own shit for over two hours.

The voices come frequently, to wake me from my dream within a dream. They're starting to sound familiar to me. The same nurses come into my room, check I'm still breathing and sleeping, then leave me alone again with my thoughts and fears. I'm not being fair; they do more than that. They turn me, I'm not sure why. I'm on my left side at the moment, which is how I liked to sleep when I had a choice in the matter. Having choices is something I used to do. Most of the shit is on the inside of my left thigh. I can feel and smell it. With my mouth forced open I can almost taste it and the thought makes me want to gag, but that's just another thing I can't do. The tube down my throat has become a part of me I barely notice anymore. I picture myself as a newly invented monster on *Doctor Who*. Part woman, part machine; skin and bones entwined with tubes and wires. I want them to clean me before Paul comes back. *If* he's coming back. The door opens and I think it is him, but the smell of white musk informs me it isn't.

"Morning, Amber, how are we feeling today?"

*Let's see, I feel like shit, I'm covered in shit, I stink of shit.*

Why do these people keep talking to me? They know I can't answer and they don't really believe I can hear them.

"Oh dear, don't you worry, we'll soon get you all cleaned up."

*Thank you.*

Two of them clean me. They've never introduced themselves, so I don't know their real names, but I've made up my own. "Northern Nurse" sounds as though she is from Yorkshire. She has a tendency to mutter quietly to herself while she works and even then her vowels sound large in my ears. Her hands feel rough and rush to do their work. She scrubs my skin as though I am a dirty pan with stubborn stains and she sounds perpetually tired. Today she is accompanied by "Forty-a-Day Nurse"—the clue is in the name. Her voice is hoarse and low and she sounds permanently cross with the world. When she stands close to me, I can smell the nicotine on her fingers, taste it on her breath, hear it in her lungs. I listen to the sound of their plastic aprons while they clean me, the slosh of water in a bowl, the smell of soap, the feel of gloved hands on my skin.

When they are done, they turn me on my right side. I don't like being on my right side, it feels unnatural. One of them brushes my hair. She holds it at the root, so the brush doesn't pull. She's trying not to hurt me any more than I already am. It reminds me of my grandmother brushing my hair when I was a little girl. Northern Nurse cleans the inside of my mouth with what feels like a small sponge, then she rubs some Vaseline on my lips, which feel dry and sore. The smell tricks my brain into thinking I can taste it. Sometimes she tells me what she is doing, sometimes she forgets. What I really want is some water, but she doesn't give me any of that. I don't know how long it has been now, but I'm already settling into my new routine. Funny how quickly we adapt. A flash of memory ignites and I think of my grandmother when she was dying. I wonder if she was thirsty. *The wheels on the bus go round and round.*

It is later, I don't know how much, when he arrives. His voice crashes through the wall I have built around myself.

"They let me go for now, but I know they think I hurt you, Amber. You have to wake up," he says.

I wonder why he didn't say hello before he started making demands of me. But then I realize I didn't hear him come in. He could have been here awhile, he could have said more, perhaps I just wasn't listening. His voice sounds as though he is doing a bad imitation of himself. I can't quite interpret his tone, which seems wrong, given that I'm his wife. Surely I should know the difference between angry and scared. Perhaps that's the point, perhaps they are the same.

I remember him leaving with the police. He doesn't talk about that, no matter how much I wish that he would. Instead, he reads me the newspaper, says the doctor thought it might help. All the stories are sad and I wonder whether he skipped the happy ones or whether there just aren't any happy stories anymore. He stops talking altogether then, and I resent the words he doesn't speak. I want him to tell me everything that has happened to him while we've been apart. I need to know. Time is marching on without me since it left me behind and I can't catch up. I hear Paul stand and I try to fill in the gaps myself. The police can't have arrested him, because he's back here, but something is wrong. He's still in the room but he's been stripped of sound. I picture him staring at me and I feel self-conscious about how I must look to him now. All I ever seem to do is disappoint him.

I start to drift when there is nothing to hold on to. The voices in my head are louder than the silence in the room. The loudest is my own, reminding me constantly of all the things I have said and done, all the things I haven't, all the things I should have. I can feel it coming. There are always ripples in the water before a big wave. I've learned already to just let it take me; far easier to surrender and let it wash me up when it's good and ready. I fear one day the dark water will swallow me down for good, and I won't always be able to resurface. Switches are either on or off. People are either up or down. When I'm down, it's so very hard to get back up and this is the farthest I've ever fallen. Even if I could remember my way back to normal, I don't think I'd recognize myself when I got there.

"I wish I knew whether you could hear me," says Paul.

I feel dizzy and as I try to tune in to his words, they crackle and distort. His tone twists into something aggressive-shaped and I hear the legs of his chair screech across the floor as he stands, like a warning. He leans over me, his face so close, examining my own, as though he thinks I'm pretending.

And then I feel large hands close around my throat.

The sensation lasts less than a second and I know instantly that what I felt wasn't real, it can't have been. A dark flash of a memory I'd rather forget perhaps, but even that doesn't make sense, Paul wouldn't do that. I try to make sense of what I just felt but I can't remember what is real anymore. Paul paces back and forth and I wish he'd be still. The effort required to listen to him walking around the room is exhausting. I don't want to be afraid of my husband, but he's not himself and I don't know this version.

Claire arrives and a brief sensation of relief is obliterated by a wave of confusion. I expect them to argue again, but they don't. I think he will leave now, but he doesn't.

*And when she was up, she was up.*

There has been a shift of gear between them.

*And when she was down, she was down.*

It sounds like they hug each other. I stop myself from hoping that she'll ask what happened at the police station. It's obvious from their conversation that she already knows.

*And when she was only halfway up,*

The plot thickens and continues on without me beyond this room.

*She was neither up nor down.*

I feel jealous of what Claire knows. I feel jealous of everything.

When Mum and Dad first brought Claire home, all she did was cry. She needed so much of their attention and behaved in a way that demanded our lives orbit hers. Mum and Dad didn't hear the tears *I* cried at night; they didn't see *me* at all after that. I became the invisible daughter. Her screams in the night would wake us all, but it was Mum who got up to be with her. It was Mum who wanted Claire in the first place. I wasn't enough for her, that's clear to me now. Our family went from three to four, even though we couldn't really afford it; there wasn't enough love to go around.

# Then

I've been shopping. Food shopping this time. I unpack the frozen items first, then chilled, then the rest, rearranging things as I go, so that everything is where it should be. The larder requires the most work. I take everything out, every tin, jar, and bottle. I wipe down all the shelves and start again, carefully arranging each item according to size, labels facing front. It's completely dark by the time I'm finished. I can see the light is on in the shed at the top of the garden, which means Paul is still up there writing. Maybe he has turned a corner. I pop a bottle of cava in the fridge—it was a small victory at work today, but one worth celebrating. Project Madeline is most definitely off to a good start. I notice the half-empty white wine bottle in the fridge door. I don't remember seeing it there before. I don't drink white wine and neither does Paul. Perhaps he used it for a recipe. I remove the offending bottle, pour myself a glass, and start cooking. It tastes like cat piss, but I'm thirsty so I drink it anyway.

When the dinner is almost ready, I set places at the dining room table we never sit at, put on some music, and light a couple of candles. The only thing missing now is my husband. He doesn't like to be disturbed when he's writing, but it's gone past eight and I want to spend what's left of the evening together. He won't mind once he knows we're having lamb; it's his favorite. I head out into the garden, the cold slapping my cheeks. The lawn is a bit slippery in places and it's hard to see where I'm going, the dim light from the shed struggling to light my way.

"Good evening, resident writer," I say in a silly deep voice as I open the door. My smile soon fades when I realize the shed is empty. I stand there for a while, looking around as though Paul might be hiding, then I glance back outside, peering around the garden in the darkness as though he might jump out from behind a bush and yell *Boo!*

"Paul?" I don't know why I'm calling his name when my eyes have already informed me that he is clearly not here. I feel panic rise up my chest and tighten around my throat. He isn't in the house either. I've been home for a couple of hours now, I would have seen or heard him. My husband who is always here has gone and I'm so consumed by myself, I didn't even notice he was missing. I must not overreact. I've always had an overactive imagination and a tendency to fear the worst in any given situation. I'm sure there will be a simple explanation for Paul not being here, but the voices in my head are less optimistic. I run back to the house, slipping and sliding on the muddy grass.

Back inside, I call Paul's name again. Nothing. I call his mobile. I hear a faint ringing sound from upstairs. Relief floods through me as I realize it is coming from our bedroom. Maybe he's having a nap, perhaps he wasn't feeling well. I run up the stairs and push open the bedroom door, smiling at my own ridiculous panic. The bed has been made and he isn't in it. He never makes the bed. Confused for a moment, I dial his number again. The familiar ringtone begins. I'm in the right room, but the sound is coming from the closed wardrobe. My hand trembles slightly as I reach for the handle. I tell myself I'm just being silly, I'm sure there is a perfectly normal explanation for all of this; Paul isn't in the wardrobe, we're not children playing hide-and-seek, and this isn't some horror film where there's a body in the cupboard. I twist the handle and open the door to his wardrobe. Nothing. I dial his number again and see the glow of the phone through the pocket of his favorite jacket. The mystery of the missing phone is solved, but not the missing husband. I spot an expensive-looking pink gift bag, partially hidden beneath the row of jeans and cotton tops that Paul calls his "writing uniform." I pull it out and stare inside, carefully unwrapping the tissue paper hiding its contents. The black satin and lace feel foreign on my fingertips, the sort of thing I used to wear. A Christmas present for me perhaps. Not the sort of thing he normally buys. The bra looks a bit small and I check the label. It's the wrong size; I hope he's kept the receipt.

I come back downstairs in a daze and make sure the oven is off. In the middle of my routine, the now-empty bottle of white wine catches my eye and produces a moment of recognition. It's one of Claire's favorites. She's been here. I put my hand over my mouth, run to the kitchen sink, and throw up. When nothing more will come, I spit, turn on the tap, and wipe my face with a tea towel. I check the oven three times, then grab my bag, quickly checking the contents. Phone. Wallet. Keys. I say each one out loud when my eyes confirm their presence, as though things are only real when we speak them. I start to leave and stop in the hallway, opening the bag again. Phone. Wallet. Keys. I say the words more slowly, my eyes resting on each item long enough for me to believe what I'm seeing. I check one last time before closing the door behind me.

Claire lives just under a mile away. It's not too far to walk, but I should have worn a coat, it's freezing. I hug my arms around myself as I march along, staring at the pavement. I get a faint whiff of gas as I pass a row of houses that all look the same. It snakes up my nostrils, then down inside my throat, making me feel nauseous so that I walk a little quicker. Claire has lived on this road for a long time. They own the house now, as well as the garage next door where David works. The street is so familiar to me that I could walk from here to her front door with my eyes closed. But I don't. My eyes are open and the first thing I see is Paul's car. It's quite distinctive. A secondhand green 1978 MG Midget, lovingly restored to its alleged former glory. He bought it with the advance for his first novel and he loves it almost as much as I hate it.

I march up the drive with a tightness in my chest, feeling like I might have stopped breathing altogether. I have a spare key for Claire's house in my handbag but feel uncomfortable just letting myself in. She gave it to me hoping it would prompt an exchange. It didn't.

I ring the bell repeatedly, wanting to get this, whatever it is, over and done with as soon as possible. The cold hurts my hands and I can see my breath. Inside, I hear a child start to cry and I see the blurry image of an adult getting bigger through the frosted glass. Claire's husband yanks the front door open and greets me with the kind of expression I reserve for door-to-door salesmen. I'm not sure why we don't get along. It isn't that we don't have anything in common; we have Claire. So maybe it's the opposite.

"Hello, Amber. Thanks for waking the twins," he says, without even the hint of a smile. He doesn't invite me in. My brother-in-law is a big man with small amounts of time and patience. He's still wearing his overalls.

"I'm so sorry, David, I wasn't thinking. This might sound a bit strange, but is Paul here?"

"No," he says. "Should he be?" He looks tired, dark circles under his eyes. Being married to my sister has aged him. She calls him David so we do too, but everyone else calls him Dave.

"His car is here," I say. David peers past me at the car on the garage forecourt.

"Yes, it is." When I don't say anything in response his frown deepens, as though it might break his face. He looks down at my feet and I follow his stare. I'm still wearing my slippers. Two grubby felt faces of pugs look up at me. Their stitched eyes seem full of equal amounts of wonder and pity. They were in the kids' section at the supermarket, but they fit and I liked them.

"Are you all right?" he asks. I think about his question and give him the most honest answer I can come up with.

"No, not really. I don't think I am. I need to talk to Claire, is she home?" He stands up a bit straighter and looks confused, then something ugly spreads across his features.

"Claire hasn't been here all day. I thought she was with you."

# Before

Dear Diary,

I've been ten for a whole month now and I'm not sure double figures feels any different really, even though Mum said it would. There's still loads of stuff I'm not allowed to do, I'm still quite short, and I still miss Nana every day. I'm so angry with Mum for lots of reasons, but especially because of what she did at parents' evening tonight. She went on her own because Dad had to work late. Mum said he might sleep there again, he's been working really hard lately. Because she didn't have Dad to talk to, she got chatting to some of the other parents at school. When she got home, she was all excited, not because of my brilliant grades like a normal human being, but because she'd met Taylor's mum and was so pleased to find out I'd made *such a good friend.* She went on and on about it, asking why I hadn't mentioned Taylor. I said I didn't want to talk about it and we sat in silence for a while.

Once Mum understood that I was in a not-talking mood, she got up from the table and made herself a mojito. I don't know what's in it, but she calls it her happy drink. She made me a lemonade with lots of ice and a bit of mint on top so that my drink looked like hers. I took the mint out when she wasn't looking. Then she got some chicken in breadcrumbs and crinkle-cut chips out of the freezer, which is my absolute favorite dinner that she makes. She got the ketchup from the cupboard and turned it upside down, then set just two places, using Nana's best plates. Because Dad wasn't there, she carried the little TV into the kitchen from his study and we watched *Coronation Street* while we ate, rather than having to try and think of things to say to each other. We were sort of having a nice time but then, just after her third Mojito (I was only counting how many in case it's the Mojitos that are making her fat), she ruined everything.

"So I've got a surprise for you, because you're doing so well at your new school," she said. Her eyes were a little bit closed, the way they are when she drinks, so that she looks really sleepy even if it's the middle of the day. I asked if it was dessert and she said no and looked all serious, asking if I had forgotten what the dentist had said about my teeth and sugar. I hadn't forgotten, but I didn't really care. Nana always made something for dessert and not from a packet, she actually made things. Chocolate cake, Victoria sponge, sticky toffee pudding, apple crumble with custard, they all tasted amazing. Now that I think about it, Nana didn't have any teeth left at all, she had fake ones that she kept in a glass by the bed when she slept. I'd still rather eat cake, even if my teeth do fall out like Nana's. Mum asked if I was listening, which she does when I'm thinking so hard about something that I don't hear what she says anymore. I nodded, but didn't reply out loud as I was still a bit cross that we weren't having afters of any description. Then she smiled, with her eyes still half closed.

"I asked Taylor's mum if Taylor could come here to play one night next week. And she said yes. Won't that be nice?" She finished her drink and put the glass back down on the table, then looked at me with a big, stupid smile on her fat face. "We'll do it on a night when your dad is at work, so it'll be just us girls. It'll be fun, you'll see!" I was so mad, I couldn't think of anything at all to say to her. I stood up from the table, without being excused, then ran up the stairs to my room, picked up the doorstop, and closed the door. I even left some of my crinkle-cut chips. I thought I was going to cry, but nothing happened.

Taylor cannot come here. I haven't decided whether we should even be proper friends yet. I'm so angry with Mum. There are so many things I hate about her but these are the three biggest reasons I can think of at the moment:

1. She drinks too much.
2. She lies all the time, like when she says we won't have to move again.
3. She wishes I was like the other kids.

I'm not like the other kids. Mum has ruined everything. Again.

# Now

*Wednesday, December 28, 2016*

My parents have finally arrived at the hospital. I hear their voices long before they enter the room. They've endured a rare breed of marriage, the kind where the love lasts over thirty years. But it's the kind of love that makes me feel sad and empty, a love based on habit and dependence; it isn't real. The door opens and I smell my mother's perfume— too floral, too strong. I hear my father clear his throat in that annoying way that he does. They stand at the end of my bed, keeping their distance as always.

"She looks bad," says Dad.

"It probably looks worse than it is," Mum replies.

It's been almost a year since we last spoke and there is absolutely no affection in their voices.

"I don't think she can hear us," she says.

"We should stay awhile, just in case," says Dad, sitting down next to the bed, and I love him for that. "You'll be all right, Peanut," he says, holding my hand. I imagine a tear rolling down his cheek, then down to his chin where it hangs in my imagination before dripping down onto the white hospital sheet. I've never seen my father cry. The feel of his fingers wrapped around my own triggers a memory of us walking hand in hand when I was five or six. Claire had yet to enter our world back then. We were going to the bank, and he was in a hurry. He was often in a hurry. His long legs took giant steps and I ran to keep up with his walk. Just before we reached the bank, I tripped and fell. There was a bloody gash on my knee and thin ribbons of blood danced their way down my leg, then joined forces to stain my white sock red.

It hurt but I didn't cry. He looked sorry but he didn't kiss it better and I can still hear his voice.

*You'll be all right, Peanut.*

Without any further words, we hurried to the bank a little more slowly.

They took much better care of Claire when she arrived. She was like a shiny new precious doll—I was already broken and scratched. My dad's nickname for me was Peanut. His nickname for Claire was Princess. I don't hate my parents, I just hate that they stopped loving me.

The air in the room is thick with silence and remorse, then the door opens again and everything changes.

"How are you?" asks my sister. I hear Paul answer and realize he's been in the room with us the whole time. It's even more awkward than I thought. Paul and my parents never did get along. Dad thinks writing isn't a real job and that a man without one of those isn't a real man. "Any update?" asks Claire.

"They said she's stable now, but it's still too soon to know what will happen," he says.

"We just need to stay positive," she says.

*Easy words for her to say.*

There are so many questions I want to ask. If I'm stable, I presume that means I'm not going to die. Not yet anyway; we all die in the end, I suppose. Life is more terrifying than death in my experience. There's little point fearing something so inevitable. Since I've been lying here, what I fear the most is never fully waking up, the horror of being trapped inside myself forever. I try to quiet my mind and focus on their voices. Sometimes the words reach me, sometimes they get lost on the way or I can't quite translate them into something that makes sense.

It's been such a long time since my family was all together like this so it seems strange that we are reunited around my hospital bed. We used to spend every Christmas together, but then that stopped. I'm the centerpiece of this family gathering but I'm still invisible. Nobody is holding my hand now. Nobody is crying. Nobody is behaving as they should and it's as though I'm not here at all.

"You look really tired," says Claire, the caring daughter. "Maybe we should go and get some food?" Nobody speaks and then my father's voice breaks the spell.

"Hold on, that's all you have to do."

Why does everyone insist on telling me to hold on? Hold on to what? I don't need to hold on, I need to wake up.

Paul kisses me on the forehead. I don't think he'll go with them, but then I hear him walk to the door and follow them out of the room. I don't know why I am surprised about being abandoned, I always have been. Claire takes everyone I love away from me.

I hear rain start to fall hard against the invisible window in my imaginary room. The watery lullaby helps distract my mind from my anger, but it's not enough to silence it.

*I won't let her take anyone else away from me.*

A silent rage spreads like a virus in my mind. The voice inside my head, which sounds so much like my own, is loud and clear and commanding.

*I need to get out of this bed. I have to wake up.*

And then I do.

I can still hear the sound of the machines that breathe for me, feed me, and drug me so that I cannot feel what I must not, but the wires are gone and the tube has been removed from my throat. I open my eyes and sit up. I have to tell somebody. I get out of the bed and run to the door, fling it open and rush through, but I fall and land hard on the ground. That's when I notice how cold I am, that's when I feel the rain. I'm scared to open my eyes and when I do, I see her, the faceless little girl in the pink dressing gown, lying in the middle of the road with me. I can't move my body and everything is still, like I'm looking at a painting.

I can see the crashed car and the damaged tree. Its thick roots come to life and snake over toward me and the child. They wrap themselves around our arms and legs and bodies and squeeze us together, pinning us to the tarmac where I fell until we are almost completely covered and hidden from the rest of the world. I sense that the child is frightened, so I tell her to be brave and suggest that maybe we should sing a song. She doesn't want to. Not yet. The rain starts to fall harder, and the painting I'm trapped inside starts to smudge and blur. It feels like the rain is trying to wash us away, as though we never were. The water falls so hard that it bounces off the tarmac into my mouth and up my nose. I feel myself start to drown in the dirty watercolor, then, just as quickly as it started, it stops.

*Stars cannot shine without darkness,* whispers the little girl.

My body is still being held in place by the roots of the tree, but I turn my head up to see the night sky. As I stare up at the stars, they become brighter and larger and more real than I have ever seen them. Then the little girl starts to sing.

*Twinkle twinkle little star, if you're down here who's in the car?*

The roots release me, an army of goose bumps line my arms, and I look over to where the child is now pointing. Sure enough, there is a shadow of someone inside the car. The driver door opens and a black figure gets out and walks away. Everything is silent. Everything is still.

The sound of a lock turning brings me back to my sleeping body in my hospital cell. Everything I could see and feel disappears. The nightmare is over, but I'm still afraid. There was someone else in the car that night, I'm sure of it. And now there is someone in my room and everything feels very wrong.

"Can you hear me?" It's a man. I don't recognize his voice. Fear floods through me as he walks toward the bed.

"I said, can you hear me?" he repeats. He's right next to me when he asks the same question a third time. He sighs and takes a step back. He opens something next to my bed and then I hear the sound of a phone being turned on. My phone. I hear the security code that I never change. Whoever this person is, he's listening to my voicemail. There are three messages, faint but audible. The first voice I hear is Claire's. She says she is just calling to see if everything is okay—her tone suggests that she already knew that it wasn't. It's followed by an angry message from Paul; he wants to know where I am. Then the stranger in my room plays the third message and it's his own voice on my phone.

*I'm sorry about what happened. It's only because I love you.*

It feels like my whole body ices over. I hear a beep.

*Message deleted. You have no new messages.*

I don't know this man. But he knows me. I'm so frightened that even if I was able to scream, I don't think that I could.

"I do hope you're not lying there feeling sorry for yourself, Amber," he says. He touches my face and I want to shrink back down into the pillow. He taps me on the head repeatedly with his finger. "In case you're confused in there by anything you've heard, this wasn't an accident." His finger slides down the side of my face and rests on my lips. "You did this to yourself."

# Then

I turn off the alarm. I won't need it. I've hardly slept at all and it's pointless trying now. The insomnia should be a symptom of my concern for my missing husband, but that isn't what I've been lying awake thinking about. I keep remembering the dead robin, its tiny lifeless body. All night long I kept imagining that I could hear its wings flapping inside the bin as though it wasn't dead. I worry that perhaps it was just unconscious, that maybe I threw it away when it was only sleeping.

I stare at the vacant side of the bed. Still no news from Paul. There's an empty red wine bottle on the floor; I tried to drink myself to sleep but it didn't work. Wine has become an overprescribed antibiotic that my body has become immune to. I consider calling the police to report Paul missing, but I feel foolish. I wouldn't know how to say what I'm afraid of without sounding crazy. Husbands don't always come home at night, I know that, I'm a big girl now.

My mind switches from Paul to Claire. When she finally returned my calls she sounded annoyed that I had accused her of knowing where he was. She said she'd been out with a friend and I had ruined her evening, then she hung up. She knows exactly what I'm scared of. I love them both but I can feel everything I've kept safe until now starting to unravel. One pull on the thread and they'll fall through an unfixable hole. It might be too late already.

It's still dark, so I switch on the light, scanning the room for anything that might resemble a clue. I remember the gift bag hiding women's underwear in the bottom of Paul's wardrobe. I retrieve it once more and take out the bra and knickers, flimsy panels of black satin, framed by lace. Definitely too small. I pull down my pajama bottoms and use my feet to step out of them, whilst pulling my top off over my head. I leave the pastel-colored pile of cotton on the floor and slip into the underwear, tags still attached, the sharp-angled cardboard edges digging into my skin. I squeeze my breasts into the too-small cups, then come to stand in front of the full-length mirror. It's been a while since I've seen myself like this. The body in the reflection isn't as bad as I had imagined. I'm not as ugly on the outside as I feel on the inside, but I still don't like what I see. My tummy is a little rounder than it used to be, but then I mostly eat what I want now. I hate this body almost as much as I hate myself. It didn't do what it was supposed to. It didn't give him what he wanted. I don't want to look anymore so I turn off the light, but I can still see the ghost of my reflection. I grab my dressing gown and hide myself again, the new underwear pinching and biting my flesh beneath. The thought that it might not have been bought for me is too loud inside my head to be ignored, so I take it off, put it back where I found it, and start the day again.

It's still dark but I know this house, I can find my way in the darkness. The shed is Paul's private place, but the tiny study at the back of the house is mine. A room of my own with just enough space for a small desk and a chair. I sit myself down and turn on the lamp. The desk was secondhand, so contains secrets that I don't know as well as secrets I do. There are four small drawers and one large one, which looks like a knowing wooden smile. I ease it open and slip on the white cotton gloves that I find inside. Then I take a sheet of paper along with my fountain pen and I write. When I am finished, when I am certain that I have written the right words and sure that I want them to be read, I fold the paper twice and slip it inside a red envelope. Then I shower, wash away any traces of guilt or concern, and get myself ready for work.

I'm earlier than usual. The main office is empty, but I can see the light is already on in Madeline's office. I take off my coat, dump my handbag on the desk, and try to shake off the fog of tiredness that has enveloped me. I need to stay alert, keep focused on the task ahead. Before I can sit down, I hear her door creak open.

"Amber, is that you? Can I have a word?" I roll my eyes, secure in the knowledge that nobody can see me. I don't need this right now, but I rearrange my face and head over to the little office in the corner, my hands screwed up into defensive fists inside my pockets.

I perform a halfhearted knock on the slightly ajar door, before pushing it fully open. There she is, dressed in black, as always. Hunched over the desk, her face scrunched up and too close to the screen so that she can read what's on it. The rumor mill is still in full flow on Twitter, churning out further speculation of her impending departure. I wonder if she's reading the new #MadelineFrost comments; there are plenty of them.

"Just a moment, I'm right in the middle of a thought." She always does this. Hers is the only time she values and she wants me to know it. She types something that I cannot see.

"I'm glad you're here early," she says. "I was hoping we could have a little chat before the others arrive."

I try not to react, willing every facial muscle I have to stay exactly where it is. She lifts her glasses off her face and lets them dangle from the pink beaded cord that hangs around her sturdy neck. I imagine tightening it and then shake the image from my mind.

"Why don't you take a seat?" says Madeline, indicating the purple leather pouf she brought back from Morocco a few months ago.

"I'm okay, thank you," I reply.

"Sit down," she says, two neat rows of veneers reinforcing the request. I make my face smile back and do what I'm told. This is what the producers have to do every morning: come into this pokey little room and sit on the pouf, waiting for Madeline to grill them about each story on that day's show. I squat down and try to balance myself. It's too low and not at all comfortable. As always, it's all about control and it's already clear I have none.

"Did you know about the meeting Matthew was having with the guests yesterday?" she asks.

"Yes," I say, holding her stare. She nods, then looks me up and down as though appraising my choice of outfit. It's another new dress but she's clearly not impressed. "I want you to do me a favor," she says eventually. "If you hear anything that you think I might want to know,

I want you to tell me." I'm starting to think she has forgotten that she's trying to have me fired, or perhaps she thinks I don't know.

"Of course," I say. I wouldn't tell her if there was a poisonous snake wrapped around her neck.

"We have to stick together, Amber. If they get rid of me, they'll bring in a whole new cast, they always do. They'll replace you too, don't think that they won't. Remember that and next time you hear something you'll come and tell me, won't you?" With that, she puts her glasses back up onto her nose and starts tapping away on the keyboard once more, to signal that the meeting is over.

I struggle to stand from the pouf, then leave her office and close the door behind me.

"Are you okay?" whispers Jo, who has just arrived. I sit back down at my desk.

"Yes, fine," I say, knowing Madeline will be watching through the window in her door.

"You don't look fine," says Jo.

"I don't know where Paul is. He didn't come home last night." As soon as I say the words, I regret them.

"Is it Claire again?" she asks. The words slap me in the face and my fear turns to anger, but there is a look of genuine concern spread across Jo's features. It isn't her fault that she knows so much about my past. I'm the one who told her.

I don't know the answer, so I give the one I want to be true.

"I don't think so."

"Maybe we should go get a coffee?"

"No thanks, I'm fine." I look away, turn on my PC, and stare at the screen.

"Suit yourself," she says, and leaves without another word.

When she's gone, I open up my e-mails. My inbox is overcrowded with obligation and invitations. It's mostly junk, discounts for things I neither want or need, but there is one message that catches my eye. My mouse hovers over the familiar name and my eyes fix themselves on the one word in the subject line, as though it is difficult to translate.

*Hello.*

I start to pick the skin off my lip with my fingernails. I should delete the e-mail, I know that's what I should do. I casually glance around the office. I'm still alone. I pick another bit of skin off my upper lip and put it on my desk. It's stained purple from last night's wine. I remember taking the business card out of my purse when I couldn't sleep last night, running my thumb over the embossed lettering. I remember typing his name into an e-mail on my phone, dithering over the subject line, composing the casual note, worrying it might look odd to send it so late at night, sending it anyway. My cheeks flush with shame, unable to remember now exactly what I said.

I open the e-mail and read it, then I read it again, more slowly this time, carefully interpreting each individual word.

*For old times' sake.*

I try on the words as I'm reading, to see if they fit. I can still picture their author if I close my eyes.

*Happy memories.*

They weren't all happy.

*A drink to catch up?*

I pull another piece of skin off my lip and examine the tiny strip of myself as it dries and hardens on my fingertip. I put it in the small pile with the others.

Catch up. Catch. Caught.

Paul is missing. My marriage is hanging by a thread. What am I doing? The thought is stillborn.

"Hello, earth to Amber?" says Jo, waving her hands in front of my face. I close down the e-mail window, brush the tiny pile of skin off my desk, and feel my cheeks redden.

"Have you been playing Space Invaders?" I blurt out.

"What? No. Why?" She smiles.

"Because you're invading my space." Her smile vanishes.

"Sorry. I heard someone say that once, thought it was funny. I didn't mean to snap at you, I was in a complete world of my own."

"I noticed. Try not to worry, I'm sure he's fine."

"Who?" I ask, wondering if she saw the e-mail from Edward.

"Paul? Your husband?" she says, frowning.

"Right. Yes, sorry. I'm a bit all over the place today."

Madeline's voice booms from her office, silencing us as she summons her PA. She looms over her in the doorway and hands over her credit card and a list of instructions. She wants some dry cleaning picked up, tells her the PIN and everything else she needs to know. The way she speaks to people makes me so angry.

I think about Edward's e-mail as we talk through the morning briefings. I think about it in the studio, during interviews, and throughout the phone-in. I barely hear anything anyone says all morning. I should feel guilty, but I don't. Paul hasn't touched me for months and I haven't done anything wrong. We're just being friendly, that's all. It's just a memory of another time and place. Memories can't hurt anyone, unless they are shared.

# Before

Dear Diary,

Taylor came to the house yesterday. I was dreading it. Dad had to work late again, so I only had to worry about Mum being embarrassing. She picked us up from school in our battered blue Ford Escort, which is basically a tin can on wheels. Taylor's family has a Volvo *and* a Renault 5. Mum made sure we were both wearing seat belts, she doesn't normally care, and then she gave us a carton of Ribena each to drink on the way home. She doesn't normally do that either. It only takes five minutes to drive home from school, so it's not as if we were going to die of thirst. I thought the car wasn't going to start, but on the third attempt, the engine coughed enough times to get going and Mum made a joke of it like she always does. *So* embarrassing.

We didn't really talk much in the car. Mum kept looking at me in the rearview mirror and asking Taylor and I stupid questions like, "How was your day?" in a silly singsong voice. I said what I always say when she asks that question, *fine*, but Taylor went into way more detail and told her about the portraits we are working on in art. That annoyed me because I'm painting a picture of Nana and I wanted it to be a surprise.

When we got home, I watched Taylor's face to see her reaction. The first thing you notice about Nana's house is the paint. Nana really liked the color blue. There's a blue front door, windows, and garage, and they all peel, like my nose when it's burnt. Sometimes I give it a helping hand. I like the way the paint feels beneath my nails. There are net curtains that used to be white in every window and a concrete driveway that always has a puddle of oil in the middle. Taylor's face stayed the same, even when she had to get out of the car on my side because her door was broken and gets stuck sometimes.

When we finally got inside, Mum said I should show Taylor my room, so I did. It didn't take long, there's not much to see. I told her that it was Nana's room and that she died there. I thought that would freak her out, but it didn't. Her face still stayed the same. We haven't redecorated, so my room still has Nana's stripy blue wallpaper with white flowers and there's a blue carpet that's completely flat from years of being trodden on. The twin beds match the wardrobe and dressing table. It's all dark brown wood that smells of Mr. Sheen. It's like living in a museum but I'm allowed to touch the stuff. Taylor said she liked my room, but I think she was just being polite. She's like that. She told me that her bedroom carpet is pink and we both agreed that might be even worse than blue.

She walked over to my bookshelves and I felt really uncomfortable. I said maybe we should go downstairs to see what microwaved delights Mum was planning on poisoning us with, but she just stood there as though she didn't hear me. I don't really like people touching my things but I tried to stay calm. Turns out Taylor reads loads, just like me. She's read some of the same books and talked about some others that I haven't even heard of, but sound cool. When Mum called us down for dinner I was actually quite annoyed, but then we carried on talking about books all the way down the stairs and while we ate our fish fingers and chips. We were still talking about books when Mum gave us a bowl of ice cream each. It had magic chocolate sauce on top, which comes out of the bottle all runny but then dries hard, like blood.

After dinner Mum said we could watch the big TV, but we went up to my room and talked instead. When Mum came up to my bedroom and said it was time for Taylor to go, it made me feel sad and I asked if she could stay a little longer. Mum raised her invisible eyebrows in that silly way she does. She doesn't have eyebrows like me because she plucked them off when she was young, so now she draws them on with a pencil and looks like a clown. She asked if Taylor would like to stay the night and Taylor said she would before I had a chance to say anything. So Mum called Taylor's mum and she said yes too because it was a Friday.

We only have three bedrooms in our house and none of them are spare. Mum and Dad used to share a bedroom in the old house, but now they each have their own. Mum says it's because Dad snores, but I know that really it's because they don't like each other anymore. I'm not stupid.

Taylor slept in my room with me, in Granddad's old bed—I don't think he would have minded.

Once we were in bed, Mum came in and said we had to turn the lamps off in ten minutes. Then she put two plastic glasses of water on the bed- side tables. This is yet another thing that Mum never normally does. She seemed very concerned about my thirst all of a sudden. She stood in the doorway before she left, smiled at us both, and said the strangest thing:

"Look at the two of you, like two peas in a pod."

Then Mum turned off the main light and started to close the door until I panicked and asked her not to. She propped it back open with Nana's robin doorstop. Once she was back downstairs, I said sorry to Taylor for her being a bit strange and that I didn't know what she meant by the peas in a pod comment. Taylor laughed and said that she had heard that ex- pression before. She said it just meant that we looked the same. I've never seen peas in anything but a plastic bag in the freezer.

We did turn the lamps off after ten minutes, like Mum said, but we talked for way longer than that. Taylor was talking with her eyes closed and then just fell asleep. I don't think it was because I'm boring. Even though everything was switched off, there was enough light from the moon peeking through the cracks in the curtain to see her face as she slept. I wasn't sure what Mum was on about at first. I'm a bit shorter than Taylor and she's very skinny, but she does look a little bit like me I suppose. We both have long brown hair.

There are three things that I have learned that I like about Taylor:

1. She's actually quite funny.
2. She likes books as much as I do.
3. She has exactly the same birthday as me.

We were born at the same hospital, on the same day, just a few hours apart. If I had been born into Taylor's family instead, my life would be so much better. I'd be picked up from school in a Volvo for starters, and Tay- lor's grandparents are still alive. But then my nana wouldn't have been my nana and that would be sad. I watched Taylor sleep for almost an hour. It was like watching another version of me. I have made a friend. I tried not to, but maybe it will be okay because we're like two peas in a pod.

# Now

Someone was in my room. He listened to the messages on my phone, deleted them, and then told me it was my fault that I'm here in the hospital. It wasn't a dream. I can't sleep now, I'm too afraid. Scared of what I know, scared of what I don't. I'm not sure how long it has been since his visit, but at least he hasn't come back. Time has stretched into something I can no longer tell. I wish someone would fill in the gaps—there are so many, as though I'm trapped inside the body of someone who lived a life I don't remember.

"Here's an interesting end to our morning rounds. Who can tell me about this case?" I hear them gather at the end of the bed. The chorus of doctors all sound the same to me. I want to tell them to get out.

*Just fix me or go away.*

I'm forced to listen while they talk about me as though I'm not here. They take it in turns to share how little they know of what is wrong with me and when I'll wake up. I have to tell myself *when*—the thought of it being *if* isn't an option I'm willing to consider. As soon as they run out of wrong answers, they evacuate my room.

I must have slept, because my parents are here again now. They sit on either side of the bed, barely making a sound, as though there is nobody there at all. I wish that they would say something, anything, but instead they seem to be taking extra care to be as quiet as possible, as though they don't want to wake me. My mum sits so close to the bed that I can smell her body lotion, and the scent triggers a memory of us on a spa break in the Lake District.

Claire had booked it as a girly treat for the three of us, but by the time we went she was quite pregnant with the twins. Her body had changed so much from my own. She was enormous and exhausted and spent most of the weekend in her room, which meant Mum and I had to muddle on without her. On the last day of the trip, when the rain had finally stopped and the sun we never saw had set, Mum and I went down to the restaurant for dinner.

We were seated at a small table, overlooking the vast Lake Windermere. I remember looking out to see the first stars appearing in the night sky above the rippled water and thinking how beautiful it was. I told Mum to take a look, the light was just perfect. She turned to glance briefly over her shoulder, then returned her attention to the wine list without a word. Claire had become the glue that held us together over the years. Without her, we had no choice but to fall apart. Mum said she didn't care what we drank so long as it was alcoholic and passed the menu to me. I ordered the first bottle of red my eyes found on the list; I felt like I needed a drink myself.

We were halfway through the bottle before our starters arrived. Mum drank quickly and I matched her pace. There didn't seem to be much else to do. Our conversation had all but dried up the night we arrived, so by now the well of words was empty. The wine changed that.

"How are you feeling, about Claire I mean? And the babies. Are you all right?" Mum's words stumbled and landed awkwardly. If she was trying to show that she cared, it still felt like a punch in the stomach. She wanted grandchildren. It wasn't a secret. I was a disappointment. Again.

When Paul and I first got together, Claire and David were already having IVF. It's really quite staggering what those three letters can do to a marriage. What they can do to a person is even worse. It changed Claire, not being able to have something she so badly wanted.

Paul was desperate for children too, everyone knew that, but I wouldn't come off the Pill until Claire had her family. I couldn't do that to her. My sister is younger than me but has always been one step ahead. First to get a boyfriend, first to get married, first to get pregnant, always winning an unspoken race. It's just who we are, who we've always been.

The third round of IVF worked for them. Claire was pregnant and I came off the Pill, thinking it was safe for us to try without upsetting anyone. It never occurred to me that we'd have problems conceiving too. We've had tests, lots of tests, but they can't find anything wrong with either of us. One of the doctors thought it might be genetic, but I know it isn't that. Something inside me is broken, I'm quite sure of it—my punishment for something that happened a long time ago.

We carried on trying, month after month. Sex became a scheduled chore. Paul wanted the baby he'd waited for, the child I had promised, but it was clear he no longer wanted me. We weren't making love anymore. We weren't making anything. I lost interest in it and Paul lost interest in me. He stuck to the script, said that so long as we had each other, that was all we needed. But we didn't have each other anymore, that was the problem. He thought I should have come off the Pill sooner, that we'd left it too late. He's never said it, but I know he blames me. He wanted a family more than any man I've ever met and I've had a ringside seat to watch his grief turn into something dark and resentment-shaped.

My mother never knew any of this. She thought I was putting off having a family because I was too focused on my career. I remember her staring at me that night, waiting for an answer I didn't know how to give, busy filling in the blanks in the meantime.

"I'm fine, I'm happy for her," I said eventually. For such carefully chosen words, they sounded all wrong. Empty and false. I suppose it was because I'd been caught off guard. When it comes to difficult conversations, I like to be prepared. I like to play them out in my head beforehand, consider all the possible lines that might be spoken and rehearse the answers I will give, until they are polished and learned by heart. Practice doesn't make me perfect, but people are more likely to believe me when I have.

We talked about Claire for a while. Mum went on about how well she was coping and what a wonderful mother she was going to be. Every compliment for Claire was also intended as an insult to me, but I didn't disagree, I knew Claire was made for motherhood; she's always been insanely protective of those she loves. With each sip of wine, the conversation that poured out of Mum's mouth seemed a little more dangerous. There is always a moment before an accident when you know you are going to get hurt but there is nothing you can do to protect yourself. You can raise your arms in front of your face, you can close your eyes, you can scream, but you know it won't change what's coming. I knew what was coming that night but at no point did I even attempt to hit the brakes. If anything, I pushed down on the accelerator.

"Do you ever wonder why I don't have children?" I asked. The words were out there. They had been born into the world because my sister wasn't there to hear them.

"Not everyone is cut out to be a mother," she replied too quickly.

Mum took another sip of wine and I took a deep breath, but she spoke before I could put my own words in the right order.

"The thing is, to be a good mother, you have to put your children first. You've always been very selfish, Amber, even as a child. I'm not sure motherhood would have suited you, so maybe it's true what they say." I felt wounded, the air knocked out of me for a moment to make room for all the thoughts fighting for space inside. I should have retreated, protected myself from further damage, but instead I invited her to strike me again.

"What do they say?"

"That everything happens for a reason." She emptied her glass and poured herself another. I remember my heart beating so loudly in my chest that I thought the whole restaurant must be able to hear it. I looked out at the lake and concentrated very hard on not crying, as her words went round and round in my head. The silence that followed was too uncomfortable, so my mother decided to fill it with some more words that might have been better left unspoken.

"The thing is, I think we are more alike than you realize, you and I. I never wanted children either." She was mistaken. From that moment on I wanted a baby almost as much as Paul, just to prove her wrong.

"You didn't want me?" I asked. Thinking that she would surely explain that that wasn't what she had meant.

"No. I never felt maternal at all. The truth is, you were an accident.

Your father and I got carried away one night and then I was pregnant, simple as that. I didn't want to be pregnant and I certainly didn't want a baby."

"But you loved me when I was born?" I asked.

She laughed.

"No, I despised you! It felt like life was over and as though you had ruined everything, and all because we'd had too much to drink and not been careful! My mother looked after you for the first few weeks. I didn't even want to look at you and everyone was worried that I would . . . not that I would have ever hurt you, I'm sure." She had hurt me so often without even knowing she was doing it. "But things got easier as you got older. You grew up so quickly, always older than your years, even then. You started walking and talking before other children your age and you being there, well, it just became normal, as though you always had been."

"What about Claire?"

"Well, it was different with Claire, obviously."

Obviously.

I hear Claire's voice, right on cue, and I am back in the present, in my hospital bed, going nowhere. The irony is not lost on me; once again I'm sitting with my mother and waiting for Claire to fix us, to teach us how to be with each other and stop us from falling apart.

"Here you are," says Claire. I picture them embracing, my mother's face lighting up at the sight of her favorite child, gliding into the room with her long blond hair and pretty clothes, no doubt. Claire sits down and takes one of my hands in hers.

"Look at these hands, just like Mum's but without the wrinkles." I imagine them smiling warmly at each other across the bed. I do look like Mum, that's true. I have the same hands and feet, the same hair, the same eyes.

"In case you can hear me, I need to tell you something," says Claire. "I hoped I wouldn't have to, but you should know that he'd be here if he could." I feel like I am holding my breath, but the machine carries on pumping oxygen into my lungs. "Paul didn't think the police were going to leave him alone and he was right. They're saying his were the only other fingerprints in the car and they seem quite sure it wasn't you driving. Then there are the bruises, the marks on your neck. Your neighbor said he heard you screaming at each other in the street. I know Paul didn't do this to you, but it's more important than ever now that you wake up." She squeezes my hand to the point where it hurts. I can feel the blanket of darkness rolling up over my neck, my chin, my face. I'm going to sleep, I can't fight it any longer, but I have to hold on. Her final words are distant and distorted, but I hear them.

"Paul has been arrested."

# Then

*Wednesday, December 21, 2016—*
*Afternoon*

I walk up our road, enchanted by the little clouds of hot breath coming from my mouth, and realize I'm smiling to myself. There is very little to smile about at the moment, so I promptly readjust my face. The sky is slowly killing itself up above while the streetlights flicker to life to show me the way home. I close the gate behind me, while the cold fingers on my other hand switch to autopilot, searching for the key inside my handbag. When they're warm enough to feel what they're looking for, I let myself in. I can hear something. Without closing the door, I stumble through the tiny hall to the lounge and see Paul lying on the couch staring at the TV. The missing husband has returned. He looks up at me briefly, before looking back at the screen.

"You're home early," he says. That is all. I haven't seen or heard from him for over twenty-four hours and that is all he has to say. I fold my arms without meaning to, like the stereotypical angry wife I've become.

"Where have you been?" I ask. My voice trembles slightly and I'm not even sure I really want to know the answer. I'm furious and yet at the same time so relieved to see that he's okay.

"At my mother's house. Not that you care."

"What are you talking about? I've been worried sick. You could have called."

"I forgot my phone and the signal is shit at Mum's house anyway. You'd know that if you ever bothered coming with me when I visit her. I left you a note and I called the landline. I thought you might make the effort to join me this time, given the circumstances."

"You didn't call me. There was no note," I insist.

"I left you a note in the kitchen," says Paul, his eyes fixed on mine. I march to the kitchen and sure enough there's a note on the counter. I snatch the piece of paper, holding it close enough to read.

*Mum has had a fall. Going to make sure she is okay.*
*Might have to take her to A&E. P x*

I try to think back to the night before. I had been preparing a meal for us both; I had to rearrange the larder. I spent a long time in the kitchen and I do not remember seeing this note. Paul stands in the doorway.

"This wasn't here. You've just put this here now," I say.

"What the fuck are you talking about?"

"The light was on in the shed. I thought you were writing. I cooked us a meal."

"So I see," he says. I follow his gaze around the kitchen, everything exactly where I left it last night, pots and pans still full of food on top of the oven. The empty white wine bottle. Everything is a mess. I can't believe I left the place in such a state.

"You haven't even asked how she is," Paul says from the doorway as I continue to survey the chaos. A pile of potato peelings are browning on a wooden chopping board, more flesh than skin because I'd used a knife to do the job. I can't stand to see the kitchen looking like this, so I start to tidy up while he continues to talk at me.

"Please can we not fight, I've had a horrible time," he says.

I don't want to fight either. Words keep falling from his lips as I clean, but I don't believe any of them. I can't stand the dirt and the lies, I just want it all to stop. I don't remember when things went so wrong, I only know that they have.

"She's broken her hip, Amber. She called me lying on her kitchen floor, I had to drop everything and go." I open the oven to find the lamb shanks I'd been cooking, dry and shriveled to the bone. "You would have done the same if it was your mother." I wouldn't have done the same for my mother because she would never have called me in that situation, she would have called Claire.

"So why was your car at Claire's house?" I say, throwing the meaty bones into the bin and turning to face him.

"What? Because my registration expired. I can't reinsure the thing until I get it sorted so Dave said he'd take a look at it for me," he says, without hesitation.

*David, not Dave, she doesn't like it.*

He has an answer for everything and all the pieces of the puzzle seem to fit. I begin to feel foolish and my own stupidity softens me.

"I'm sorry," I mutter, not sure that I should be.

"I'm sorry too."

"Is your mum going to be okay?"

We leave the dirty kitchen behind us and sit and talk for a while. I play the caring wife he needs me to be and he tells me what a wonderful son he has been, which only seems to highlight his failings as a husband. There is no time for me to practice my lines, so I'm forced to improvise. It's not an award-winning performance, but enough to satisfy the audience of one. I've never been fond of Paul's mother. She lives on her own in a dated, drafty bungalow near the Norfolk coast. I hate the place and have only been to visit a few times. I always get the impression that she sees straight through me and doesn't like the view.

Paul talks about his night at the hospital, and I listen for any holes in his story, but there are none. I watch his mouth as it forms his words and will them to be louder than the running commentary in my head. I want to believe him, I really do. My mobile is on the coffee table and I can see now that there is a missed call . . . maybe Paul had called to tell me where he was and I just hadn't noticed.

"Do you fancy some wine?" I ask. Paul nods. I pick up my phone as I head out to the kitchen and listen to the message, but it isn't my husband's voice that I hear.

# Before

*Saturday, December 14, 1991*

Dear Diary,

Last night I stayed at Taylor's house and I didn't want to leave. She lives in the nicest home, and has the kindest parents. She was born in that house, they've never moved, not like us. There are even marks on the larder door, showing how tall Taylor was every year since she was born. A larder is a really big cupboard just for food. They need one because they have a lot of it and none of it is frozen. When I grow up I want a house with a larder too.

Taylor said her parents were just as weird as mine, but that is so not true. Her mum was really nice to me and her dad didn't have to work late. When he came home we all ate dinner at the table together and it was delicious. It was a lasagna that Taylor's mum cooked herself, in the oven, not the microwave, from scratch. Her parents didn't argue once and her dad was actually quite funny, cracking silly jokes the whole time. Taylor rolled her eyes, maybe she'd heard them all before, but I laughed.

After dinner they said we could either go hang out in Taylor's room, or watch a film with them. They have the biggest TV I've ever seen. I think Taylor wanted us to go up to her room, but I said I'd like to watch the film. Her mum made popcorn and her dad turned all the lights off, so that the only things we could see were the Christmas tree lights and the glow from the television. It was like being at the pictures. Her parents sat on the sofa and Taylor and I shared a giant beanbag on the floor, as if we were a proper family. I didn't really pay much attention to the film, I kept looking around the room. Everything was so perfect, I wish I lived there.

Taylor had fallen asleep by the time the film was over, so I thought maybe I should pretend to be asleep too. Her mum picked her up and I was a bit scared at first when her dad picked me up in his arms, but then they carried us upstairs like we were still babies and put us to bed. Taylor only has one bed in her room, so we were sharing. The sheets smelled so nice, like a meadow. Taylor really was sleeping, but I couldn't, it was the best night ever and I didn't want it to end. I looked up at her bedroom ceiling and saw hundreds of stars. I knew they were only stickers that glowed in the dark, but they were still beautiful. I reached up and if I held my finger in the right place and squinted my eyes, it was like I could touch them.

Even when I heard Taylor's parents go to bed, I still couldn't sleep. The thoughts in my head were too busy. I got up to go to the bathroom and when I got there I noticed the three toothbrushes in the cup. I'd asked Taylor about them earlier and she'd explained that hers was red, her dad's was blue, and her mum's was yellow. She said they always had the same colors. Then she said maybe I could get a green toothbrush and then I could be part of their gang. I didn't want a green one though. I wanted to be red.

I crept back to the bedroom, where Taylor was still asleep. I did something bad then. I didn't mean to, it just sort of happened. I walked over to the dressing table and picked up her jewelry box. She'd asked me not to touch it earlier, which made me really want to. I opened it slowly and watched the tiny ballerina twirl away inside. There should have been something for her to dance to, but someone had broken the music. I watched the little doll spin round and round, dancing in the silence with a tiny strawberry-colored smile painted on her face. Inside the box there was a gold bracelet. I held it up close so I could see it properly and noticed that it was engraved with Taylor's date of birth. It could have been mine, it's my birthday too. On the other side it said *my darling girl* in tiny joined-up letters. I didn't mean to take it. I just wanted to see what it felt like. I'll give it back.

After that, I climbed into the bed and wiggled my body so that my face was right next to Taylor's and our noses were almost touching. Even though she was sleeping, she looked like she was smiling, probably because she's so lucky. I bet even her dreams are better than mine.

There are three things that Taylor has that I don't:

1. Cool parents.
2. A nice home.
3. Her very own stars.

I'm glad that Taylor and I are friends now. I'll give the bracelet back, I promise I will. And I hope we don't ever move house again because I really would miss her. I wish I lived in a house that smelled of popcorn and had stars on the ceiling.

# Now

My family is not like other families. I think I knew that even as a child. I've always wished my parents would love me the way other parents loved their children. Unconditionally. Things weren't perfect before Mum brought Claire home from the hospital, but things were better than they became. Nobody was there for me then and nobody is here for me now.

Paul has not returned. Every time the door opens I hope it might be him, but the only people who have been to visit me since morning rounds are paid to do so. They talk to me, but they don't tell me what I need to know. I suppose it's hard to give someone the answers when you don't know the questions. If Paul really has been arrested, then I need to wake up more than ever before. I have to remember what happened.

Evening rounds are brief—I'm no longer the main attraction. I'm old news now. Someone more broken than I am has come along. Even good people get tired of trying to mend what can't be fixed. Forty-a-Day Nurse was talking about her upcoming holiday with one of the others earlier. She's going to Rome with a man she met on the Internet and seems happier than usual, a bit gentler. I wonder what her real name is. Carla, perhaps? She sounds like she could be a Carla. She's not my favorite, but I'll still miss her while she's away; she's part of my routine now and I've never been fond of change.

In my new world, I am dependent on complete strangers: they wash me, they change me, and they feed me through a tube in my stomach. They collect my piss in a bag and they wipe my shitty arse. They do all these things to look after me, but I'm still cold, hungry, thirsty, and scared. I can smell dinner on the ward outside my room. I feel the saliva congregate inside my mouth in anticipation of something that will not come. It slides its way around and down the tube in my throat, while the machine that breathes for me huffs and puffs as though bored of it all. I'd give anything to taste food again, to enjoy the feel of it on my tongue, to chew it up and swallow its heat down into my belly. I try not to think about all the things I miss eating, drinking, doing. I try not to think about anything at all.

I hear someone come in, a man I think, based solely on the faint smell of body odor. Whoever they are, they don't speak, and I can't tell what they are doing. I feel fingers touch my face without any warning and then someone opens my right eye, shining a bright light into it. I'm blinded by white until they let my lid close again. Just as I start to calm down, they do the same to my left eye and I feel even more disoriented than before. Whoever it is leaves shortly afterwards and I am glad. I never would have thought lying in bed could be so uncomfortable. I've been on my right side for over six thousand seconds. I lost count after that. They should turn me soon. Nothing good ever happens when they leave me lying on my right side. I think it might be unlucky.

I feel something drip on my face, something cold. Then it happens again. Tiny drops of water, landing on my skin. It feels like rain but that doesn't make any sense. I instinctively open my eyes and see the night sky above me. It's as though the roof has been lifted right off and it's raining inside my room. I can open my eyes, but I can't move. I look down to see that my hospital bed has become a boat floating on gentle waves. I tell myself not to be afraid, this is a dream, just like the others. The rain falls harder and the sheets that are pulled over my limp limbs start to feel damp and cold. The body that I am estranged from starts to shiver. Something moves beneath the sheets and it isn't me. The girl in the pink dressing gown emerges from the covers at the foot of the bed and sits herself up so that we mirror each other. Her hair is already dripping wet and she still doesn't have a face. She can't speak but she doesn't have to—silence is our common language. She chose it; I live with her choice. She points up at the black sky and I see the stars, hundreds of them, so close that I could reach up and touch them, if I could move. But they're not real. They're assorted luminous stickers, which start to peel off and fall down onto the bed, pointy corners of white plastic curling up at the edges. There are star-shaped holes in the sky now. The little girl starts to sing and I wish she wouldn't.

*Row, row, row your boat, gently down the stream.*

She takes her hands out from under the sheets and I see a flash of gold on her wrist.

*Merrily, merrily, merrily, merrily.*

She grabs the sides of the bed that has become a boat and starts to swing from side to side. I try to tell her not to, but I cannot speak.

*Life is but a dream.*

I close my eyes before she tips us over completely. The water is cold and dark. I cannot swim because I cannot move, so I sink helplessly deeper into the black like a flesh-colored stone. I can still hear her distorted voice beneath the waves.

*Life is but a dream.*

There is a loud beeping sound and a lot of watery noise but I'm no longer underwater. There are voices I recognize and faces I don't.

My eyes are open.

I can see the doctors and nurses fussing around me.

This is real.

Then the voices are silent, except for one.

"That's VF, we need to shock."

Those aren't my initials.

"Stand back."

The faces disappear and all I can see is the white ceiling.

*Everything* is white.

I close my eyes because I'm scared of what they might see. Then I hear my dad's voice at the end of the bed.

"Hold on, Peanut," he says. It's like hearing a ghost.

I open my eyes again and he smiles at me. I realize that I really can see him. He looks so old to me now, so frail, so tired. Everything else is white, it's just me and my dad, and I feel the tears start to roll down my cheeks.

"I'm sorry about what happened," he says. I want to tell him that it's okay but I still can't speak. I want to hold his hand one more time, but I still can't move.

"If I had any idea that that would be the last time we would speak, I never would have said those things. I didn't mean them. I love you, we both do. We always did. Life is but a dream." He turns to leave and he doesn't look back. I am her again—that little girl desperately trying to keep up with her father. He's slower than he used to be, but he still leaves me behind.

# Then

*Thursday, December 22, 2016—*
*Morning*

And if you've just joined us on *Coffee Morning*, welcome," says Madeline. "So far today we've been talking honestly and openly about adultery. We'll be discussing here in the studio why some women feel they could never turn a blind eye to a cheating partner, while others have chosen to forgive and forget. We'll also be talking to women who cheat. I'm joined now by Amber, who says that you can never really know a person, including yourself. Amber, tell us more," says Madeline, before rolling her eyes and checking her script to see what's next on the show. She looks up at me then. "Well? What have you got to say for yourself?" Her voice changes with each word, as though her batteries are dying. Then she is sick all over the desk in the studio. She looks up, wipes her mouth, and carries on.

"Amber?" Paul's voice is now coming out of Madeline's mouth.

"Amber?" I sit up in the bed. "You were having a nightmare," says Paul.

I blink into the darkness. My skin is covered in sweat and I don't feel right.

"You're okay now," he says.

But I'm not. I pull off the duvet and run to the bathroom. I grip the toilet bowl with one hand and hold my hair out of my face with the other. It doesn't last long. I hear Paul get out of bed and I close the bathroom door.

"Are you okay?" he asks from the other side of the pine border.

"I'll be fine. It's cold, go back to bed, I'll be there soon," I lie. It isn't long before he retreats without protest.

I flush the toilet, wash my face, and watch myself brush my teeth in the mirror. A crazy woman stares back so I look at the floor instead. I spit out the toothpaste, tiny bits of red mixed in with white, then wipe my mouth. My index finger and thumbs come to meet and my hands move up to my face. I pull at each of my eyebrows in turn and sprinkle tiny bits of hair into the sink. Only when I can count ten tiny black pieces of myself on the white porcelain do I stop. There always have to be ten. When enough time has passed I turn on the cold tap and wash myself away.

I open the door as quietly as I can and check on Paul. He's already gone back to sleep, gentle snores escaping from his open mouth. I take my dressing gown from the back of the bedroom door and creep along the landing to my little study. Everything is neat and tidy, just how I left it. I take out my white gloves and my fountain pen and stare at the blank sheet of paper. I'm too tired to think of what to write and then I remember Mrs. MacDonald from school and her three things rule. The words come and I smile to myself.

> *Dear Madeline,*
>
> *I hope you've been enjoying my letters so far. I know how much you like reading letters from your fans.*
>
> *I am not a fan.*
>
> *There are three things you should know about me:*
>
> *1. I know you're not the woman you pretend to be.*
>
> *2. I know what you did and what you didn't.*
>
> *3. If you don't do what I ask, I'll tell everyone who you really are.*
>
> *I'll keep writing until you get the message. Ink doesn't last forever of course, so let's hope we don't have to hear from each other for too much longer. If the ink runs out, I'll have to find another way to make you listen.*

"What are you doing? Why didn't you come back to bed? What's with the magician gloves?"

Paul is peering round the study door in just a T-shirt and his boxer shorts. I've been caught.

"I couldn't sleep. Thought I'd make a late start on the Christmas cards but my hands were cold," I stutter. He gives me a strange look.

"Okay. Well, Mum has just texted, she thinks the doctors are trying to kill her. I'm going to have to go back up there."

I didn't think she knew how to text.

"Now?"

"Yes, now. She needs me."

"I'll come with you," I offer.

"No, it's all right. I know how worried you are about work at the moment. I won't be away long."

He retreats from the door before I have time to reply. I hear the shower being turned on and the boiler rumble to life. He's not in too much of a hurry then. I fold my letter, place it in the red envelope, and put my white gloves back in the drawer. I walk past the bathroom. The door is a little ajar and steam is already billowing out in a bid to escape. I peer through the damp cloud and see my husband, naked in the shower. It's been a while since I have seen him this way and I feel a curious mix of rejection and relief. I move quickly toward our bedroom and take his phone from the side table next to the bed. 06:55. I hadn't realized how late it was. It still feels like the middle of the night. I type Paul's password into his phone. I remember the first time I tried to guess it a few months ago, putting in our wedding anniversary, my date of birth, and then finally his. Of course it was all about him. I open his text messages. The last one was over twenty-four hours ago, from me. There are no texts from his mother. I hear the shower stop. I put the phone down, climb back into bed, and face the wall. I listen as he dries himself, gets dressed, sprays himself with deodorant, does up his belt, and refills the pockets of his jeans with loose change.

"How will you get there? Train?" I ask.

"No, quicker to drive."

"I thought the car needed its registration renewed?"

"Dave says it's ready now. I'll just collect it from the forecourt. I've got the spare key."

"Did he text you too?"

"No, he called last night. Why?"

"No reason."

He has an answer for everything.

He kisses me good-bye and tells me that he loves me. I tell him that

I love him too. Well-worn words that have shrunk and lost their meaning. I lie perfectly still as I listen to the sound of my husband leaving me. It doesn't last long. When the front door closes, I get out of the bed and watch him walk away from behind the bedroom curtain.

I follow in Paul's footsteps, head down to the kitchen, and turn on the light. My throat is dry so I pour myself a glass of water to take back upstairs. I stop in front of the oven and check that it is off twelve times, clicking my fingers with my empty left hand. I notice the red light of the answering machine flashing away on the sideboard in the hall. The only people who have ever used the landline are my parents, and even they don't call this number anymore. My index finger hovers reluctantly over the Play button, almost too scared to make contact, as though it might burn me. I swallow a gulp of water, letting it wash away my fear, then I push the button. It's Paul from two days ago. So he did call to tell me he was at his mum's. I don't know how I missed the machine flashing, I walk past it all the time. I delete the message and then pause over the Play All button. I shouldn't need to hear his voice again, but I do. I close my eyes as the familiar sound of my father's voice fills my heart and ears. *Hello, it's me, Dad. Call me back when you get this, Peanut.* He hasn't called me that for such a long time. The tears I have been managing to suppress fall freely from my eyes. They make tracks down my cheeks and cling to my chin for as long as they can, before dropping down onto my nightshirt to form damp stains of sadness. I've saved this message for so long now. Paul says it's morbid; he doesn't understand. Out of some instinctive curiosity, I pick up the phone and hit the Last Number Dialed button. After several rings, I hear a click and then a prerecorded message speaks in my ear. I slam the receiver down, glaring at it as though it's to blame. I've never called Claire from this phone.

# Then

I'm a few minutes late for work. Madeline is already in, but it doesn't matter, not today. I still feel disorientated, as though I might be dreaming within a dream. I checked the bottom of Paul's wardrobe after he left. The pretty pink bag and its black lacy contents were gone. He'd taken them with him. I doubt they were a gift for his mother.

I sit quietly at my desk as the rest of the cast assembles. Colleagues say *good morning* and I nod back; it's like listening to a stuck record. I don't feel like making conversation today, polite or otherwise, and my morning hasn't been particularly good. When I think nobody is looking, I study the faces of the women in the office. They all look blinkered, a little weary, a lot lost. A collection of people treading water, trying to stay afloat in an unpredictable sea. They're not my friends, not really; we'd all push each other under if it meant we wouldn't drown. I conclude I have nothing to worry about—they can't see the real me, they can't even see themselves.

Madeline comes out of her office to bark at someone and I catch her eye. She's talking to them, but she's staring at me, and for a moment I'm convinced that she knows. There's a terrible taste in my mouth that I just can't get rid of. The nausea rises up through my throat once more and I head for the toilets, doing my absolute best to appear calm. As soon as I'm inside, I burst through a cubicle, flush the toilet, and lean my head over the bowl just in time, hoping that nobody will hear me. It's just bile, I haven't eaten anything. I wonder if it's nerves or guilt or both. Either way I need to fix myself and fast, I don't have time for this. I hear Jo's voice outside the door. She thinks I should pop to the chemist before we go on air, there's one not far from our building. I think she's right. I wait awhile, to be sure that it's over, then I open the door and wash my hands, relieved to see that I'm alone again.

I feel much better after the show. Madeline, however, is not feeling at all well. She's been waddling back and forth to the toilets throughout the morning and is covered in sweat. She thinks it must be food poisoning. I think it is far more likely to be the laxatives I put in her coffee just before we went on air. Madeline likes coffee, she drinks a lot of it, never says no, as long as it's black. She also likes to drive to and from work. She thinks public transport is "dirty and full of germ-ridden commoners." She's in no fit state to drive herself home now, so I offer to, much to her surprise and Matthew's approval. I don't think she's going to go for it at first, but after another impromptu visit to the lavatory, she seems to come round to the idea and I am glad.

I carry her bag as we leave the office because she "feels too weak" and I pretend not to know which car is hers when we reach the parking lot. She unlocks the black VW Golf, then passes me the key before folding herself into the backseat, as though her car has metamorphosed into a taxi. She barks her postcode at me as I tap it into the satnav, then warns me to "drive bloody carefully" and "watch for foreigners on the road."

She sleeps as I drive and I decide I like her a lot better like this. Silenced. The poison is trapped inside her while she sleeps, opposed to seeping from her lips when she is awake.

I hate driving in London. It's too busy and loud. There are too many people on the roads and all of them are in a hurry, though few of them have anywhere they really need to be. It's better once we're out of the city center. The roads seem to widen and are less crowded.

When the satnav suggests we're only ten minutes away from our destination, the car makes a warning sound and an angry red symbol glows on the dashboard.

"You're almost out of petrol," I say, observing the narrowing eyes of my passenger in the rearview mirror. Awake again.

"I can't be," she says.

"Don't worry, I'm sure there's enough to get you home."

"Do I look worried?" We make eye contact in the mirror again. I hold her stare for as long as seems sensible when driving at forty miles an hour, then look back at the road ahead.

We don't speak again after that, not until I turn left into the road where she lives. She barks at me again then, telling me where and how to park, but I don't really hear her. I'm too busy staring up at the house she says is hers, unsure how to feel about what I'm seeing. I recognize this place. I've been here before.

# Before

*Easter Sunday 1992*

Dear Diary,

Taylor is on holiday with her parents for the whole of Easter and I feel miserable. I haven't seen her since the last day at school and I won't see her again until next Tuesday when we go back. She sent me a postcard. Mum barged into my bedroom with a big grin on her face to give it to me a couple of days ago. She thought it would make me happy. It didn't. Taylor seems to be having a lot of fun without me and I don't think she misses *me* at all.

I'm not going on holiday this year, not even somewhere in England. Mum says we can't afford it. When I pointed out that Dad has been working loads, so we should have lots of money, she just cried. She's always crying lately and she's not fat anymore, I wonder if maybe she's too sad to eat. One night last week she was too sad to make lunch or dinner. I'm not allowed to touch the oven, so I just ate crisps and biscuits. I asked Mum if she was still sad about Nana and she said she was sad about everything.

Mum said she'd take me to Brighton again one day next week if I was good. I asked her where she would take me if I was bad, but she didn't laugh. I've reminded her that I'm ten and a half now, so I'm a bit old for the kids' rides, but I don't mind walking along the pier and I like the sound of the sea. Now that I am older, Mum has started looking for a part-time job, like Taylor's mum. She hasn't got one so far, even though she's applied for loads. Every time she gets an interview, she wears her hundred-year-old black suit, puts on too much makeup, then comes home and drinks all afternoon. I wouldn't give her a job either, she's too sad and lazy. I had to wear the same shirt for school three days in a row before the holidays.

She said it didn't matter and that nobody would notice, then sprayed some disgusting perfume on me so that I stank of her all day.

My packed lunches have also taken an interesting twist. Part of Dad's job is to fill up the sweet machines where he works. One of the perks of his job is being able to bring home boxes of free chocolate and crisps. Last week, he brought home a box of forty Kit-Kats. We ran out of bread before the last day of term, so Mum gave me two Kit-Kats for my packed lunch instead of butter-and-crisp sandwiches, which was fine with me. But then the lunch monitor spotted what I was eating and thought I'd forgotten my lunch, even though I told her that I hadn't. She sent me to join the kids who have hot meals, which was great, because that's what Taylor does.

She was sitting alone, as usual, so I sat down at her table. But then there was a fuss because apparently Mum hasn't paid the school for the last time I had to have a hot lunch. In the end, I think Mrs. MacDonald felt sorry for me or something, because she paid for it herself and told me not to worry. By the time I got my fish and chips, everyone else had been sent out for playtime. I could see almost the whole school on the field while I ate my lunch. I spotted a group of girls from my class and saw Taylor standing in the middle of them. They pushed her between them as though she was a rag doll and she didn't look like she was enjoying it. When she tried to leave, they joined hands and closed the gaps between them, pushing her back to the center of their circle. I left my chips and said that I didn't want any of the dessert either, even though I was still hungry. I ran to the playing field but I couldn't find Taylor or any of the other girls. I ran to the quadrangle where she sometimes sat on the steps on her own, but she wasn't there either.

I went back to our classroom even though it was still break time, but it was empty. Something caught my eye, something out of place. I walked over to the class fish tank and looked at the dead goldfish floating on the surface of the green-tinged water. Taylor and I had helped clean the tank a few weeks ago. Mrs. MacDonald taught us that you empty the liquid by putting a piece of hose in the water and sucking the other end. The water rushes out by itself if you do it right, and you can collect it in a bucket. It's all to do with gravity. Like the moon and the stars. I got a mouthful of fish tank water the first time I tried it and Taylor laughed at me. I don't think anyone has cleaned it since.

I knew the fish was dead and I couldn't decide how I felt about that. I had a goldfish that died when I was little. Nana flushed it down the toilet and I was sad. But that was mine, it had belonged to me. This fish wasn't mine and while I tried to find the right feelings to feel about it, my hands did their own thing and opened the lid of the tank. I don't know why I wanted to hold it. It was wet and slippery and cold. Taylor came into the classroom then. She looked at the dead fish, then she looked at me. She took the fish from my hands, put it back in the tank, and closed the lid. She took a tissue out of her sleeve, like a magician takes a rabbit out of a hat, then she dried my hands before drying her own. I was glad that she was all right.

Last year I had two Easter eggs. One from Mum and Dad and one from Nana. Nana's was better because it had sweets inside the chocolate egg. I counted them and there were thirteen sweets, which I remember because it was lucky and unlucky all at the same time. This year I've only got one Easter egg, but that's okay because it's from Taylor. I didn't get her anything, but I will. I might give her some of the Kit-Kats, we've got loads.

# Now

My parents are dead. I don't know how you forget a thing like that, but I did. They were here in my hospital room, as real as anyone else, and yet they weren't here at all. They can't have been; they've been gone for over a year now. The mind is a powerful tool, it can create entire worlds and it's certainly more than capable of playing a few tricks in order to aid self-preservation. We weren't even on speaking terms when they died. I remember the last words my dad said to me. I can still hear him speaking them, a cruel stuck record of a memory.

*"Listen to me, Amber. Any distance that exists in our relationship was created by you. Ever since you were a teenager you withdrew into your own little world. You didn't want us there and we wouldn't have been able to find you even if we tried. I know because we did try. For years. The world does not revolve around you. If you'd had children of your own you would have learned that by now."*

They didn't call again after that and neither did I.

Claire was the one who called to tell me that they were gone. It was a coach crash in Italy. I'd seen it on the news but even when the presenter talked about the British tourists feared dead, I had no idea that the voice from the TV was speaking directly to me. We never knew what happened, not really. There was speculation that the driver of the coach had fallen asleep at the wheel. It was on the news for a day or so and then our parents were forgotten again by everyone who wasn't us. Something bad happened to someone somewhere else and that became the new news while we carried on watching our story alone. They'd written Claire's name as their next of kin in their passports, not mine. Even in death, they chose her over me.

Claire did everything: arranged to bring them home, organized their funeral, dealt with the solicitor. I cleared out their home, disposed of their things, distributed parts of their lives to other people in other places. Claire said she couldn't bear to do that.

I'm still shocked by how very real they seemed to me in this hospital room. I must have wanted to share my solitude with someone so badly that my mind obliged by returning my parents to me as living memories. The dead are not so very far away when you really need them; they're just on the other side of an invisible wall. Grief is only ever yours and so is guilt. It's not something you can share. Claire was genuinely heartbroken when they died. She cried on the outside for weeks; I cried on the inside forever. I'm starting to question everything my mind presents to me now, trying to sift through what is real and what might be a dream.

The door opens and someone pulls up a chair. He takes my hand and I know it's Paul just from the way he holds it. His hands are mostly soft, except for a lump of hard skin on his middle finger where he grips his pen too hard when writing. He's back. The police must have let him go. We sit in silence for a long time. I can feel him staring at me. He doesn't say a word, just holds my hand. When the nurses come to turn and change me, he waits outside as requested. When they leave me, he is there again. I want to know what happened to him, I want to know what the police said, what it was they thought he had done.

A nurse comes in to tell him that visiting hours are over. He doesn't reply but his face must have said something to her, because she says it's fine for him to stay as long as he wants. Whatever the police thought he did, the nurses clearly think he's a good husband. We sit in silence for a while longer. He can't find the right words and mine have been taken away.

"I'm sorry," he says.

Just as I'm wondering what for, I feel him lean over me and the routine panic sets in. I don't know why I am afraid and then there is that flash of memory again, a man's hands around my throat. It feels like I can't breathe despite the machine forcing oxygen into my lungs. Paul's hands are on my face, not my throat, but I don't know what he is doing. I want to cry out as he pushes something into both of my ears. The soundtrack of my world deflates a little and I don't like it at all; hearing is all I have left.

"What are you doing?" asks Claire, and I am shocked to hear her voice. I don't know how long she has been here; I didn't know that she was.

"The doctor said it might help," says Paul, taking my hand in his again.

"The police let you go?"

"It would appear so."

"Are you all right?" she asks.

"What do you think?"

"I think you look like crap and smell like you need a shower."

"Thanks. I came straight here."

"Well, it's over now."

"It's not over, they still think that I . . ."

But it's over for me because I can no longer hear them. My ears are filled with music, which pulses and bleeds down into my body, diminishing all other sensation until it is all that I know. Everything else, everyone else is gone, and I am taken away from this place by a series of notes culminating in a memory: this is the song I walked down the aisle to when Paul and I got married. The lyrics about trying to fix someone you love pull me back in time. Even back then he wanted to fix me, when I didn't know I was broken. He's still trying.

The memory is a little torn around the edges, but it's something real, so I slow it right down and hold on to it. I can see Paul in the corner of the memory, sliding a ring onto my finger. He is smiling at me and we are happy. We were happy then, I remember now just how much. I wish we could be that version of us again. Too late now.

It was a small ceremony; I've never had many friends. The truth is I just don't like many people, not really. Everyone you meet is inevitably flawed. Once I know someone well enough to see all the cracks and blemishes, I don't really want to spend time with them anymore. I don't avoid broken people because I think I'm better than them, I just don't like looking at my own reflection. Besides, everyone I've ever got close to gets hurt in the end—that's why I don't bother to make any new friends anymore. I've learned it's best to just hold on to what you've got.

The track stops and I'm back. The music replaced by the rhythm of the ventilator accompanied by a less familiar beeping sound. A nurse has joined us. I can tell by the *Shh* of her plastic apron as she sashays past the bed. The apron has got its wish: the room is silent. I paint my life by sounds, not numbers now, my overworked ears holding the brush. The beeping stops. When the nurse leaves, Paul and Claire resume their conversation and I can't help wondering about the words I missed.

"You have to stop blaming yourself, Paul. It was an accident."

"I should never have let her go."

"You've got to keep it together. She needs you and right now you're a mess. You need to wash and rest and get your head sorted."

"They still think I was driving the car, that I'm some guy who beats his wife when he's drunk and then forgets about it. I'm not that guy."

"I know."

"They hate me. They won't give up, they'll come back, I know it. I'm not leaving her again. You go if you want to."

When I want them to speak the most, they stop. Someone else *was* driving the car, I'm sure of it. But not Paul. I'm relieved that Claire believes him too.

"I'll stay awhile, keep you company if you like?" she says.

"Suit yourself."

They settle themselves down into the silence. Paul plays me another memory: a song we fell in love with on our last holiday. There are more songs, more memories, but then the music stops, the silence resumes, and it's so much louder.

"Do you want to talk about the baby?" asks Claire.

*What baby?*

"No," says Paul.

"Did you know?"

*Know what?*

"I said I don't want to talk about it."

*I want them to talk about it.*

But they don't. The ventilator huffs and puffs, echoing the frustration in the room.

"Right, well, I'm going home. It's late," says Claire. "I can give you a lift or I can pick up some clean clothes and a wash bag for you, if you want to give me your house keys?"

*Don't give her the keys.*

"I'll take a lift home, then come back in a couple of hours."

"You need to rest."

"I need to be with Amber."

"Okay."

Claire kisses me on the cheek and I can smell her peppermint shampoo. I wonder what my hair must look like having not been washed for so long. Paul kisses me too, then tugs the tiny speakers out of my ears. I don't want him to go and I feel my mood darken as the door closes behind them, leaving me alone with my silence and machinery. I hear the door and think that Paul has changed his mind and come back to stay with me, but it isn't Paul.

"Hello, Amber," says a man's voice. I hear a lock turn and I know it's him, the man who was here before, the man who deleted my voicemail. "I just bumped into your husband. Rather disheveled chap, not sure what you see in him. I hear from one of my colleagues that we nearly lost you? But you found your way back, so no harm done there then."

*Colleagues.*

He works here?

"Did you know that one of the drugs we use to keep people in a coma is the same drug they use in America for the death penalty? That's why I'm so surprised to see you tonight, because that dose *really* should have killed you. I got the maths wrong, you see."

*This can't be real, this isn't happening. Wake up. WAKE UP.*

"Everyone makes mistakes. The important thing is to learn from them. I'm going to do a much better job of looking after you from now on."

*This is not a dream.*

"You're welcome. I know you'd thank me if you could."

*I know this man.*

He strokes my face.

*I remember him now.*

He leans down to the bed and kisses me, then slowly licks my cheek as though tasting my skin. I shrivel inside of myself. He moves my breathing tube to the side and kisses my mouth, pushing his tongue inside my lips, his teeth gnashing against the tube and my own. His hand slides along my body, cupping my breast beneath the hospital gown. When he is finished he puts me back how he found me.

"You're right, we should take it slow," he says, and leaves the room.

# Then

I'm not doing this because Paul isn't coming home again tonight. And it isn't because of the disappearing bag of black lace—there could be a perfectly reasonable explanation for that. I'm doing it because I want to and that's okay. Plenty of people are friends with their exes. It doesn't have to mean something and I'm not doing anything wrong. I encourage the words to repeat themselves in my head until I might believe them. Every step forward feels like I'm going in the wrong direction, but I carry on regardless down my chosen path.

The Southbank is alive with people wearing each other's smiles. The Thames dances in the moonlight and the buildings rise up majestically in the distance, snaking around the river's shores. I love the city at night: you can't see the dirt or the sorrow in the dark.

I spot him straight away at the bar, his outline still strangely familiar even after all these years. He has his back to me but I can see he has a glass of something in his hand already. It isn't too late. I could just turn around and walk out the door, forget the whole thing that never happened.

*It's just a drink.*

My heeled feet seem stuck to the floor until the nausea rushes up through my body, screaming at me to run. I see a neon sign for the toilets and push my way through the early-evening drinkers, fearful I won't make it in time. But the feeling passes as soon as I'm inside a cubicle, just nerves perhaps. I wash my hands. I don't know why, they're not dirty. I take a paper towel and roughly dry them, my attention suddenly focused on the wedding ring on my left hand. I take a deep breath, exhale, and then stare at my reflection in the mirror, grateful that there is nobody else here to see this me. The eyes that stare back look tired and far away but overall things are satisfactory. My new little black dress looks good, flattering my neglected body, and the heels, although uncomfortable, give me confidence. I've tamed my brunette mop of hair and painted my face and nails. I don't know why it matters so much, but I want him to see me looking good.

I try to reassure my reflection with a smile, but she responds half-heartedly. I return my features to neutral. The quiet stillness that calmed and embraced me smashes as the door bursts open. The loud chaos of the bar floods the space and sucks the air out of the tiny room. I struggle to keep my head above the noise and grip the basin, white knuckles pointing at the exit. Two women, slightly worse for wear, stumble inside, laughing at something I'm not privy to. They look younger than me, though I suspect we are probably the same age. Their skirts are short, their lips are red, and their paper hats remind me that it is Christmas. It doesn't mean anything anymore—Christmas. The chatter spilling out of the women is just loud enough to drown out the voices in my head telling me to walk away, so I take a deep breath and head for the bar.

I stand right next to him, breathing in his smell, already so familiar and forbidden. He doesn't seem to notice me at all.

"I'll have a glass of Malbec, please," I say to the barman. In my peripheral vision, I see Edward's head turn, his eyes drinking me in from top to bottom, the way they always did.

"Hello, Edward," I say, turning to face him. I do my best to keep my voice and my expression level. He smiles back. Time has changed me, but clearly left him alone. More than a decade of life seems to have only improved him. I can't help noticing the tanned skin, white teeth, and mischievous brown eyes that seem to dance with delight as he stares at me.

"I'll get that, and another pint of Amber Ale, I like the name." He takes a crisp twenty-pound note from his leather wallet and places it on the bar. His white cotton shirt looks almost too small for him as it struggles and strains to hide the muscles beneath. He was always at the gym when we were students and clearly still works out now. "So, you came."

"I did," I reply. His stare feels too intense and I struggle not to look away.

"It's good to see you." Something about the way his eyes hold mine makes me shrink a little. The wine arrives and I am greedy for it.

"Well, I had a couple of hours free this evening and thought it might be nice to catch up," I say.

"A couple of hours? Is that all I'm getting?" he says, passing me my glass.

"No, I've only got ten minutes to spare with you, then I've got another date with some cool people."

He smiles, a fraction too late.

"Another *date*?" he asks.

I blush.

"I see. Well, I had better make the most of the time I have with you then. Cheers." He raises his glass to mine and continues to hold my stare as we drink. I look away first and swallow down more of the wine than I should.

Things quickly become comfortable between us. The alcohol oils our conversation and both flow freely. It feels easy and natural to be in his company again, despite the missing years. Three days before Christmas and the bar is uncomfortably full, but I barely notice. The strangers that surround us are regularly replenished, cushioning me from the dangerously sharp edges of who we used to be. I return Edward's smiles, compliments, and light touches, only too aware that it would take just a tiny tear to rip through the fabric of the life I have now. After two drinks I'm already feeling slightly more intoxicated than seems wise. I haven't managed to eat much today.

"I don't know about you, but I'm starving," he says, as though reading my mind. "Do you have time to get a quick bite to eat?" I consider the proposal. I'm hungry, I'm having fun. *I'm not doing anything wrong.* In my albeit brief search, I can't find a reason to say no.

"Somewhere nearby?" I ask.

"Sounds good to me," he says, then stands to help me into my jacket. After fighting our way through the masses, he pushes the door open ahead of me. "After you." I'd forgotten what it was like to be out with a gentleman; it's like being with someone from the past, my past.

The air is soberingly cold, but Edward says he knows a place not too far away. I'm out of practice walking in heels on cobbled streets. The second time I stumble he takes my arm and I let him, aware that we must look like a couple and I don't think that I mind. We stop at what looks like a residential town house and I'm confused when he releases my arm and knocks on the intimidating black door.

"What are you doing?" I whisper. I feel like a schoolgirl.

"Finding somewhere for us to eat, unless you aren't hungry anymore?"

Before I have a chance to reply, the large, glossy door swings open, and a middle-aged man in a black suit appears in the doorway. He's uncomfortably tall, like someone has stretched him, and he has the face of someone who's received too much bad news. "Any chance of a table for two?" asks Edward. To my surprise, the man nods.

"Of course, sir, step this way."

I feel like Alice in Wonderland as I follow the suited man down a long, marble-floored hallway. I look over my shoulder to make sure Edward is still following behind. He looks pleased with himself and I realize this was probably all part of his plan for the evening. I don't mind. It's not as though he forced me to come. We turn through a small door on the right and enter a large, candlelit dining room, where we are shown to the only remaining empty table. Four other couples are already seated. They don't look up.

"I will get you the wine list, sir," says the suited man before retreating with our coats through a curtained doorway.

"Well, this is impressive," is all I can manage to say.

"Thank you, I like it. It's members only."

His tanned hands pick up the white cotton napkin on the table in front of him, carefully unfolding the cloth as though he's handling the Turin Shroud, before placing it on his lap. I do the same with my own napkin, then wonder what is taking so long with the wine list. I worry that we might have already exhausted all avenues of interesting conversation without it.

"How's the new job going?" I ask.

"Well. Very well, in fact. It was supposed to be temporary, but they've offered me a permanent post and I've decided to stay a little longer."

"Congratulations, which hospital?"

"King Alfred's."

"That's near me," I say. He smiles.

"And your girlfriend, does she work in London too?"

"She does, but in the city center. What with my shifts and her work schedule, I don't get to see her as often as I'd like. There's no food menu here, you get what you're given I'm afraid, but it's always good."

"What if I don't like what I'm given?"

"I'm pretty sure that you will."

I listen to him talk about his work. He always wanted to be a doctor and now he is. I think it was one of the things I found so attractive about him when we first met. He wanted to help people, wanted to save them. He doesn't talk about it for long, he's too modest for that, he keeps changing the subject back to me. My stories seem shallow and empty in comparison. What I do doesn't save lives. I do what I do to help myself.

The meal is the nicest food I've eaten for a long time, but as my wineglass is refilled, I can't stop myself from prodding at the perfect evening.

"Does your girlfriend know you're out with an ex tonight?" I ask.

"Of course! Doesn't your husband?"

I don't say anything and he laughs at me. I don't like it.

"That was a long time ago. We've both moved on and grown up a lot since then," he adds. I feel foolish and old, past my "best before" date.

He says no to dessert, so I do the same. As he talks, I can't help remembering when we were together. He struggled to keep his hands off me then but that was over ten years ago. He might look the same, but I don't. Despite the new clothes and makeup I'm still the old me and not the one he remembers.

"I'll walk you to Waterloo," he says.

"There's really no need, I'm perfectly capable of getting there myself."

"I'm sure you are, but I'm new around here, remember? I might get lost, so I'd appreciate the company."

He offers me his arm as we leave the restaurant and I see no harm in taking it. I can feel the warmth of him through his coat and notice the way women seem to stare at him as we stroll to the station. We walk along the concourse and I scan the departure boards through tired eyes, anxious not to miss the last train home.

"Platform thirteen for me. Thank you so much for a lovely evening." I kiss him on the cheek.

"We must do this again sometime."

"I'd like that," I reply, not entirely sure that I would.

He takes my hand in his and I feel instantly uncomfortable.

"I have to go," I say, trying to retrieve my fingers from his grip.

"No you don't. Come for one last drink. You can get the next train. . . ."

"I really can't, I think this might be the last one."

"Then stay with me. We can get a room at one of the best hotels London has to offer." His grip on my hand tightens and I see a look in his eyes that I'd deleted from the memories of us. I pull my hand away.

"Edward, I'm married."

"You're not happy. You wouldn't have come tonight if you were."

"That's not true."

"Isn't it? I know you."

"The version of me you knew is several years out of date."

"I don't think so. We both messed up before, but we can move on from that. I didn't know what I had back then, but I know now, and I want it back. I think you do too. That's why you came."

"I'm really sorry if I've given you the wrong impression. I have to go."

I walk away. I don't need to look back to know he's still standing there or that I've made a big mistake.

# Before

*Wednesday, October 14, 1992*

Dear Diary,

Today was my birthday. I am now eleven years old. It was also Taylor's birthday, but we did not spend it together. Today was officially the worst birthday I've ever had. Everything is broken and I can't think of a way to fix it. Things went very wrong, very quickly, and then just kept getting worse. It wasn't my fault, it really wasn't.

I've been wearing Taylor's bracelet to bed at night, the one with our date of birth engraved in the gold. It sounds silly, but wearing it felt like she was with me somehow and that made me happy. I was so excited this morning that I forgot to take it off before coming downstairs. It was a stupid thing to do.

Mum said I had to eat breakfast before I could open any presents. She thinks about food all the time and has got fat again, so fat this time that she had to cut the top of her leggings with the kitchen scissors because they were too tight. She saw the bracelet when I reached for the cereal and was calm at first, just asked what it was and where I got it. She looked at the inscription and read the words out loud. *My darling girl.* I didn't want to get in trouble on my birthday, so I told her it was a gift from Taylor's mum.

It was just a little white lie and I promised God that if he existed and made Mum forget about it, I would definitely give the bracelet back the next day. But God doesn't exist or wasn't listening. Mum just lost it and went nuts. Even Dad, who had called in sick again, told her she was overreacting, but that just seemed to make things worse. She told me to take it off, so I started pretending to fiddle with the clasp. Then she walked away and I thought it was over, but she picked up the phone on the wall at the other end of the kitchen.

Dad poured me a bowl of cereal but I couldn't eat it. I knew she was calling Taylor's mum and that this was going to be bad. My cereal crackled and popped while I watched Mum snap. Sometimes it's hard to understand a conversation when you can only hear one side of it, but sometimes you can fill in the blanks as though you've heard the whole thing. She told Taylor's mum that we would be returning her gift. Mum said she didn't appreciate Taylor's mum spending more money on her daughter than she could afford to, and that a child wearing jewelry was a decision for the child's parents.

*I'm not a child.*

Mum went quiet then. It was as though the conversation had ended, but she was still holding the telephone to her ear, the red cord tightly twisted around her fingers. Then she looked up at me and I knew that she knew I had told a lie and it wouldn't matter whether it was white or not. Her mouth hung open as though she was silently saying the letter O for a very long time. Then she said "good-bye" and "sorry" and I knew I was in trouble. She put the phone down and very calmly told me not to lie. Then she asked me if I had stolen the bracelet.

I said no.

Sometimes I lie. Sometimes everybody lies.

Mum told me to take it off again. I shook my head and she started marching toward me, so I ran. Mum's pretty fast when she hasn't been drinking, even though she's let herself go. She's won the parents' race twice on sports days, but she didn't catch up with me until we got to the top of the stairs. She put her face right in my face and yelled at me to stop lying, bits of her spit landed on me, then she asked again if I had stolen the bracelet. As soon as I started to say the word no, she slapped me really hard on the cheek. Mum was yelling at me and Dad was at the bottom of the stairs yelling at Mum, then she grabbed my wrist and yanked the bracelet.

It was only thin gold.

It snapped and fell to the floor.

It was an easily broken thing.

I didn't mean for what happened next to happen. I just wanted her to get away from me and stop ruining everything so I pushed her.

I didn't mean for her to fall down the stairs, it was an accident.

Everything seemed to slow down and her eyes changed from small and cross to wide open as she fell backwards. She landed at the bottom and didn't move and everything was quiet. At first I really thought she might be dead. I didn't know what to do and I don't think Dad did either because he just stood there for what felt like a really long time. Then she moaned and it was horrible. She didn't sound like Mum anymore but the sound definitely came from her. Dad looked really worried and said he would call an ambulance, but Mum said it would be quicker for him to drive her to the hospital in the car. I wondered if it would start and hoped that it would. Dad helped her up and she kept just moaning about the baby.

I'm not a baby, I'm eleven.

They didn't say anything to me, not even good-bye. They just walked out the front door and drove away without looking back.

I picked up the broken bracelet and went downstairs.

There was a patch of bright red blood on the carpet where Mum had landed. She must have cut herself quite badly. I went into the kitchen and picked up the phone. I hit last number redial, I was hoping to wish Taylor a happy birthday, but nobody answered. My birthday cake was on a plate on top of the oven. Nana would have baked a cake herself, but Mum just got one from the supermarket. It was pink with a dancer made from icing and it reminded me of Taylor's jewelry box, which made me want to cry.

I leaned on one of the buttons on the cooker by accident and jumped back when I saw the sparks. I'm not supposed to touch the oven. Silly really, because it won't catch fire without matches, I watched Nana do it hundreds of times. I pushed the ignition button again and again, just because there was nobody there to tell me not to.

By lunchtime I still hadn't had any breakfast. My cereal was too soggy to eat by then but I was hungry, so I went to the top drawer and took out the biggest knife I could find. Then I cut myself a really big slice of cake and ate it with my fingers at the kitchen table. I blew on it first with my eyes closed and made a wish, even though there was no candle. I have to keep my wish a secret or it won't come true.

When I had finished my cake, I looked at the small pile of presents and decided Mum would be even more cross with me if I opened them while they were out. I opened one card, because it had Taylor's writing on the envelope. It didn't say much.

*Happy Birthday!!*
*Love from,*
*Taylor*

Underneath her name, she'd drawn two green circles with smiley faces. I did cry then, proper big tears that rolled down my cheeks and wouldn't stop. I don't think we'll be allowed to be two peas in a pod anymore.

# Now

You're here already?" says Paul.

"I couldn't sleep," Claire replies.

"Me neither."

*Me neither; our insomnia seems contagious.*

"I'll go, so you can have some time together."

"No, stay. If you want to. I don't mind."

Hours seem to go by without either of them saying a word. The nurses come to change my position, but the outlook stays the same. I want to tell them about the man who is holding me hostage in my sleep. I'm not sure they'd believe me, even if I could. I remember who he is now but I don't know why he is doing this to me. All I did was say no.

My husband and my sister sit on either side of the bed—my broken body forms the border between them. The stretched-out time the three of us endure is coated in the silence of unspoken words. I can feel walls of them, each letter, each syllable piling up on top of one another to form an unstable house of unanswered questions. Lies form the mortar, holding the walls together. If there weren't so many lies, the walls would have collapsed by now. Instead we've built ourselves a prison.

Paul doesn't hold my hand today and he doesn't play me any music. Pages turn, time rolls onward, and the ventilator punctuates each moment with the effort it takes to breathe for me, until the room is so fat with silence, one of us has to burst it. I can't, she won't, but he does.

"It was a girl."

The four words stab me in the stomach and punch a hole in the muted existence we've become accustomed to.

*It was a girl.*

I was pregnant.

*It was a girl.*

Past tense.

*It was a girl.*

I'm not pregnant anymore.

Now that the memory is complete, I don't want it. I want to give it back.

There was a baby growing inside of me but I killed it with my mistakes and now I can't even remember what they were, only what I've lost as a result.

"You could always try again," says Claire.

We weren't really trying anymore. We'd given up.

She was an accident.

A beautiful, fucked-up miracle of an accident.

I imagine Claire putting her arms around Paul, pushing her body up against his to comfort him. Even my grief for my unborn child is no longer my own, she's taking that from me too. The thought sparks a rash of jealousy that spreads itself all over my immobile body, an emotional gravity pushing me down, farther into my worst self.

*I would have kept her.*

*We would have loved her.*

*Now I've lost her as well as us.*

Northern Nurse comes into the room, smelling of tea and completely unaware that she's interrupting something I can barely comprehend. I feel all of my hate direct itself at her, but she remains oblivious, pottering about the place as though the world didn't just end.

*Get out and leave me alone!*

I feel myself letting go, my grip on reality loosening. Something is being pumped into me, something I don't want. I can feel it snaking below the surface of my skin, paralyzing my mind, squeezing the life out of me. For a moment I think it might not be a bad thing to die now, to just slip away. For a moment I don't want to wake up. Nobody would really miss me if I was gone, they'd probably be better off for it. I think I cry, but the nurse is wiping my face with a flannel so she doesn't notice. She's not as gentle as the others. Perhaps she can see all the dirt that hides just below my surface. The wet flannel slaps me in the face and I open my eyes.

I see them standing over me, all dressed in black. I'm not in my hospital bed anymore, I'm in an open coffin. They're all there: Paul, Claire, Jo, even *him*. He's shoveling soil onto me and I don't understand why they don't make him stop. It's in my hair, my mouth, some gets into my eyes. I scream at them to stop him but they don't listen because they cannot hear me.

*I'm not dead.*

He smiles at me, then leans right down to the coffin and whispers in my ear.

"Yes, you are, but don't worry, you'll have company."

He lifts up the little girl in the pink dressing gown and lays her in the coffin next to me. She wraps her arm around my waist. Everything turns black as the coffin starts to lower down into the earth. I start to cry and she starts to sing.

*Silent night. Holy night. All is calm. All is bright.*

She points up at the starless sky and I stare at the moon.

*Round yon virgin, mother and child.*

She squeezes me tight.

*Holy infant, so tender and mild.*

She turns to face me, her finger lifting to where her lips should be. *Shh.*

*Sleep in heavenly peace.*

*Sleep in heavenly peace.*

She reaches up and pulls an invisible cord. I hear what sounds like my bathroom light as she switches off the moon, plunging us into the unforgiving dark. Then the dirt starts to rain down on us faster. I scream at them again to stop, but if they can hear me, they're not listening. The hole is too deep for me to climb out of, but I have to do something. I scratch at the walls of earth, trying to find anything to hold on to, my nails clawing at the dirt. It starts to rain and water and soil fall down hard on top of me until I give up and roll myself into a ball. I hide within my fear and make it my home. A coin lands near my feet as though I'm at the bottom of a well where people make wishes. Neither side of the coin has a face.

"If you want to get out, just point at the exit," says the little girl. She's standing over me now, clumps of wet soil in her tangled hair. I follow her stare to a green neon emergency exit sign buried in the dirt beneath my feet.

"Just point when you want to get out, that's all you have to do."

I look down at the sign, half covered in dirt already, and try to point at it, but I can't move my hands. I'm crying again when the pain comes. Then there is blood. Blood dripping down on the emergency exit sign, blood on my hospital gown, blood on my hands as I hold them between my legs, trying to stop the life falling out of me. I close my eyes with the pain and when I open them and look up, the only face I can still see is Claire's. The little girl reaches for my hand and helps me to point my finger at the sign beneath my feet. It takes every last bit of strength I have.

"Did you see that?" says Claire's voice in the distance.

"What?" asks Paul.

"Look! Her hand, she's pointing her finger."

"Amber, can you hear me?"

"What does it mean?"

"It means she's still here."

# Then

I flush the toilet and wipe my mouth with the thin strip of recycled paper. I rub my lips harder than I need to, letting the rough edges sand my skin. I take a moment to breathe, grateful that none of my colleagues have seen me like this. It's the last show before the Christmas break, just one more day to get through, then it's done. Just a few more hours, I can manage that. I take a breath mint from my handbag and pop it in my mouth. I'm well practiced at hiding hangovers, but that isn't what this is.

I checked my diary on the train this morning: thirteen weeks and I hadn't even noticed. It isn't like we do it very often and I just presumed that this was never going to happen. All that time we spent trying and now, when I'd given up, now I'm pregnant. It doesn't make any sense and yet somehow it does and I'm sure that I am. I'll get a kit after work, that's what I'll do. I feel certain that I already know but I need to be sure.

I can't hear anything, so I flush the toilet once more and open the cubicle door. I think I'm alone, but I'm wrong.

"There you are. Are you quite all right?" asks Madeline. I feel my cheeks redden. I've never seen her in here before, seems out of place somehow. I thought she had a commode under her desk or something.

"What have you done to your head?" she asks, staring at my forehead. I look in the mirror and brush my hair over the bruise with my fingers.

"I tripped over something in the hall when I got home last night, it's nothing." It's the truth and yet the words leave an unpleasant taste in my mouth.

"Late night, was it? Drowning your sorrows?"

I turn on the taps to wash my hands and don't reply.

"Well, better that than morning sickness. Nothing like a pregnancy to ruin a girl's career!"

I don't react, just keep washing my hands over and over. She seems different somehow, like she's torn up the script. She's improvising and I can't keep up. The lines I've rehearsed don't make sense anymore. I turn off the tap, take a paper towel, and turn to face her. Sometimes saying nothing says too much, but the words won't come.

"I'm so glad I caught you," she says.

I want to run. My heart is beating so hard now that I'm sure she can hear it.

"I need to know that this conversation is going to stay within these walls," she continues, as though we are old friends conspiring and I can be trusted. I still can't force the words out just yet, so I nod. She reaches into her handbag and pulls out a collection of red envelopes. "I want to know what you know about these."

I look at them. Then I look her in the eye.

"Christmas cards?"

"They're not Christmas cards. As I'm sure you're aware, someone is spreading rumors about me on the Internet. I've also received some threatening mail in the office and at home this week. I'm sure the two things are linked and I want to know whether you have seen anything or anyone unusual hanging around."

"No, I don't think so."

"And you haven't opened anything unpleasant yourself?"

"No." I smile. I didn't mean to.

"This isn't a joke, this is serious. I think whoever wrote these letters has been inside the building."

That's when I spot it, the thing that has changed about her. This is what Madeline looks like when she's frightened, I've just never seen it before.

"This last one was on my desk this morning, before I arrived," she says, holding up the top red envelope.

"What does it say?"

"It doesn't matter what it says."

There is a gap for words we don't speak.

"Have you told Matthew about the letters?" I ask.

"No, not yet."

"Well, maybe you should." She sizes me up.

"I'll see you out there," she says, and leaves. I stay a while and wash my hands again.

I watch Madeline a little more closely during the show. I hate her, but she is good at her job, even if she doesn't deserve to be here. I study her face, still looking for a resemblance I can't see. She nods when I excuse myself to pop to the bathroom, as though she understands how I feel, as though she cares. I rush out, leaving my mobile in the studio. Jo comes to find me in the toilets to see if I'm okay. She makes me splash some water on my face, and it helps a little.

"You just have to get through the show, it's not much longer now. You're doing so well, it will all be all right," she says.

I wish I believed her. I wish the words were real. She heads back to the studio without me, giving me a moment to catch my breath. I walk back, stopping briefly at Matthew's desk. The office is empty when we're on air and he always leaves his phone out here. It isn't as though anyone would steal it, I suppose—his mobile is so old it doesn't even require a passcode. It takes less than thirty seconds to send the text and then delete it from his sent items.

They're halfway through a prerecorded Christmas feature when I get back to my seat. The mics are off, I've got a couple of minutes.

"You don't look at all well. I can finish the show without you if you need to go," says Madeline.

"I'm fine, thank you," I manage, and take my seat. The screen on my mobile is still lit up with the unread message I just sent from Matthew's phone.

*Dinner booked for you, me, and the new presenter next week. M x*

One look at Madeline's face confirms that she's already seen it and I offer an apologetic smile. I watch her neck and chest redden as though the anger burns her skin.

The phone-in is all about families at Christmas. I listen patiently to Kate in Cardiff who doesn't want to visit her mother-in-law and Anna in Essex who hasn't spoken to her brother for over a year and doesn't know what gift to buy him. It's all just nonsense, utter bullshit, all of it. These people have nothing real to worry about. It's pathetic. The nausea bubbles up once more when Madeline talks about the importance of forgiveness.

"Christmas is about being with family, whoever they are," she says, and I struggle not to vomit all over the desk. How would she know? She doesn't have any family left.

When the show finally draws to a close, I feel exhausted, but I know there is so much more work to be done today. It's my last chance and I'm just getting started.

Madeline is not a fan of watching television, but the one thing she likes more than the sound of her own voice on the radio is seeing herself on a TV screen. As the face of Crisis Child, she's required to do the odd TV interview speaking on behalf of the charity, and today is one of those days. The news program I used to be a reporter on has booked Madeline for an interview on their lunchtime bulletin, to talk about children living in poverty at Christmas. All it took was one phone call pretending to be from the charity, offering their celebrity spokeswoman and the mobile number for her PA if they were interested. The rest took care of itself.

There's an enormous satellite truck parked on the street ready and waiting down below. When I look out the window I can already see a camera set up on a tripod in front of the Christmas tree outside our building. As soon as the debrief is over, we head downstairs.

"How much longer is this going to take?" Madeline barks at one of the engineers.

"Not long, just have to find the satellite and mic you up," says John, an old colleague of mine. He turns and sees me standing behind her, a wide smile spreading itself across his face. "Amber Reynolds! How are you? I heard you were working here now." He hugs me and I'm surprised by the show of affection. I make myself smile back and try not to look too awkward, unable to return the hug and willing him to let me go.

"I'm good, thanks. How are the family?" I ask when he finally does. He doesn't get a chance to answer.

"Why are you out here? Nobody wants to interview you," Madeline says, glaring in my direction.

"Matthew asked me to come with you."

"I bet he did."

John's smile fades. He's been working in the business for over thirty years. He's met plenty of "Madelines" in his time. Celebrity ceases to impress when you subtract humility.

"If I could just . . ." John tries to attach the mic but it's hard to find a suitable place amongst all the rolls of black fabric she's wearing to attach the clip and hide the battery pack.

"Take your hands off me," snaps Madeline. "Give it to her, she'll do it. She used to be on television, after all; they'll let anyone call themselves a journalist now."

John nods, rolls his eyes when she isn't looking, and hands me the mic.

"I still can barely hear the studio," says Madeline, fiddling with her earpiece once I'm done.

"I've turned it right up," I say to John.

"I'll go and see if I can adjust it in the van," he says, taking off his headphones and leaving the camera. "Do you mind?" he asks me. I can see he's glad of an excuse to step away.

"Not at all, may as well make myself useful." I borrow his headset so I can hear the producer at the other end and cue Madeline when it's time to speak. She's not fazed and easily adjusts herself into caring ambassador mode when she thinks the world is watching. The answers roll off her tongue, one lie after another.

"I think that's it," I say, taking off the headset.

"You sure? Didn't last long."

"Think so, they're talking to another guest now." Her fake smile promptly falls from her face. "I'm sorry you saw that text earlier," I say.

"Poppycock." She looks agitated and checks her watch.

"If you do leave *Coffee Morning,* at least you'll have more time for your charity work."

"I'm not going anywhere, I've got a contract and charity starts at home, did nobody ever teach you that? Is that gobshite coming back or can I go?"

"I'll just double-check that you're done," I say, popping the headset back on. I can hear the program loud and clear. "It must be rewarding though, raising awareness of vulnerable children?" We've had this discussion so many times before, I know her thoughts on the matter.

"Vulnerable, my arse. Most of these kids are little shits and it's the parents I blame. There should be some sort of IQ test to identify people who are too stupid to have children and then those with low scores should be sterilized. Too many stupid people populating the land with their mentally retarded offspring is a big part of what's wrong with this country." I see John step out of the sat truck parked just down the street, frantically waving his hands above his head like he's trying to land a plane in a hurry.

"I think you can definitely go now," I say.

"Good, about time," Madeline replies. I couldn't agree more. She swivels on her heel and marches back inside the building. I follow her, unable to take my eyes off the battery pack still attached to the back of her giant black pashmina. She jabs her finger on the button to summon the lift, then turns to me and smiles. "And then there are the sluts who get pregnant by mistake, often with someone they shouldn't. That's why God invented abortions. Sadly too many of the dumb bitches don't have them." The lift doors open. "Are you getting in or what?" I shake my head. "Oh, I forgot, you're scared of lifts." She tuts, rolls her eyes, and steps inside, repeatedly stabbing the button to make sure the doors close before anyone else can get in.

By the time I've climbed the stone steps to the fifth floor, it feels like I've missed an episode of my favorite drama. Everyone is staring in the direction of Madeline's cupboard office. Matthew is in there with her and they are both shouting, so that every word of their supposedly private conversation is public, despite the closed door.

"What's going on?" I ask nobody in particular.

"Madeline's mic was still on. They did a guest in the studio, then went back to her. Everything she just said went out live on national television."

I do my very best to look surprised.

# Before

*Friday, October 30, 1992*

Dear Diary,

Mum came home from the hospital today, which seems fitting as it is Halloween tomorrow and she is a witch. Things have been better while she wasn't around. I thought that Taylor's mum would be really cross with me after what happened with the bracelet, but she's been even more kind to me than normal, taking me to school and picking me up afterwards for two whole weeks because Dad was working.

I tried to give Taylor her bracelet back and said sorry for accidentally borrowing it for such a long time, but she said it was okay and told me to keep it. She even fixed it for me by hooking a small safety pin through the broken links. I think it looks cool, even better than before. I think she was just really grateful after what happened at school last week and that was her way of saying thank you.

I really don't know what it is about Taylor that makes the other girls dislike her so much. She's pretty and kind and clever but those aren't reasons to be mean to her. I'm glad I found her when I did in the girls' toilets. There were two of them. Kelly O'Neil and Olivia Green. They were holding clumps of wet tissue in their hands and they were laughing. They stood on the toilet seats in the cubicles either side of Taylor, looking down at her over the wooden walls. I could hear her crying behind the closed door in the middle. Kelly told her to stand up and give them a twirl. The other girl whistled. "We'll go away if you let us see," she said, and they laughed again. "Don't be shy, show us." The crossness started to churn inside my tummy and I kicked their toilet doors. Kelly glared down at me, then turned back to look at Taylor over the wall. "Your girlfriend is here and she's getting jealous. Better pull your knickers up."

The bathroom door swung open and Mrs. MacDonald appeared, telling us we should all be outside. Kelly and the other girl left, both smiling at me as they walked past. I said I had to use the bathroom and would be straight out after that. When they were all gone, I knocked on the door of the cubicle in the middle, but Taylor still wouldn't come out. So I climbed up on the toilet next door, exactly the same way as Kelly had done, and looked down at her. She was sitting on the toilet seat, her pants around her ankles. She was covered in wet toilet roll—balled up like people do when they want to throw it on the ceiling. I don't think it had landed on her by accident. I told her to unlock the door and this time she did.

I climbed down and gently pushed the door open. She just stood there. Her eyes were all wet, her cheeks were red, and her pants were still around her ankles, so I bent down and pulled them up. We don't talk about that day. I'm not sure I should have even written it down. We stick together at all times now and the other girls keep away from us, which is fine by me.

Until Mum came home, things were pretty perfect. I was so happy when I got out of the Volvo this afternoon that I danced all the way up the driveway. Taylor's mum has been bringing dinners for me and Dad to heat up in the oven too, things she's cooked herself that smell and taste amazing. Dad hasn't been drinking as much as he sometimes does and I've been allowed to stay at Taylor's house for loads of sleepovers when he's been working late or visiting the hospital. Mum didn't want *me* to visit her. Nobody told me that, I just know. I didn't want to go anyway, hospitals remind me of Nana dying. Dad said Mum had to have a small operation on her tummy, which is why she didn't come home for such a long time. He said she's been feeling very poorly. He said it wasn't my fault.

I knew she was coming home today, but I guess I forgot. So when she was standing at the top of the stairs when I got back from school, it sort of made me jump and I felt scared. She didn't say anything at first, just stood there looking down at me in her big white nightie, like a ghost. Her eyes had even darker circles underneath them than before and she looked really skinny, like she'd forgotten to eat while she was at the hospital.

I didn't know what to say, so I went into the lounge to watch the big TV. The remote doesn't work anymore, so you have to push a button beneath the screen and then wait a little while for the picture to blink itself alive. A cartoon I don't like came on, but I was already sitting on the sofa so I watched it anyway. I was still wearing my hat and gloves because it is always cold in our house since the radiators stopped working. We've got a fireplace and we have a real fire on Sundays, but I'm never allowed too close and today isn't Sunday.

I could hear her coming down the stairs really slowly, like Granddad used to do when his hip had gone somewhere. A bit of me wanted to run away, but there was nowhere to run to. I went to bite my nails but the gloves got in the way, so I sat on my hands and swung my legs instead, as though I was on a swing instead of the sofa.

She stood in the doorway and asked me if I had anything to say to her. I shook my head and carried on looking at the TV. The cat in the cartoon chased the mouse but it got away again, clever mouse. I laughed, even though it wasn't very funny.

"It's happening again, isn't it?" she said.

The mouse took some matches and stuck them between the cat's toes. The cat didn't even notice, it was too busy looking in the wrong direction. Then the mouse lit all the matches and ran away. The cat could smell the smoke, but didn't see the flames until it was too late. I laughed again, a pretend loud laugh, hoping she would just go away and leave me alone.

"I said, it's happening again, isn't it?" She spoke in her cross voice, the one that means I'm in trouble.

I shrugged my shoulders, stood up, and walked out to the kitchen. My coloring things were still on the table from the night before, so I started doing that while Mum followed me and sat down on the chair opposite. I didn't look up. My pencils were too blunt, all of them. I looked at her then and asked if she would sharpen my pencils for me. I'm not allowed to do it myself. Our eyes spoke but her lips didn't move. She shook her head to say no. I wanted to use the red pencil even more then, but it was so blunt it hardly left a mark. I pushed harder, making a pattern of clear, jagged dents in the paper. Mum tried to take my hand to stop me but I pulled it away. She said we needed to talk, but I didn't have anything to say to her, so I just carried on pretending she wasn't there and picked up the black pencil, which still had some color left in it. It was hard to stay inside the lines with my gloves on, so the black pencil went all over the picture until I couldn't see what it was anymore.

Mum told me to look at her. I didn't. She said it again but broke up the words so they were on their own.

Look. At. Me.

I still didn't look up, but I whispered something very quietly. She asked me what I had said and I whispered it again. Then she stood up so quickly that her chair fell backwards, making me jump. She leant over the table and grabbed my chin, forcing my face up to look at her. She spat in my eyes a little bit as she asked me again what I had said. She was hurting my face, so I told her.

I. Hate. You.

It was the opposite of a whisper.

She let go of me and I ran out of the kitchen and up to my bedroom. I still heard what she yelled up the stairs, even though I'd closed my door and put my hands over my ears.

"You're not to see Taylor anymore. I don't want her coming to this house."

She can't stop me seeing Taylor, we go to the same school.

I tried reading for a while, but I couldn't concentrate, I kept reading the same sentence without meaning to. I threw the book on the floor and took Taylor's broken bracelet out from the drawer next to the bed where I hide it. I unfastened the safety pin and tried to put it on, but the end of the chain kept slipping off my wrist. I wanted to go trick-or-treating tomorrow night, but I know there's no point even asking now that she's back. I can hear her down there, shuffling about, scraping the contents of casserole dishes into the bin and ruining my life.

# Now

*Friday, December 30, 2016*

I'm flying feet first and it takes a while for me to remember that I am in the hospital. I still can't move or open my eyes, but I can see the light shifting above, like I'm going through a tunnel. Subtle changes from light to dark. Then dark to light.

I realize I'm tucked into my bed and they're moving me somewhere. I'm not sure what that means and I wish someone would explain. I ask the questions in my head but nobody answers.

*Am I moving to a ward?*

*Am I better?*

*Am I dead?*

I can't shake the last thought from my mind. Maybe this is what dead feels like.

I don't know where I'm going but it's much quieter than before. The bed stops moving.

"Here you are then. I'm off shift now, but someone else will be back to collect you in a little while," says a stranger. He speaks to me as though I'm a child. I don't mind though—him speaking to me at all means that I must still be alive.

*Thank you.*

He leaves me and it is so quiet. Too quiet, something is missing.

The ventilator.

They've taken it away from me and the tube in my throat has gone. I panic until I realize that I am breathing without it. My mouth is closed but my chest is still inflating with oxygen. I'm breathing on my own. I *am* getting better.

I hear footsteps and then there are hands on my body and I'm afraid again. They are lifting me off the bed and I'm scared I will fall, frightened they will drop me. They lay me down on something cool. The surface chills the skin on my back through the open gown. I'm lying flat, with my hands by my side, staring up at nothing, unable to see beyond myself. They leave me there and it is the most quiet it has ever been. For a while.

Whatever I'm lying on lifts me up and backwards, headfirst again, swallowing me inside itself. The quiet is silenced by a piercing noise, like a muffled robotic scream. I don't know what's happening. Whatever it is, I want it to end. The relentless whirring is loud and strange and seems to be getting closer. Finally it stops.

As my body rides back out into the brighter gloom, I hardly notice. The mechanical screams have rendered themselves into the sound of a baby crying and it's so much worse. I feel wet and realize I have pissed myself. There was no bag attached to collect my liquid shame. The smell smothers me and I switch myself off.

The sound of whistling brings me back to somewhere a little less dark. I hate whistling. I am on my bed again and someone is pushing me feetfirst down another series of endless, long corridors. The shadows rise and fall overhead once more as though I am rolling beneath a conveyor belt of lights. The bed stops and turns and stops again several times. I feel like I've become a hoover, moving back and forth trying to suck up all my own dirt. We come to an abrupt stop and the whistled tune concludes at the same moment.

"I'm so sorry to trouble you, could you remind me where the exit is, I always get lost in here," says the voice of an elderly woman.

"Don't worry, happens to me all the time, it's like a warren. Back where you came from and take the first right, that's the main exit to the visitor parking lot," says a voice I don't want to hear. I tell myself it isn't him, that I'm imagining things.

"Thank you."

"You're welcome."

It is him. The voice of the man who is drugging me to sleep. I'm sure of it.

He starts to whistle once more and it triggers something, dislodges a forgotten memory. He used to whistle all the time when we were students. It irritated me then and it terrifies me now. I've been telling myself I was mistaken, confused, but any remaining doubts that were giving me hope crumble. The man keeping me here is Edward. I know that now. I just don't know why.

We're on the move again and I panic, wondering where he is taking me. Surely someone will stop him, but then I remember that he works here. Nobody would question a member of the staff pushing a patient around a hospital. I feel sick. Doctors are supposed to help people, not hurt them.

*Why are you doing this to me?*

The bed on wheels makes its final stop and the whistling is replaced by something worse. I hear the door close.

"Here we are, just the two of us. Alone again at last."

# Then

The whole team is meant to be enjoying a Christmas lunch together before the holidays, but two people are missing. Madeline and Matthew. Given the latest Category 5 social media storm and the story being picked up by several other broadcasters, I'm not surprised. The whole interview has been posted on YouTube and #FrostBitesTheDust is more popular than ever on Twitter, albeit for slightly different reasons than before. I wonder if she's even had time to notice my final blackmail letter tucked inside her handbag. Not to worry, it can wait.

Madeline and Matthew are busy having crisis talks with the station bosses on the seventh floor. I can't imagine how this story could possibly result in a happy ending for either of them. Matthew told the rest of us to head for lunch without him. He's booked a small Italian restaurant round the corner, because nothing says Christmas like meatballs in tomato sauce.

The restaurant owner looks scarily happy to see us. There's one long table, like we're sitting down to a medieval banquet of napkins and crackers and paper crowns. The others discuss leaving the seat at the top of the table free for Matthew when he arrives, I guess because he is the head of this dysfunctional work family. I seat myself at the end of the table nearest the exit and feel a moment of relief when Jo sits down in the empty seat next to me. Thank goodness she's here.

"*Vino rosso?*" she asks, before reaching for an open bottle of house wine on the table.

"Not for me, thank you." She pulls a face but I can't even tell Jo the truth, not until I'm sure. "I'm fine, I just had a bit too much to drink last night."

"With Paul?"

"No, an old friend."

"A friend who isn't me?"

"I do have other friends, you know," I say, realizing that I don't, not anymore. We've received even fewer Christmas cards than I've written this year.

One of the producers leans over with a cracker, trying to get my attention. I smile back at her and wrap my fingers around the edge of the shiny gold paper. I pull hard but nothing happens and we both laugh. I pull harder and the cracker snaps, making me jump even though I was expecting it. I've won. I put the paper crown on my head and read the joke out to the rest of the team.

"What lies at the bottom of the sea and shivers?"

I look around at their expectant faces. I doubt I'll see them again.

"A nervous wreck."

A few smiles and a groan but nobody laughs. Someone reads out a better joke.

Jo points out the red plastic slither of a fish that has fallen from the cracker. I pick it up and lay it flat on my open palm. I remember these from when Claire and I were children. "Fortune Teller—Miracle Fish," reads the packaging and I smile at the memory. The fish's head curls up in my hand. I can't remember what that is supposed to mean, so I read the tiny square of white paper covered in instructions, scanning it for the translation.

Moving head = Jealousy.

I remove the fish from my hand and the smile from my face. I am jealous. I've got every right to be.

The restaurant door opens and a cold burst of air rushes in, stealing some paper hats from heads, blowing them onto the floor. Matthew has arrived. Madeline is not with him.

He makes a performance of taking off his coat and sitting down at the table. Then he clinks his glass of prosecco with his knife, which really wasn't necessary; the restaurant is completely empty apart from our table, and the polite conversation of sober colleagues has already dried up, despite everything we've had to gossip about.

"I want you all to enjoy your Christmas lunch and a well-deserved afternoon off. . . ." He pauses for dramatic effect and I want to throw my plate at his head. I unfold my paper napkin and place it on my lap. "But before we do that, I have some sad news." Now he has my attention. "I know you're all aware of the unfortunate incident with Madeline's microphone on the lunchtime news today."

I sip my glass of lemonade. It's more ice than drink and hurts my teeth.

"What I'm about to tell you has absolutely nothing to do with that."

Liar. I put down my glass and push my hands together beneath the table in a forward-facing prayer, trying to stop myself from picking the skin off my lips in public.

"I'm sorry to tell you that Madeline has sadly decided to leave the program for personal reasons and will no longer be presenting *Coffee Morning*."

Now the gasps come, including my own.

*Ding. Dong. The witch is Dead.*

"I'm telling you now because the bloody papers will have it by tomorrow and I wanted to reassure you all that the show will go on, your jobs are safe. We'll have some guest presenters in the New Year. Amber, I hope you'll help them as much as you can, and then we'll look for a new long-term solution." I nod. It's his way of letting me know I'm safe now.

The chatter and gossip escalate again. Now that we have something new to talk about, there is only one topic of conversation. Matthew said that Madeline's reasons for leaving were personal. I expect I'm the only person at this table who knows just how personal it is.

Our "Christmas garlic bread" arrives looking dry and unappetizing. I'm wondering how to extract myself from the situation when I hear a knock on the restaurant window behind me. I turn and can see the outline of someone, but the fake snow makes it hard to recognize the smiling face staring back.

"Do you know him?" asks Jo.

I can't speak at first. I'm too busy trying to understand what he is doing here. Edward smiles back at us both.

"Excuse me for a moment," I say to nobody in particular, and walk away from the table. I step out onto the street, the cold wind reminding me that I should have brought my coat.

"Hi," he says, as though him being here is somehow acceptable.

"What are you doing here? Are you following me?"

"Whoa! No, I'm sorry. It probably does look like that, but I'm not stalking you, I promise. You said last night that you were coming here for your Christmas lunch today."

*Did I?*

"I had a meeting down the road and when I spotted you in the window, I had an impulse to say hi."

I don't believe him.

I notice that he hasn't shaved. A dark shadow of stubble has grown over his tanned chin and he is wearing exactly the same clothes as yesterday, his white shirt visible beneath the long woolen coat. He waits for me to say something and when I don't he tries again.

"I'm lying. I'm sorry, I shouldn't do that. You see straight through me anyway, you always did. There was no meeting. I remembered you were coming here and I just had to find a way to see you again. . . ."

"Look, Edward . . ."

"To say sorry. I was mortified when I woke up this morning and remembered last night. I just wanted the chance to apologize, that's all. I don't know why I said the things I did, it must have been the wine. Not that I don't think you're great, but that's all in the past. I won't keep you from your Christmas lunch, I'm so sorry, I just wanted to clear the air and reassure you that I'm not a psycho."

"Okay."

"It's freezing, please go back to your friends. I fear I've made things even worse. I won't trouble you again, Amber. I'm really sorry for how I behaved."

He does look very sorry, so much so that I'm starting to feel a little sorry for him; it's hard living in a city where nobody really knows you. I look over at the restaurant and can see Jo in the window, beckoning me to come back inside. I feel like I ought to say something but I can't seem to find the right words. I'm cold and it's awkward, so I settle for the wrong ones.

"Happy Christmas, Edward. See you around," I say, before turning back toward the restaurant, leaving him out in the cold.

# Before

*Friday, December 11, 1992*

Dear Diary,

It's happened again. I've been suspended, but it really wasn't my fault. I didn't want to go to school at all today. I didn't feel well, and if Mum had let me stay in bed then none of this would have happened. So it's her fault really, just like everything else, but I expect she won't see it that way when she finds out. Sticks and stones, Nana used to say, but Taylor could have been really hurt if I hadn't done something.

We were in science and using the Bunsen burners for the first time. I'd always wondered what they were, but we hadn't been allowed to touch them until today. I liked the smell of gas when we turned them on, it reminded me of Nana's old oven. Mr. Skinner taught us what to do. Bunsen burners all have a hole and that's important. When the hole is closed it makes a yellow flame, but when it is open it makes a hot blue flame. Basically it's all about combustion. Gas can be dangerous, though, and so can flames obviously, so when I came back from the toilet and saw Kelly holding the flame up close to Taylor's hair, I had to do something.

They said her nose was broken this time. I don't even remember doing it really, I just wanted to get her away from Taylor. Mr. Skinner pulled me off her and asked what happened and I said I didn't know. He yelled at me not to lie and that he'd seen me, but I wasn't lying. All I can remember is Taylor and Kelly's faces too close together. It was like something just snapped inside of me. I love Taylor. I won't let anyone hurt her. I didn't have a choice.

Mr. Skinner dragged me by my blazer to the headmistress's office. I hadn't been inside of this one yet but I wasn't scared. They're all the same and they can't do anything to me, not really. It was all very dramatic, like I was in a film or something. Except that if it had been a film, I would have been the hero. Instead, because it was real life, I was the bad guy who had to sit on a hard chair in the corridor and wait there while they called Mum.

Taylor appeared with the nurse. She'd bumped her head when I pushed her out of the way to save her. She didn't look very happy. Her face was all red and puffy from crying, but she was all right, thanks to me. The nurse told her that her mum would be there soon to pick her up. The nurse didn't say anything to me and neither did Taylor. We've never run out of words to say to each other before and it made me feel sad. I asked her if she was all right but she just stared at the floor. I was about to ask her again when she spoke.

"You shouldn't have done that," she said.

Which I thought was very ungrateful.

"Why not?" I asked her.

"Because you have to use this," she said, pointing to her head, "not these." She held up her hands. "What do you think they'll do to me if you're not here? You've ruined everything."

Her words made me feel sad and cross at the same time. I could see she was upset, so I just kept quiet and stored up my crossness. There was so much inside me that it made a pain in my tummy.

Taylor's mum arrived and gave Taylor a big hug. I was really worried that she'd be upset with me too, but she gave me a hug as well, so I knew that she still loved me. I think she does love me. Not as much as she loves Taylor, but quite a lot. She asked me if Mum was coming to get me and I said that I didn't know. Taylor's mum and my mum don't really talk anymore since the bracelet incident.

Taylor's mum spoke to the headmistress in her office. We could hear every word through the glass door, which made me think that the PRIVATE sign on the outside was pretty stupid. The school couldn't get hold of my mum or my dad and in the end they let Taylor's mum take me home.

Taylor didn't talk to me as we walked out of the school or as we got in the Volvo or even when we arrived outside my house. Taylor's mum looked at me in the backseat as though she didn't understand what I was still doing there, but then I asked her if she could come with me and explain to Mum what happened because I was scared. Her face changed then, like it went all soft and her big green eyes looked sad and kind at the same time. She told Taylor to stay in the car, not that Taylor had even taken her seat belt off, she was just staring out the window. She didn't even say good-bye.

Taylor's mum followed me up the path and knocked on the door—the doorbell hasn't worked for a while. When nobody came I looked up at her and she smiled down at me. She's so pretty and kind and her outfits always match as though the clothes she wears are meant to be worn together. She knocked again. Then when nobody came, she asked if I had my door key. I said I did but told her that I was still scared, which wasn't even a lie because I was a bit. I knew Mum and Dad would be really angry. I'd also made a promise to Nana that nothing like this would ever happen again. Now that she's dead, I don't know whether it means I broke my promise or not.

I called out for Mum once we were inside but nobody answered. Then I saw her. Just her feet at first, sticking out from behind the sofa, as though she was hiding but not doing a very good job. When I got closer, I saw that she wasn't hiding. She wasn't moving. Her eyes were closed and her face was in a big puddle of sick on the carpet. I screamed for Taylor's mum because I was genuinely scared. Mum looked like she was dead for real, just like when she was all broken at the bottom of the stairs. There was a horrible smell too. The sick was all down her chin and on her clothes. Taylor's mum said not to worry and that Mum wasn't well but would be okay. I had to help her get Mum upstairs, then she told me to go and get Taylor from the car. I could tell Taylor didn't want to come in but she did. She still wouldn't talk to me though.

We sat on the sofa and Taylor's mum told us to put the TV on and to stay downstairs. I turned it on, but neither of us really watched it. The sound was too low to block out the noise coming from above. Taylor's mum took my mum into the bathroom to clean her up. Mum cried very loudly and then she started shouting all kinds of things.

The three things she shouted that I remember the most are:

1. Fuck you. (She said that a lot.)
2. Get out of my house, you bitch. (It's not her house, it's Nana's.)
3. I don't need your bloody help.

The third one was the silliest of all because clearly she did need help from someone.

I've never heard Mum speak to anyone except Dad like that before. She also called Taylor's mum a snob. A snob is someone who thinks they're better than you. I don't think Taylor's mum thinks that, even though she is a much better person than my mum, she's the best mum ever. It was a horrid afternoon, but a little secret part of me was pleased because it meant we'd all forgotten about me being suspended.

Taylor and her mum didn't leave until Dad got home. He said "sorry" and "thank you" a lot, like he didn't know any other words to say. Then when they left he asked if I wanted chicken nuggets for dinner. We ate sitting on the sofa in front of the big TV, which was still on but still not being watched. Dad forgot the ketchup but I didn't say anything. He didn't make Mum any dinner and I think I know why. While we sat there not watching TV and eating our chicken nuggets without ketchup, I realized for the first time that Dad probably wishes Mum was dead just as much as I do.

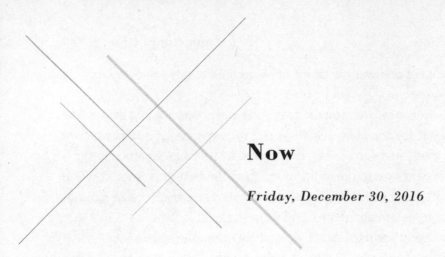

# Now

How are we doing, Amber? Still got some fight in you, I see. I like that."

My hospital room seems a shade darker than before. I want to scream as Edward touches my face. I want to disappear so that he can't see me or ever find me again.

"And breathing on your own now, that's such good news, well done you."

His fingers slide over to my right eye and he opens it. I can just make out the fuzzy outline of a person looming over me before he shines a bright light into my eye, leaving me completely blind. All I see now is white with a shower of moving dots. He does the same with my left eye and then my world returns to black.

"I think you're progressing a bit too quickly. Maybe we just need to slow things down a little."

I can hear him doing something but I don't know what. Just when I run out of hope and accept my fate, I hear the door open.

"How's she doing?" asks Paul. I don't understand why he is so calm about finding this man in my room, but then I remember that all he sees is a medical professional.

"I'm afraid I'm not really the best person to ask," says Edward.

"I'm sorry, I've met so many people . . . haven't we spoken before?"

"I don't think so. I'm just the night porter. . . ."

The *porter*? I don't understand.

". . . and this is the start of the night shift, so you really shouldn't still be here now."

"Should you?" asks Paul.

It's silent for a moment and I'm scared of what will happen next.

"I've just brought your wife back from a scan. Just doing my job."

*You didn't tell him you were my husband. Think, Paul, think.*

"I'm sorry, that was rude of me. I'm very tired, I apologize. You must see all sorts, working nights in this place," says Paul.

"You'd be amazed the things that go on here after dark," Edward replies. "I don't mind if you want to stay a little longer, say your good-byes, but you'll need to leave soon. Hospital rules, hope you understand. Don't worry though, we'll take good care of her while you're gone."

Edward leaves and Paul and I are alone. He drags a chair closer to my bed and sits down. I have to find a way to tell him that the man he just spoke to is keeping me here. I don't understand why Edward said he was the night porter or why Paul believed him. Claire comes into the room and for once I'm glad. She's smart, she'll figure this out.

"Who was that?"

"Just some porter guy, he said we need to leave."

"He's probably right, it's late," she says, sitting down next to Paul, no longer on opposite sides.

"She moved her finger, you saw it too, she was pointing at something, I know it," he says.

*I remember now. I pointed at the exit sign. I thought it was a dream but they saw me!*

"I saw her finger move, yes, but you heard what the doctor said earlier. There are coma patients who move their hands, open their eyes, even speak, but they're still in a coma. Her moving is just like someone twitching in their sleep when they're having a bad dream."

*This is more than just a bad dream.*

"I think we need to stay positive, see what they say when the rest of the results come back. . . ."

"I think we need to be realistic," interrupts Claire.

Nobody says anything for a while.

"For what it's worth, I don't believe them either," she says eventually.

"You think the doctors are lying to us?"

"Not lying, I just don't think they're listening. It did seem like she was trying to communicate and they don't know her like we do."

"Then why hasn't she done it again?"

"Have you even asked her to? What if she's lying there hearing every word of this?"

Claire takes my hand. Her fingers are icy cold.

"Amber, if you can hear me, squeeze my hand."

"This is stupid."

"Maybe that's too difficult." She lets go of my hand and puts it back down on the bed. "Okay, Amber, we're watching your right hand. If you can hear me, move your finger, just a tiny bit." I want to, I try so hard to, but he's done something to me, I know he has. I focus all of myself on my right hand. I feel as though I must be panting with the effort, but nothing happens.

"I'm sorry," says Claire.

"Don't be," says Paul. "I know you're just trying to help. You're probably right about getting some rest too, we should go soon."

*Please don't.*

"Five minutes, then we'll go."

The three of us sit in silence for a while. I wish they would talk. I can feel myself slipping away to somewhere else and I could really do with something to hold on to. Claire speaks first.

"We're going to need to get some help if this is going to be a long-term situation."

"It isn't."

"I hope it isn't too, but if it is, we can't do this on our own."

"Yes we can, we'll just take it in turns to watch her."

"For a few more days maybe, but then what? David is going nuts looking after the twins, it's not like when my parents were around to help out. Are there any of her friends we can call?"

Paul doesn't reply.

"She still has friends, doesn't she?" Claire persists.

"She talks about Jo at work, they go out sometimes."

Their conversation stumbles and I feel sick. Claire recovers her composure before I do.

"A friend called Jo?"

"Yes, a woman."

I can almost hear her thinking.

"Have you ever met her?" she asks.

"No. Why?"

"No reason. Well, maybe she can help."

"I don't have her number."

"Well, it will be in her phone, won't it?"

I hear Paul open something and then picture him going through my handbag. The room starts to spin one way and my bed turns in the other direction. I can hear her singing in the distance, the little girl in pink, but I have to stay here, I have to stop this from happening. Paul cannot go through my phone, there are things he must not see. I think I remember something bad. Something I shouldn't have done that would make any husband angry if he found out. The memory feels real and is joined by another. Strong hands tightening around my throat again, fighting for breath, for the first time I think I remember why. The fears brick themselves up inside my head so that nothing else can get in or out.

"The battery is dead," he says. The room slows down again but doesn't stop spinning completely. "I'll take it home tonight and charge it."

# Then

I can't believe I just did that," I say.

"Neither can I but I'm glad you did," Edward replies.

"They'll all be talking about me now, running off with a stranger halfway through the Christmas lunch."

"I'm hardly a stranger."

We walk into the bar and sit at the same table I sat at with Jo a few days earlier. I like this place—it feels safe, familiar, like nothing bad could ever happen here.

"Things have been a bit difficult at work recently. I'd rather have a quick drink with an old friend instead of making polite conversation over warm prosecco." I pause for a moment, knowing I need to say more. "That's all this is though, two friends having a drink to clear the air."

"Understood," Edward replies. "What can I get you?"

"I'll get them," I insist, taking my wallet out of my handbag and leaving it on the chair. It's heavy with all the things I didn't want to leave behind at the office, things I might need.

"A pint of whatever pale beer they've got on draft in that case."

"A pint it is. I'll be back in a bit."

The bar is busy and I find myself staring at the black-and-white photos on the walls while I wait. My eyes find the date on the frame nearest to me, 1926. The place looks exactly the same. The world keeps on spinning, repeating itself over and over until something changes, which it doesn't because we can't. I do the math and realize that the faces of the dead are smiling back at me. I look away. When I'm finally served, my feet seem to stick to the ugly patterned carpet, holding me back. I negotiate my way through the crowds toward the table, a pint of beer in one hand, pint of lemonade in the other, and two packets of cheese-and-onion crisps between my teeth. Edward's expression alters slightly as I sit down. I can't interpret the look so I ignore it.

"Cheers," I say, raising my glass.

"Cheers."

"So what are your plans for Christmas?"

"Working, sadly. I drew the short straw and have got a run of nights from Christmas Day until New Year's."

"Ouch."

"It's okay. Staying up all night isn't as bad as people think." A memory, loosened by his words, rises to the surface.

"Do you remember my graduation?" I ask, and watch his face argue with a smile.

It's easy for a while, almost comfortable. We talk about holidays and countries we've visited during the years we didn't know one another, safely navigating around mutual memories to stories that aren't shared. Creating a little distance, restoring order. I think we might be in safe territory and start to relax a little.

"Are you happy?" he asks. His hand finds a place to rest on the table that is a little too close to my own. I withdraw both my hands to the safety of my lap and ball them into conjoined fists.

"I love my husband."

"That isn't what I asked."

"Edward." I won't see him again; this is the last good-bye. He knows it too, but still persists in asking the question.

"Are you? Happy?"

I decide I'll give him the answer, then I'll finish my drink and go home.

"No. I'm not especially 'happy' right now. But that's not because of my marriage."

"What then?"

"Just life, I suppose. It's hard to explain."

"Try."

"I've made mistakes and now I'm paying for them."

# Then

I wake up with a pounding headache and can't understand where I am or what has happened to me. The last thing I remember was chatting with Edward in the pub. I sit up. The sudden movement makes the room sway as though I'm on a tiny boat in rough seas, but I'm not on a boat, I'm on a bed. The room I'm in is dark, the curtains closed. The dimly lit sight and smell of the place are foreign to me, a mix of stale belongings and sweat. I still don't know where I am but I soon realize that I'm naked.

Time stops for just a moment while I look down at my pale white body. Every single part of myself that is usually covered, hidden away, is now exposed. Things get very loud, very quickly inside my head. The bedroom I'm in is not my own. I stare down at the unfamiliar navy blue sheets, I hear the sound of a shower in the distance, and I try to decipher the strange taste in my mouth. I look around for my clothes and see them on the floor. I wasn't even drinking, I only had lemonade. I didn't do anything, I wouldn't do this.

*I can't remember.*

I try to move, pull myself up from the bed. I feel as though I'm in slow motion as I attempt to stand. Again the room starts to tilt and twist around me. I am liquid mercury trapped inside a maze. No matter what I do, I can't seem to flow in the right direction. I bend my body forward, willing it to respond to my commands, and the farther I bend the more I fear I will snap. I hear a man whistling somewhere in the distance, the sound diluted by the crash of water being pushed out of a power shower. I feel sick. This cannot be real. I'm not the sort of person who would do this.

I force myself to stand and I feel the ache between my legs. I don't know whether it is real or whether I'm just imagining it. I try to shake the thoughts and the feeling and take a step closer toward the pile of clothes I recognize as my own. The room shifts again, trying to unbalance me. I look down at my bare legs and see a tattoo of blue-green bruises on both my knees. Something very bad has happened.

*I must try to remember.*

My mind races through a catalog of recent memories but every file is blank until I am back at the pub. I only drank lemonade, I'm sure of it. I went to the bathroom, I came back, and I was going to leave soon. But then . . . nothing.

My eyes search the room again. I see a framed photo next to the bed and my body forgets how to breathe. My own younger self looks up at me, laughing at how foolish I have been. A young Edward has his arm wrapped around her shoulders, pulling her a little too close, although she looks as though she doesn't mind. I remember the photo being taken. It was my graduation. A few days before I broke up with him. I didn't want to, I had to. He's kept it all this time. The boy in the photo has grown into a man I don't know. A man I'm now very afraid of. And somehow I'm in his flat and my clothes are on his floor.

*I don't want to remember.*

This isn't right. I have to get out of here but I don't even know where I am. I've been such a fool. I pause my self-revulsion momentarily to take in my surroundings. Everything has a look of filth about it. There are newspapers on the floor, unopened post, an empty bottle, unwashed clothes, dirty plates, an open pizza box on the carpet with some chewed bits of crust. The musty air is stifling and I can see a thick layer of dust on every surface. There's a machine in the corner. I'm not sure what it is at first, but then I recognize its outline as an old-fashioned sunbed. None of this makes any sense.

My eyes find my own clothes once again, abandoned on the stained carpet. My body feels bruised and persistently protests as I cover myself up with the clothes I can find, forgetting the ones I can't. I spot my handbag and search inside for my phone but it isn't there. Instead I find the unopened pregnancy test kit and feel the nausea rise up my throat. I look around again, scanning through the debris of a life I'm unfamiliar with and spot my phone on a table. I check the date and time—it's still Friday. The sound of the shower stops and I freeze. My legs switch to autopilot and start to move, forcing me to stumble toward the only door in the room.

I turn the handle and pull it open to reveal a long, narrow hallway. I can hear him whistling behind a door at the other end. The dirty brown carpet is almost completely hidden by stacks of old newspapers and there's a strong smell of damp. I notice the two large corkboards on the walls and I recognize them instantly. He had them in his room at university. They were covered in photos of the two of us back then and they still are, but more recent pictures have been added to the collage now too, this time just of me. Me outside work, me reading a newspaper on the tube, me sipping coffee at a café down the road from my home less than a week ago; I recognize my new coat. There must be over a hundred photos and my face stares out from every one. I make myself look away. I have to get out. Now.

I see what looks like a front door between the room I am in and where he is. I know I'm running out of time as I stagger along between the wall and the highly piled detritus. It's an effort to steady my hands enough to unhook the chain and let myself out into the blacker darkness. I'm outside but high up, some sort of walkway within a large block of flats. I turn briefly to look at the number on the navy blue door I have just walked through, then I start to back away. I don't even stop to close it behind me. I enjoy the shock and pain of the cold air. I feel it sneak inside my sleeves, down my top, up and under my skirt. I blink back the tears. I don't deserve anyone's pity, not even my own.

# Before

Dear Diary,

We're all at home together now, Mum, Dad, and me. I'm still suspended, not that anyone cares. Dad has stopped going to work. He says it's so he can look after Mum because she's not well, but he sits downstairs all day watching TV while she stays up in her bedroom. He says I'm old enough to be told the truth and that Mum was pregnant before she fell down the stairs and that the baby died. That's why she drank so much she was sick and why she was shouting at Taylor's mum that afternoon. I thought people only shouted rude things when they were angry, but Dad says some people do it when they are sad.

I didn't know Mum was pregnant but I'm glad that she isn't anymore, it's disgusting. I asked Dad if she would get pregnant again and he said no because they had to remove something from her tummy in the hospital. I was pleased about that. They can't even look after me properly, so it doesn't make any sense at all for them to have another child. I'm a bit worried that they might adopt a fake brother or sister to make Mum happy again. I don't want one of those either.

Dad is always having to pop out for this or that, but sometimes he comes back with nothing at all. I think he should start making lists so he doesn't keep forgetting things, that's what Nana used to do. He asked me to keep an eye on Mum while he went out to get some bread, milk, and a lottery scratch card. That was tricky, because I didn't want to look at her. The bedroom door was slightly open so I decided to keep watch from there with one eye closed like Dad said. I thought she might like to hear me singing, seeing as she missed the Christmas concert this year. So I made up a funny song, which I sang to her from the landing.

*What shall we do with the drunken mother?*
*What shall we do with the drunken mother?*
*What shall we do with the drunken mother?*
*Early in the morning?*

I even made up a little dance to go with it, miming drinking from lots of bottles. She didn't laugh, so maybe she was still sleeping. She sleeps a lot. Dad says the sadness tires her out.

When Dad got back he said we needed to have a little talk. He had forgotten the milk again but I didn't tell him because he already looked very worried about something. We sat at the kitchen table and at first I thought he'd forgotten what he wanted to talk about, but then he pulled a face and said we have to move house again. I told Dad that I don't want to move again but he said that we have to. I asked if it was my fault, for getting suspended, and he said no. He started to explain but his words got all jumbled up on the way to my ears because I was crying without meaning to.

It's something to do with a man called Will. Nana was supposed to talk to him before she died, but she forgot to and now we have to move because people keep forgetting things. Dad said Mum's sister is very cross about Nana not talking to Will. I didn't even know Mum had a sister. Dad said I met her a few times when I was really little but I don't remember her at all. Dad said Mum's sister hadn't spoken to Mum or Nana for years, but when Nana died she decided she would like half of her house. I asked if we could still live in the other half, but Dad said no, it didn't work like that. I asked if we could stay if he matched three things on the lottery scratch card. He said he'd already scratched it and we hadn't won.

This all made me feel very sad, so I asked Dad if I could go upstairs and read in my room for a while and he said yes, so long as I was quiet, and not to disturb Mum. He said we had to take very good care of Mum because she was even more upset about all of this than we were. I don't see why I should take care of her at all. She was meant to look after Nana and she didn't do a very good job because the cancer killed her. I can't help thinking lately that if someone better, like Taylor's mum, had looked after Nana when she was ill, she would have got better and still been alive now. Every-thing would still be good and we wouldn't have to keep moving house. This is all Mum's fault, even if Dad is too stupid to see it. Mum has ruined everything for everyone and I'll never forgive her.

# Now

*New Year's Eve 2016*

The sound wakes me. I've heard it before. My bed is tilting me backwards, so that my feet are pointing up toward the ceiling and the blood rushes to my head. They lift me a little farther toward the very edge. I'm scared I might fall and that nobody will catch me, but then they carefully let my head lean right back and I feel the warm water and gentle fingers on my scalp.

I'm having my hair done today, and I didn't even need to book an appointment! I can smell the shampoo and picture the suds and if I try really hard, I can convince myself for a few seconds that I'm at the hairdresser's, that life has been restored to my version of normal. I try to extract some pleasure from the experience, I try to relax, try to remember what that means.

I think about time a lot since I lost it. The hours here stick together and it's hard to pull them apart. People talk about time passing but here, in this room, time doesn't pass at all. It crawls and lingers and smears the walls of your mind with muck-stained memories, so you can't see what's in front or behind you. It eats away at those who get washed up on its shores and I need to swim away now, I need to catch up with myself downstream.

"That should feel better, all the dried blood gone," says a kind voice before wrapping a towel around my head. I imagine blood staining white porcelain and an ever-decreasing red orbit until another part of me is washed away.

"I'll do that, I imagine you must be very busy, I don't mind," says Claire. She's been watching, so quiet I didn't even know she was here.

The nurses like her, I can tell. People do tend to like the version of her she lets them see. They put the bed back upright and leave us alone. Claire dries my hair, then plaits it the way we did for each other when we were children. She doesn't say a word.

"You're here early," says Paul, coming into my room just as she's finishing.

"Still can't sleep," says Claire.

It looks like I'm sleeping all of the time, but I'm not, and even when I do sleep, people are always coming and going. Turning me, cleaning me, drugging me. Edward hasn't come back for a while, at least I don't remember him being here. I tell myself that he might leave me alone now, then maybe I'll wake up for real, for good.

"Something weird happened last night," says Paul.

"Go on," replies my sister. I preferred it when they had the rule where he arrived and she left. They're spending too much time together now and nothing good can come of that.

"I charged Amber's phone, but there was no contact number for anyone called Jo."

"That's strange."

"I called her boss, thinking he'd be able to give me her number. He was very nice at first, but then got all agitated and said he couldn't give it to me, because he doesn't know anyone called Jo."

"I don't understand," says Claire.

*I know that she does.*

"Nobody at *Coffee Morning* is called Jo. I asked him if maybe it was a nickname or something, told him that she was definitely a friend of Amber's from work. Then he got all flustered and tried to find a polite way to tell me that Amber didn't have any friends at work."

*Please stop.*

"How strange."

"I'm starting to understand why she quit, the guy sounded like an arse."

*Please stop talking.*

"She quit?" asks Claire.

*Don't say any more.*

"Sorry, she told me not to tell you, I forgot."

"Why?"

"She just wasn't happy there anymore."

"No, I mean why didn't she want you to tell me?"

"I don't know."

# Then

I can't make eye contact with the taxi driver as we pull up outside my home. I could see him repeatedly looking at me in the rearview mirror as he drove me away from the block of flats, unable to tell whether it was disgust or concern in his eyes. Maybe it was both. I hand over the cash and don't wait for the change, mumbling my thanks before climbing out and closing the door. The first thing I see as the cab drives away is Paul's car parked outside. He didn't tell me he was coming back tonight. He's hardly been in touch at all.

I search inside my handbag for a mint and spray myself with a spritz of perfume. I find my small compact mirror and examine different parts of my face in the glow from the streetlight outside the house. It's the first time I've had to look myself in the eye since I woke up in someone else's bed. Most of my makeup has rubbed off but my mascara has bled down my face. No wonder the cabdriver was staring at me. I lick my fingers and rub the skin beneath my eyes before checking my reflection once more. I still look like myself, even though I am not.

I step from the pavement onto our property, crossing an invisible border and closing the gate behind me, cementing the decision to proceed with caution. The air is so cold that the frozen wood needs persuading to shut all the way and burns the tips of my fingers in protest. I force myself to walk toward the house, leaving all the truths we haven't shared out on the street. I survey the front of our home as I trudge up the gravel path. The place looks tired, unloved, in need of some attention. White paint has flaked in places, peeling away like sunburnt skin. Everything in the garden looks dead or dying. A thick trunk of wisteria ascends and divides into a network of dry brown veins all over the front of the house, as though it will never blossom again. I try to tell myself that maybe I haven't done anything wrong, but the guilt of what I can't or won't remember slows my steps. Madeline has been dealt with but now I fear I'm facing something so much worse.

I search for my keys in my bag, but I can't find them so I ring the bell. I wait a while, then the cold nudges my impatience and I ring it again. Paul opens the door. He doesn't say anything and we both just stand there as though I'm waiting to be invited into my own home. It's cold so I step inside, pushing past him without meaning to.

"You're home late," he says, closing the front door behind me.

"Yes, Christmas party. How's your mum?" I ask.

"Mum? Yes, she's fine. I think we need to talk."

*He knows.*

"Okay. Talk." I force myself to look up and face him.

"There's something I need to tell you. Maybe it's better if we sit down."

*He doesn't know but it doesn't matter. I'm too late.*

"I might get a drink first, do you want one?" I ask.

He shakes his head and I retreat to the kitchen. I take a bottle of red, doesn't matter which one. I hesitate as I reach for a glass, then I overrule my apprehension—one glass can't do any harm. It's all been for nothing anyway. He wants to tell me that it's over, all that's left to do is listen. It doesn't even matter what I have or haven't done, he's already decided for both of us.

I find the bottle opener and hold on to it, trying to steady my hands as I start to twist down into the cork, tearing it from the inside out. As my wrist turns, the irony snakes up around my arm, across my shoulder to my throat, strangling me so that the words can't get out and the air can't get in. Her name screams itself over and over inside my head. I need Claire. I need her so badly right now and I hate her at the same time. I thought today was a victory, but now it feels like I've been playing the wrong game. The sound of the cork being pulled from the bottle is less satisfying than normal. I hold it in my fingers for a second. From some angles it still looks perfect, you'd never know it was so damaged on the inside.

Paul is sitting on the sofa that is normally for guests. I pause for a moment, then sit down opposite him in the seat that is habitually mine. I feel dirty and damaged but he doesn't seem to notice.

"I'm not sure where to begin," he says. He looks nervous, childlike. I used to find it endearing, but now I just wish he'd grow up, get on with it and spit it out. I don't say anything. I won't make this easy for him, regardless of where I have just come from or what I might have done.

"I've been lying to you," he says. He still doesn't look at me, just stares at a spot on the floor.

"What about?"

"I wasn't at Mum's yesterday. I was before that, she did have a fall, but when I left yesterday morning that wasn't where I was going."

I take a sip of wine. I realize now that I've been looking the wrong way before crossing a busy road. My patience expires and I need this performance to come to an end.

"Who is she?" He looks at me then.

"Who?" he asks.

"Whoever you're having an affair with." My hands are still trembling slightly so I put down my glass. Paul shakes his head and laughs at me.

"I'm not having an affair. Jesus. I was with my agent."

I take a moment to process the unexpected information.

"Your agent?"

"Yes. I didn't want to tell you until I was one hundred percent sure. I didn't want to get your hopes up and let you down again."

"What are you talking about?"

"I've written another book. I didn't think it was any good, didn't think anything would ever be any good ever again, but they've sold it, they've sold it everywhere. I found out there was going to be an auction when I was in Norfolk. My head was so all over the place with Mum that I didn't really believe it myself. But it's real and they're talking about a lot of money. They love it, Amber, there was a bidding war in the States too and things just got crazy, thirteen territories so far. And the best bit, there's talk of a film deal. It hasn't all been completely signed off yet, but it's looking pretty good." He's smiling, really smiling, and I realize I can't remember the last time he looked this happy.

I'm smiling too; it seems infectious and I can't help it. But then I re-member something I cannot forget.

"There was underwear in your wardrobe. Now it's gone."

"What?"

"You bought lacy underwear for someone else. I found it. It wasn't my size."

For a moment I can't tell whether he is angry or amused by what I have said.

"I bought underwear for *you*. It was the wrong size, yes. So I took it back. If you go upstairs right now you'll find the same bag contain-ing what I thought I'd picked up the first time, hidden in the same place. Or at least it was supposed to be hidden until Christmas. You didn't really think I was having an affair, did you?"

I start to cry. I can't help it.

"Darling, I'm so sorry," he says, then he holds me and I let him. "I know things haven't been great for a while, but I love you. Only you. I know I've been inside the book for the last few months and I'm sorry if I've been distant. We've been through so much and of course I'm gutted about the baby stuff, but you are the only person I want to spend my life with and that's never going to change. Do you understand?"

I could tell him right now that I might be pregnant. I shake the thought from my mind almost as soon as I think it. I haven't done the test yet. I can't tell him until I'm sure. Really sure. Can't get his hopes up. I've been such a fool.

He kisses me. Really kisses me, like he hasn't for so long. I don't want it to stop, but when it does I open my eyes and he's smiling at me again. I'm smiling back. The happiness I'm feeling is real.

"There's just one catch," he says. The mirrored smiles fade fast.

"What?"

"I'll need to go to America for a bit. Part of the deal includes doing some promotion and if the film happens I might need to spend some time in L.A. I know it's something we should have talked through first, but . . . I said yes."

"That's it? That's what you were worried about telling me?"

"I'm not sure how long I'll be gone for, it could be a couple of months, and I know things haven't been great recently. I have to do this. I know you've always said you can't be too far from your family and I know you can't just give up your job, but you could come out to visit and I'll fly back when I can. I just know we can make it work if we both want it to."

I nod quietly and take a moment to let it all sink in.

"And I know you get scared when I'm away." I give him a look. "Okay, not scared, just anxious, like when you thought there was someone in the back garden in the middle of the night last week. I've been thinking about that too and I want you to feel safe while I'm away. I've seen these mini security cameras you can get now, activated by movement, no wires, no fuss. I'm going to order them and put them up at the back of the house. You'll be able to stream the footage to your phone if you want and see for yourself that there's nobody there."

"I quit today."

"What?"

"I handed in my notice. I told Matthew before I left the Christmas party."

"Why?"

"I had the most awful week at work. It's a long story. It was time to go. So if you really do want me to come with you, then I will."

"Of course I do, I love you!" He means the words, they're real, and the tears they inflict on me are real too. We're not acting, we're just us, and it feels so much lighter. A smile so wide I think it might swallow him takes over his face. I want to smile back but a thought pushes its way in and spoils things. I think about where I woke up. The dull pain between my legs, the still-unopened pregnancy test kit in my handbag. I think about Claire. So much of my own news that I cannot and will not share. I need to shower. I need to wash whatever happened away. He sees my face change.

"What is it? What's wrong?"

"We can't tell anyone about this, not yet."

"We'll have to tell some people."

"Not yet, please. Not even family."

"Why?"

"Just promise me?"

"Okay, I promise."

# Before

*Friday, December 18, 1992*

Dear Diary,

It's been a whole week since I've seen Taylor and I've got so much to tell her. I wrote a lot of it inside her Christmas card, but I couldn't fit it all in, even though I did really small writing. I know she's got it, I hand-delivered it myself because Dad forgot to get stamps. I knocked on her front door but nobody answered so I pushed it through the letterbox. I'm hoping she'll call later because I really do need to talk to her.

Strangers have been coming to our house and I don't like it. A tall, thin man with no hair at all on his head came to talk to Mum and Dad. He said his name was Roger and he had a white smile that wasn't real. Roger is an estate agent and he wears suits that are shiny. He said he thought it would be best if none of us were home when he showed people the house. He didn't say why, but I expect it's because of Mum being such a mess now, he probably thought she'd scare people away.

Dad told me he didn't think anyone would want to buy Nana's house so close to Christmas, but he was wrong. People came first thing this morning, before I was even dressed for a viewing, that's what Roger calls it. Sometimes he knocks on the door, but sometimes he just lets himself in because he has his own key. He talks about Nana's home as though he lives here, but he's never lived here and he keeps getting it all wrong.

I didn't mean to lose my temper. Dad had a job interview this afternoon, he's decided to get a new one. Mum had popped to the corner shop to get a can of baked beans, so I was here on my own when Roger let himself in. I crept out of my room and could see the top of his shiny head through the banisters. He was talking very loudly, like an actor on stage in one of the plays Nana used to take me to see. Actors do that so that the people in the cheapest seats right at the back of the theater can still hear. Roger was shouting at a fat couple even though they were standing right next to him. I wondered if they were hard of hearing like Granddad was. They waddled around the hall like ducks who've been fed too much stale bread and I didn't like the look of them.

Roger was talking so loudly that I picked up the robin doorstop and quietly closed my bedroom door, but I could still hear them. I tried to read my book, but I couldn't concentrate knowing they were poking around down there where they shouldn't. They came up the stairs, which creaked even more than usual, and then spent ages looking at the bathroom. It's not a particularly big bathroom, has all the normal things in it, so I'm not sure what took so long. It was like listening to burglars walking around our home, the only difference was that Mum and Dad had invited them in.

They went into what used to be Mum and Dad's room. They were right on the other side of my bedroom wall and I listened as the fat man talked about our house being a "fixer-upper," wondering what that meant. Only Mum sleeps in that room now and I hate her, but I still didn't like the idea of them being in there and touching her things. The fat woman started to speak. She hadn't said much before that and it was her, not Roger or the other man, that made me really angry.

The three things she said that made me lose my temper were:

1. Nobody in their right mind would want to live here.
2. It needs knocking down, really.
3. It's such an ugly little house.

I felt my breathing get faster and things inside my head got really loud, the way they do when I'm very upset. I couldn't believe that anyone could be so rude and stupid. I didn't know what I was going to do, I didn't plan it, but I had to do something. I didn't want the horrid fat couple to buy Nana's house. I didn't mean to do something bad, I think I just wanted them to get out.

It all happened very quickly. I heard them leave Mum's room and walk along the landing, then Roger opened my bedroom door and I just screamed as loud as I could for a really long time. The fat woman looked terrified and Roger looked a bit scared too. The fat man was already bright red in the face from walking up the stairs and I thought he might have a heart attack.

"Calm down, little girl," said Roger. That made me even more cross, I'm not a little girl. Then he said that they hadn't meant to scare me, which was stupid. They hadn't scared me, I'd scared them. I wanted them to leave then, so I said what Mum said to Taylor's mum when she wanted her to get out. I shouted, "Get out of my house, you fucking bitch," really loudly over and over again. Even when they got to the bottom of the stairs, I stood on the landing still screaming at them. Then I threw the iron doorstop at Roger's head but it missed, hit the wall instead, and landed on the carpet. I was glad when they were gone. I was scared I had broken the robin, but it was exactly the same, not even a scratch, unlike the wall, which had a beak-shaped dent. Funny how something so small can do so much damage and still look exactly the same.

When Mum came home with the baked beans I didn't tell her what had happened. The phone rang and she answered it in the kitchen, so I couldn't hear very much or tell who she was talking to. She called me downstairs a little bit later and said that Roger had called. She told me to sit down on the sofa and I thought I was in trouble. But then she sat down next to me and when I looked at her I saw that she was wearing her sad face, not her angry one. She told me that someone who came to look at the house first thing this morning had bought it and we'd have to move out very soon. I cried, I couldn't help it, then she cried a bit too. She went to hug me, but I pushed her away and ran up to my room.

A little later she came upstairs. She knocked on my door, but I ignored her. I knew she wouldn't come in without me saying it was okay, not after what happened last time. She stayed there for ages before eventually just whispering *Good night* like a ghost and walking away. I replied too late, I don't think she heard me, it was a rhyme she taught me herself.

*Night night.*
*Sleep tight.*
*Don't let the bedbugs bite.*
*And if they do, squash them.*

I rolled over and put my pillow over my head. I held my breath for as long as I could but eventually it pushed its way out of my mouth and I didn't die.

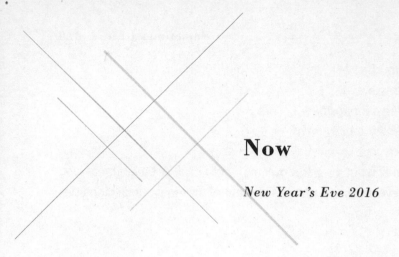

# Now

*New Year's Eve 2016*

How you doing?"

I open my eyes to see Jo sitting at the end of my hospital bed and I'm so happy to see her, even if she hasn't come alone.

"If you didn't want to come back to work after Christmas, you could have just said so; you didn't need to crash a car into a tree and put yourself in a coma, you know." She smiles and holds my hand. She looks so young. I wish time had been as kind to me as it has been to her. I can see my room and it's so much nicer than I imagined, so bright and colorful. The window is wide open, framing a clear blue sky as birds provide us with a little background music.

"Do you remember what happened yet?" she asks. I shake my head. "You do know it wasn't Paul, don't you? He'd never hurt you. Not like this." I nod because I know now that she's right. The truth has got a little tangled and twisted while I've been lying here, but the strands are starting to unravel and straighten out.

"It wasn't an accident, was it?" I ask. It feels strange to hear the sound of my own voice out loud again.

"No."

I nod again. The pieces of the puzzle are starting to show themselves, but still don't fit together.

"Why did you do it?" asks Jo. She's no longer talking about the crash.

It's so good to see her. She's the only one I can be completely honest with, no secrets, no lies. I try to sieve the truth from my memories.

"You know why," I reply.

"I don't know why you resigned, you didn't need to."

"I only took the job to get to Madeline, you know that."

"I also know having that job was good for you, something of your own."

"It was a shit job."

"Being a presenter on a top radio program, listened to by millions, is not a shit job."

"No, but I wasn't really the presenter, was I? We just made that up for fun," I say. Jo frowns.

"Did we?"

"Yes. I was just Madeline's PA."

"Were you?"

"Yes, Jo, you know this."

"Maybe I do. I think I forgot. Things get muddled in my head sometimes."

"No, that's me, things get muddled in *my* head," I say, and she lets go of my hand.

The air rapidly darkens and it starts to rain outside. The sound of birds has been replaced by an impatient wind, blowing the curtains and bedsheets about the place. The room seems to have faded, like I'm watching a remastered color version of an old black-and-white film. I can tell something is not quite right. The scene no longer seems authentic and it reminds me that I'm lost. I sit up and reach for Jo.

"Please find me, I want to be found."

But the little girl in the pink dressing gown stands up and takes Jo's hand before I can reach it. She pulls her toward the door. The room starts to fall apart, huge jigsaw-shaped pieces of it falling down into the darkness below. I have to hold on. I so badly want to knit the pieces of my life back together, but I don't know how.

"Do you have to go?" I ask.

"I think so, don't you?" Jo says, and they leave my room together, closing the door behind them.

# Then

There is never a good time to lose someone you love, but the death of a loved one at Christmas is a truly terrible thing. Both our parents died at Christmastime and it was never the same after that. It's something we'll always have in common no matter how far we drift apart. Spending Christmas Eve together was Claire's idea, not mine, but I couldn't say no, it has become a morbid tradition of ours. She said we should try to remember what we've got, not what we've lost. I'm trying. I know she sees them in me. Sometimes it feels like she's trying to extract any last fragments of our parents from my DNA just by staring at me. I have the same eyes as our mother. I sometimes see her too, looking back at me in the mirror, always disappointed by what she sees.

Kingston High Street was my choice; it's always busy. The twins are a welcome distraction from the day ahead, a pair of terrible twos. Claire pushes them around in the biggest double buggy I've ever seen. They both grip on to their own toys in their tiny fists; they never have to share. A boy and a girl, she has her own perfect little family now, it really should be enough. She loves the twins more than she loves me, more than she loved any of us, which is how it should be. I'm going to tell her today. Not all of it, just what she needs to know when the time is right.

"That's far too small for them now, silly," says Claire.

"I know, just thought it looked pretty." I put the 0–6 months dress back on the rail. I did the pregnancy test this morning while Paul was still sleeping. It was positive. I think I already knew that it would be. I don't know how I am pregnant now after trying for so long. I think it's a sign, it must be. It's time for me to move on and start living my life with Paul. Just Paul. A family of our own that nobody can take away from us. I want to tell him first before I share the news with anyone else. I've rehearsed the scene in my head. He's going to be so happy. I'll tell him tonight.

I buy the twins some clothes that Claire picks out, may as well get them something she likes, they won't even remember this Christmas, let alone what they were wearing. I wonder if they'd remember me if I were to disappear from their lives sometime soon. I looked it up the other day, the term "godmother." "A female arranged to be the legal guardian of a child if untimely demise is met by the parents." *Untimely demise*. I can't get that phrase out of my head. Being their aunt and a godmother hasn't really meant an awful lot yet, but it will. I plan on doing a lot more for them when they're older. They won't remember what happens this Christmas, it won't count.

The number of last-minute shoppers bustling and hurrying along makes it almost impossible to progress from one shop to the next. I find it strange that the people we pass, saddled with bags and debt, all look so happy. Sometimes I feel like everyone is happier than I am, as though they're all in on a secret I'm not privy to. The wide smiles on their faces are too loud. I find myself hating them, hating everything. The Christmas lights, songs, fake snow, all the things I used to enjoy, leave me cold. Claire isn't enjoying the experience either. We're more alike than I care to admit and I can see her already sinking down into a bad mood or worse. It's probably better to share my news sooner rather than later if I'm to prevent her from going somewhere too dark for me to follow.

I steer our little herd toward a small Christmas market—Claire likes this sort of thing. She stops by a stall selling scented candles. She lifts each one in turn, holding them up to her face and breathing them in. Each has a different name. Love. Joy. Hope. I wonder what hope smells like.

"That friend from university you said you bumped into . . ." she says, still looking at the candles. I freeze to the spot I am standing on and the busy Christmas market seems to quiet.

"He's not a friend, he's an ex," I manage to say.

"Whatever." She picks up a diffuser, its sticks spiking outward like a stretched hedgehog. "I remember him now, it came back to me last night."

*Last night when I woke up in his bed.*

The words were definitely in my head but I'm still scared she somehow heard them. She carries on without looking at my face and I'm glad; I don't trust it not to give me away.

"He was a medical student, wasn't he?" she asks.

"Yes."

"Wouldn't leave you alone when you split up with him, do you remember?"

"I remember. He was upset. He didn't understand why I broke it off. I couldn't explain to him that you made me."

"I didn't make you. He just wasn't right for you. He was pleasant to look at but something wasn't quite right up here." She taps her temple with her index finger. "You do remember him calling you nonstop when you ended it? Waiting outside your flat in the middle of the night?"

"Like I said, he was upset."

"Did you never wonder why he stopped harassing you in the end?" She turns to face me, her eyes shining with delight, before returning her attention to the items on sale.

My mind whirrs into overdrive. The pieces of a puzzle I didn't know I needed to solve start to slot into place.

"What did you do?" I ask.

"Not much. I wrote some letters, that's all. It's a shame people don't write to one another anymore, don't you think?"

She doesn't look up, just casually makes her way along the stall, picking up pastel shaped lumps of wax, lifting them to her face and breathing them in.

"Tell me what you did."

Finally she turns to face me.

"I wrote some letters to the head of the medical school from women who wanted to complain about his conduct. Your ex. I wrote them all on different paper, using different handwriting. It was really very clever." She smiles. "Then I rang him from a pay phone and said the letters would only stop if he left you alone." Her smile erupts into laughter.

"That isn't funny, Claire. You could have ruined his career."

"What does he do now?"

"He's a doctor."

"No harm done there, then. Getting yourself all worked up over nothing as usual. I'm only telling you in case you happen to 'bump' into him again. I wouldn't advise it."

"Why?" I ask, fearing I already know the answer.

"Because I think I might have said the letters were from you."

# Then

The market starts to spin a little and I need something to steady myself. The smell of mulled wine rises above the stench of candles, spices, and people. I have to calm down. I try to make myself focus on what I came here to say. I push Edward to somewhere dark at the back of my mind and lock him away inside a box there. I've hidden memories in boxes inside my head before. Sometimes it's the only way to deal with things.

"Shall we get a drink?" I ask.

"Go on then," says Claire.

I queue up at the counter while she finds us a table. I see her giving the twins some crisps to keep them quiet. They shouldn't be eating that crap but I won't say anything. I hear someone taking a photo behind me and I spin around, my mind replaying the recent photos of myself I saw in Edward's hallway. I half expect to see him in the crowd, taking pictures of me again right now. I have to stop thinking about him, need to deal with one thing at a time, but I can't shake the image of how my face looked when I thought nobody was watching. Photographs like that capture the way we hold ourselves up when life tries to drag us down. A paper rectangle revealing how we might unfold.

I put our drinks down on the table, warming my hands by wrapping them around the hot glass. It burns a little but I don't mind the pain. Claire takes a sip of the velvety liquid and I watch her mood cool down as she warms up. Her thermostat restores her to a less volatile version of herself but it still feels awkward between us. Dangerous.

"Don't be cross. It was years ago," she says, taking another sip.

"I'm not cross."

"Then what's wrong?"

The question catches me off guard and I feel like I might slip out of my seat. "Nothing."

"Come on, spit it out. I know you, remember?" She smiles. She still thinks she's in control. "You've got something to say, so say it."

I look around. There are a lot of people here.

"I've done what you asked," I say.

She puts her glass down.

"Madeline?"

"Yes."

She smiles again. I'm not surprised that she doesn't already know. She's spent most of her life living in a Claire-shaped bubble. She has no interest in social media, doesn't even e-mail, she only uses the Internet for online shopping. She doesn't watch the news now that I'm not on it, prefers a surplus of soap operas and endless hours of reality TV.

"Well, it's about bloody time. Don't know what took you so long. Tell me everything," she says, her eyes as eager as a child's on Christmas morning.

"All that matters is she's gone. She quit."

"Good. I wish her a very unhappy retirement."

I've always known where I stood with Claire. She doesn't pretend to be someone she's not with me. She knows what I know and it never seems to bother her. Katie starts to cry. Claire doesn't even glance in her direction.

"How did she look?"

"What?"

"When you told her?"

Katie is crying louder now. I can see people throwing irritated glances in our direction, but Claire just stares at me, her face so familiar and yet impossible to read.

"I don't really want to talk about it."

"I do."

"I did it my way. All that matters is it's done."

Both children are screaming now, but it's as though we can't hear them.

"Thank you," she says. The conversation feels like a forgery.

"I didn't exactly have a choice. Now that I've done what you asked, leave Paul alone." She gives me a look when I say this, a warning look. A glass smashes on the stone floor a few tables away and it feels like something between us has also broken. I know I shouldn't say any more, but a drawer has opened in my mind and the words that were neatly folded away for so long tumble out.

"I mean it, Claire. Leave Paul alone or I'll disappear, you'll never see me again."

"Has something happened?" she asks, sitting up a little straighter in her chair.

"No."

"I don't believe you. You're not yourself. You're not . . . balanced. Has he hurt you?"

"No!"

She studies my face and I look away. Too late. She's seen something.

"Has someone else hurt you?"

"No," I reply again. Not fast enough. For a moment I want to tell her everything. I want to tell her that she's right, she's always right. Someone has hurt me but I still can't remember how I ended up in Edward's bed. When I recall my naked body on the navy sheets I worry that it was all my fault.

"It's okay. You'll tell me when you're ready. You always do. Paul is no good for you though, not anymore. He's lost his way in life and you can do better. Mum and Dad knew it too."

"Leave him alone."

"Don't be silly."

"If anything ever happens to him, I'll kill myself."

The corners of her mouth turn upwards.

"No you won't," she says, through her smile.

*Run rabbit, run rabbit. Run! Run! Run!*

The twins are screaming and I'm crying now too. Claire is the only one left at our table who isn't.

"We had an agreement," I say. "If people knew what you . . ." Claire reaches across the table and takes my hand. Her grip is so tight that it hurts.

"Just be careful, Amber."

# Before

*Saturday, December 19, 1992*

Dear Diary,

I haven't been talking to Mum or Dad since I found out we are moving again, but I'm not sure they noticed. I told Dad this morning that I wanted to go to the park and he said that I could. Then, when him and Mum were arguing upstairs, I called Taylor. Her mum made her come to the phone. She didn't say much, but I told her to meet me there if she could. The park is exactly halfway between our houses. I left at 12:47 because I know it takes thirteen minutes to get there and I told Taylor to meet me at one o'clock. I don't have a watch, but I must have walked very quickly because I was waiting on the swings for a long time.

Just when I was about to give up, I saw the Volvo on the street outside. Taylor's mum waved and smiled. I waved back at her but I didn't smile because I wanted her to know how sad I was. I thought it was strange that Taylor hadn't walked there by herself, it isn't far. She took ages to get out of the car and when she finally did, she didn't look like herself. She's had her hair cut into a bob, so now we don't look the same anymore.

The playground is for little kids really, so there are bars all the way round the outside to keep them in, to keep them safe. Taylor came and stood on the other side of the bars, so it looked a bit like she was visiting me in jail. It felt strange at first, not easy and comfortable like before. I told Taylor I was moving and she said that she knew that and did a funny shrug of her shoulders. Then she said that she had heard her parents say that Dad had been fired for stealing. I told her that wasn't true and explained that Dad left his job to look after Mum, I'm not sure she believed me. I said maybe we could talk on the swings instead of through the bars and she came round.

I asked her about school and she said I hadn't missed much before the end of term. It seemed really difficult to talk to her and I felt like she didn't understand how terrible it was that I had to move house, so I cried a little bit on purpose. She was much nicer after that, like the old Taylor even though she looked different. I asked her if she'd been okay at school without me and she shook her head. She took off her coat and rolled up the sleeve of her jumper. There were two round red scars on her arm. I asked who did it to her but she wouldn't tell me. I asked if I could touch it and she nodded. I was very careful, feeling the smooth skin on her arm and then circling the inflamed red craters in a figure of eight. I told her I was sorry I wasn't there to stop it from happening. When I took my finger away she pulled her sleeve back down and put her coat back on. I knew that was her way of saying she didn't want to talk about it anymore.

She stood up and walked off and I was scared I had upset her and that she was leaving but she didn't. She stopped at the roundabout and lay down inside one of its quarters. She looked silly, so I laughed. Then I ran over and started to push as fast as I could, running alongside, and she started to laugh too. When the roundabout wouldn't go any faster, I jumped on and lay down in the opposite quarter to Taylor. We were both still laughing and I reached my hands up to touch hers through the bars. We held on to each other, laughing and spinning until I was dizzy, but I didn't care. I wish we could have stayed like that forever.

Later, when we had stopped spinning but were still lying there, Taylor told me this funny story about her friend Jo. She said Jo was really good at going to new places and meeting new people, that she was brilliant at listening and keeping secrets. I started to feel a bit jealous of Jo. I think that as Taylor and I are the best of friends, she shouldn't really need anyone else. I didn't like the sound of Jo much at all actually, until Taylor told me that she wasn't real, she was an imaginary friend. I laughed so much then, but Taylor didn't laugh, she was serious. She said I could borrow Jo when I moved if I wanted, that Jo would keep me company when I was scared or lonely and that I'd always have a friend wherever I went. I told her I didn't need any other friends so long as I had her but it was like she didn't hear me. She said Jo could come home with me for the night, just to see if we could be friends too. I said no thanks. Taylor got all weird then and said that Jo was sitting on one of the empty swings and not to hurt her feelings.

I looked over at the swings. There was nobody there. I started to think Taylor was a nut job, but when it was time to go home I agreed that Jo could come with me, just to keep Taylor happy. Jo is here in my room now, watching me write my diary. She's got blond hair and blue jeans and we like all the same stuff. She keeps whispering things in my ear. I don't know whether we're going to be friends or not yet, but she can hang around for now.

# Now

*New Year's Eve 2016*

Paul leaves my room and I wait for Claire to say something. Even if she doesn't believe I can hear her, I know she won't be able to resist.

"Thirty-five years old and you're still making up stories about your imaginary friend? Seriously?" Her laugh is unkind. "I suppose the real question is who have you really been with when you've been telling Paul you're with Jo?"

The door opens and I'm so grateful for the interruption.

"I'm sorry, I didn't mean to startle you," says Edward.

My sense of relief dies instantly.

"You must think I'm crazy, sitting here talking to myself," says Claire.

"You might be crazy, but you're not talking to yourself, you're talking to your sister. It's good to talk to coma patients. Good for them and good for you."

"I don't think we've met before. How did you know I was her sister?" asks Claire. She's got him; Claire can see through anyone.

"You look like sisters," says Edward. "I just need to . . ."

"Of course. Doctor . . . ?"

"Clarke."

*I thought he told Paul he was a porter.*

I listen for a while, as my captor and sister make polite conversation. She doesn't like him, I can tell by her tone. I try to hold on to the shapes of the words, no matter how mundane. Their voices become quieter, as though someone is turning the volume of my world down until I can barely hear anything at all. I don't know what it is, but I know that it's coming. The silence always chooses me back because I chose it first.

Time slows itself down. I can still hear Claire in the distance, but only just. My eyes and mouth are closed, so the quiet fills my ears until I am completely deaf as well as dumb and blind. When I can no longer hear her voice, I open my eyes and see Claire standing right in front of me. We're in her hallway and she is frozen still, like a living statue. It's as though she has been paused mid-sentence, horror etched on her face, refracting off her glistening eyes. I follow her stare and look down. I can see blood running up my legs until it disappears completely, as though I imagined it. I already know I don't want to see any more but I can't close my eyes now that they are open. I want to hit Stop, but instead my mind continues to rewind the image. Claire is shouting at me, I can't hear what she's saying, everything is mute. I reverse through her front door, walk backwards down the drive, and see her close the door as I get into the car. She had been waiting, she was expecting me. Before I can process what that means, I turn on the engine and drive Paul's car backwards down familiar streets and then I'm outside our own home. Paul is standing on the driveway shouting as I reverse to a halt. I open the car door twice before getting out, my cold, wet fingers clinging onto the key so hard it hurts my palm. I crouch down on the gravel, ignoring the pain as it engraves the skin on my knees and let go of the key beneath the shadows of the car. Things seem to unravel in reverse. I stand up to face Paul while we shout at each other in the rain. I can't hear what we're saying, but I watch the shapes his mouth is making. He's waving his hands in the air, but my initial interpretation is wrong, his face translates into fear, not anger. It's raining hard and everything slows down again until time is almost still.

I can see it all so clearly that my surroundings start to feel real. Because they are real. This is a memory, not a dream, I'm sure of it. I look down and see that my new cream dress is soaked and clinging to my skin, but there is no blood and I know that the baby is still there, she's still alive inside me. I place my hand on my stomach. I wonder why I'm not wearing a coat and realize that I must have left in a hurry. Paul shakes his head and walks backwards into the house. I stand alone in the rain. I'm quite sure that this part is wrong. I didn't stand in the rain like this, but now it seems important that I should be frozen in time and space until I can remember, until it makes sense. The rain is so heavy now that it hurts my face. My vision blurs and I realize that some of the water on my face is my own. I hear Paul's voice pouring down with the rain from the night sky above me.

"She's crying."

The black sky runs down over the house and spills over the top of the car. The memory is being painted over, but I need to hold on to it, I have to remember what happened. I sense her presence before I see her. The girl in the pink dressing gown stands next to me and slips her little hand into mine. I can see her face now; I know who she is.

"Look, she's crying," says Paul again, from behind a tree, and I realize that I am.

The little girl starts to cry too and I pull her close to me, knowing that I must never let her go. She couldn't have stopped it from happening, it wasn't her fault. The picture darkens, stripping away the memory until all that remains is black. It is only then that everything becomes clear. She chose silence and now I must endure it. The little girl holds me tight. Over two decades fall away and I look down at the girl I used to be. She's traveled a quarter of a century through time and space to remind me who I was then and tell me who I must be now.

Some people are ghosts before they are dead.

# Then

*Christmas Eve 2016—*
*Afternoon*

My hands are still shaking when I arrive home. I left Claire at the Christmas market, walked away without turning back. The sky is dark with unfallen rain and I just want to get inside and shut the world and my mistakes out for good. I take the keys out of my bag and realize I've picked up Paul's set instead of my own. It's not like me to be so careless. I need to calm myself down, keep it together, stay focused. I feel better as soon as I'm inside. I lean my back against the door and encourage my breathing and thoughts to slow down. I close my eyes for a moment and try to think clearly but I still don't have the answers when I open them. It's hard to see something that isn't there.

I peel off my coat in the hall, hang it on the rack, and bend down to take off my shoes.

"I'm home," I say without cheer or expectation.

There's no response.

I untie the second set of laces.

"Paul?"

Nothing.

I've never been fond of being touched by others. I've trained myself not to flinch or pull away, but I've always thought it was pointless to hold on to someone when you know you'll have to let them go. Despite all of that, I'd like to be held right now. I'd like to hold on to someone and let them hold me back.

I can feel that I've burnt my tongue on the mulled wine and I'm thirsty, so I head to the kitchen and get myself a glass of water from the tap. I look around as I gulp down the cool liquid and spot it straight away. I put down the glass and stare at the oven. The dial farthest to the left is not in the correct position. I straighten it until it is completely turned off, then stare at it, as though it might twist itself out of shape again before my eyes. I look around for an explanation and feel a surge of anger that Paul could be so careless, today of all days. I hear a floorboard creak in another room and allow my anger to bubble to the surface.

"You left the oven on!" I yell at no one as I march from room to room, looking for someone to blame. But Paul is not here. I come to a standstill in the front room, which is empty apart from an enormous Christmas tree in the corner. It wasn't there when I left this morning—we'd agreed not to bother with decorations this year—but there it is, taller than me and covered in tiny white twinkling lights. Almost every branch of the tree has a decoration that Paul and I have bought together over the years: a miniature little brown bag from Bloomingdale's from a trip to New York, a tiny greenstone angel from New Zealand, a white lace snowman from Germany. We used to travel so much. We'll lead that life again now that he's written another book. I stand there transfixed by the memories hanging from each branch and realize that I'm smiling without an audience, I'm happy just for the sake of it. I switch off the Christmas lights. I've read about them catching fire when left on for too long, houses burning to the ground.

I hear a floorboard creak upstairs and try to shake off any remaining irritation as I climb the stairs in search of Paul. He's done a nice thing so I must forgive the other. I walk from room to room—there aren't many so it doesn't take long—but he isn't here either. I retrace my footsteps back to our bedroom. Something seemed different about it, something was out of place. I scan the room and spot the offending wardrobe doors, which are ever so slightly open. They should always be closed. I'm breathing faster than normal and the hairs on my arms are standing to attention but I tell myself I'm just being silly. I walk over to shut them and notice that my clothes have been moved, they're not in the right order. I always hang things up according to size and color. I have a system and this isn't it.

Something is wrong.

I'm sure of it now.

I'm not imagining it.

I stand perfectly still and listen for the smallest sound. Nothing. I creep along the landing, peering around doorways, scared of what I might see. Even my breathing seems too loud. I stop at the bathroom door. Now that I'm looking properly, I can see the medicine cabinet is slightly ajar and the towels are not lined up how I like them. Paul would never do this, he knows it would make me crazy. Someone else has been here.

Claire.

Claire would do this to punish me, to teach me a lesson. I don't understand how she got back here before me, or how she got in without a key. I hold my breath until my thoughts are suffocated and I can be sure they won't be heard.

I have to find Paul. I need to know that he is safe. I hear him then, walking around downstairs. He must have come in from the garden. The relief that he is okay permits me to abandon the chaos up here for now and run down the stairs. I just want to see his face. He isn't in the kitchen, where I was expecting him to be. I double back along the hallway toward the front room and paint a smile on my face as I open the door I don't remember closing.

The Christmas tree lights have been switched back on again, but that isn't the first thing to catch my eye when I enter the room. The thing I spot first is Edward, sitting on the sofa. He looks up at me as though he has been waiting, as though we had arranged to meet, as though it is perfectly normal that this man from my past is sitting in my lounge. I want to shout, but more than that, I want to run. He smiles up at me.

"Hello, Amber. You look tired, why don't you sit down."

# Before

Dear Diary,

Dad put up our Christmas tree today. It's not a real tree, it's made of plastic and it isn't really ours, it was Nana and Granddad's, but I don't suppose they would have minded. It's a funny color green, like it faded and would like to be gray instead. I was allowed to decorate it. The lights don't work and there are no presents underneath, but I like it anyway. Jo said it looked good when I was finished. I quite like having her around for company.

Dad has got a new job, which should have been good news, but wasn't. His new job is in Wales which is nowhere near here. Wales is so far away that it's a completely different country. They even have their own language, which sounds like people talking backwards, Dad played me a cassette. Taylor told me that she's been on holiday to Wales before and they speak English as well as Welsh, but I still don't want to go and live there.

There are three big reasons why we shouldn't move to Wales:

1. I'll have to change school, again.
2. I'll miss Taylor too much.
3. Nana won't be there.

Nana isn't here either, but because all her things are, it's quite easy to pretend she still is.

Dad has been packing our lives away into boxes. Little bits of our history are stacked up all around the house, a maze of forgotten old things we won't need carefully wrapped and packed as though they are precious. We still had the old boxes up in the loft from when we moved last time, that's when Dad found the tree. He asked Mum to help with all the packing but she's not very well, so he's been doing it on his own. Mum doesn't even get dressed anymore, just wanders round in her pajamas. The doctor gave her some sleeping pills, which seems a little odd to me because she spends all day in bed already.

Dad says that I'm old enough to pack my own things this time. He put thick brown tape on the bottom of two boxes and put them up in my room, then he told me to fill them up before dinner. He found a ten-pound note in one of the kitchen drawers and said we could have fish and chips as a treat, just me and him. I'm glad he found some money, I think we've almost run out. A man came to the door asking for Dad yesterday and I heard him say we hadn't paid our water bill. I checked the taps in the kitchen and bathroom and they still work. Dad said that if anyone else comes to the door we have to pretend not to be home and hide under the windows so they can't see us if they look in.

I have tried to fill up the boxes in my room, but it's harder than it sounds. I put some of my books in one of them, but it just felt wrong, so I took them out again and put them back on the shelf. I don't think my books want to leave this house, it's their home and they should be allowed to stay here as long as they want. I put my clothes in the boxes instead. I don't need many clothes anyway, I've been wearing the same thing for two days now and it's fine. I've also stopped showering to save the water we haven't paid for but nobody seems to have noticed. I sealed one of the boxes with the brown tape, then left the roll dangling from the box. I'm not allowed scissors in my room.

The fish and chips were the best ever! I had salt and vinegar and ketchup on mine and I felt so full but I finished them anyway. I think Dad liked his too. We were having a nice time just the two of us, but then he started drinking red wine out of a box and got all moody. I asked him why the wine was in a box, not a bottle, and he told me I asked too many questions and said to be quiet. I don't think Dad should drink so much, it makes him into a not very nice person. He pretends to be nice with Christmas trees and fish and chips, but he doesn't like me really. I watched him for a while after dinner while he watched the big TV. His beard had bits of food in it and his lips had pieces of dry skin on them, which were stained purple from the wine. I don't think I look like him at all, I'm not even sure I believe that he's my dad. I hate him when he drinks too much. HATE HIM.

I spotted the scissors when I went to get a glass of water from the kitchen. I know I'm not supposed to touch them, but I am eleven now. I decided to close the boxes in my room properly with the tape. But then a funny thing happened when I got to the top of the stairs. My feet came up with a different plan without telling me and walked into the bathroom. I turned on the light and Jo was standing in the bath, she gave me a proper fright. She told me to close the bathroom door, so I did. Then I looked in the mirror so I could see what I was doing.

There was lots of my hair on the bathroom floor when I was finished. Cutting it into a bob was Jo's idea. When I squinted my eyes in the mirror, I could pretend it was Taylor looking back at me and that made me feel happy. I smiled and she smiled too. I asked Jo what she thought and she said I'd done something very clever because it means that so long as they have mirrors in Wales, I can take Taylor with me.

# Now

I wake up to the sound of a cork popping in the distance. Someone somewhere is celebrating. A flash of something comes back, Champagne at Christmas, the clinking of glasses, the twins crying upstairs. I struggle to retrieve more, but the rest of the file is blank. I don't think I was drunk but I honestly can't remember and the mere possibility feeds the shame that has been growing inside me. Our parents used to drink and the alcohol changed who they were. I never wanted to be like them, but history has a way of repeating itself whether you like it or not. I hear laughter down the corridor and wonder what there can be to laugh about in a place like this.

Paul takes my hand in his. He's here; he hasn't given up on me yet.

"Happy New Year," he says, and kisses me ever so gently on the forehead.

*New Year.*

So I've been here a week. Time here seems to stretch like an accordion: sometimes it's all squashed together, sometimes it feels as though my folded-up existence is infinite, tucked away between the creases of life-shaped cloth and cardboard. I'm a little confused and a lot lost.

I think back through the New Year celebrations of my past. I can't think of a single good one, not really, although I suppose they must all have been better than this.

"Just move your finger if you can hear me," says Paul. "Please."

I picture him staring intently at my fingers, willing them to move. I wish that I could do this one small thing for him.

"It's okay, I know you would if you could. They said I could stay until midnight, so long as it was just me. It's 12:03, so . . ." I hear him zipping up his jacket and I panic.

*Please don't go.*

"Don't worry, I'll still be watching over you. Just between us, I've set up a little camera in your room, the one I was going to put up at the back of the house. I'm going to put it right here, where nobody will notice. It's activated by movement, so if you get up and start dancing in the night, I'll be able to see you on the laptop at home. I know that you're in there, Amber. They don't believe me, but I know. You just have to hold on, I'll find a way to get you out." He kisses me again, then switches off the light before quietly closing the door behind him, like a parent putting their child to bed. I'm alone. Again.

So this is 2017. It sounds so futuristic in my head. When we were little we thought that there would be flying cars and holidays to the moon by now. Things have changed since we were children, perhaps not as much as we might have liked, but the world is a different place. Faster, louder, lonelier. Unlike the world around us, we haven't changed at all, not really. History is a mirror and we're all just older versions of ourselves; children disguised as adults.

# Then

*Christmas Eve 2016*

What are you doing here? How did you get into my house?"

Edward sits calmly on my sofa, smiling up at me. As though this is normal, as though any of this makes sense. He's even more tanned than before and I remember the ancient-looking sunbed in his flat.

"Calm down, Amber. Everything is fine, why don't you have a glass of wine? Unwind, tell me about your day?" he says. I spot the bottle of red on the coffee table and two glasses. Our glasses, mine and Paul's. Our wine.

"I'm calling the police," I say.

"No, you're not. Unless this is how you want your husband to find out that you've been seeing another man?" He picks up the bottle and pours two glasses. I try to stay calm, to think, to understand what is happening. "You wanted me to come here, that's why you left your keys at my flat." He puts them on the coffee table and I feel a brief moment of relief. I need those keys, not all of them belong to me. And then the penny drops.

"You took the keys from my bag last night. . . ."

"Now why would I do a thing like that? By the way, it was very rude of you to leave my flat like that without saying good-bye."

"You put something in my drink," I stammer.

"What are you talking about?" he asks, his perfect white smile still fixed on his bronzed face.

"You must have. It's the only thing that makes sense."

His smile fades. "Don't play games, Amber. We're too old for that now. You wanted to come to my flat. You wanted me to take your clothes off. You wanted all of it."

I feel myself start to crumble.

"I didn't." My words seem to be coming from someone else, someone small and far away. He stands up and I take a step backwards. His eyes darken before the smile returns to his face.

"May I?" Without waiting for an answer, he reaches down and picks my phone up from the coffee table. He unlocks it without needing to ask for the code, then holds the phone up to my face so I can see what he's looking at. "Does it look like I'm making you do something you didn't want to?"

Everything stops. I want to look away but I can't.

He scrolls through various pictures of a woman who looks a lot like me, but I've never seen myself like this before. My naked body. My open mouth. A look of pure pleasure on my face. I close my eyes.

"You wanted to go all the way, but I'm too much of a gentleman for that. We must be patient and wait for the right time. I want you to end things with your husband first. I'm not going to share you with him. We've wasted too many years apart but now we've got so much to look forward to." He takes another step closer, I take another step back.

"You're crazy." I instantly regret my choice of words as he slams my mobile back down on the table.

"Don't worry, there are plenty more pictures on *my* phone. I have a favorite. I was thinking of sending it to *Paul*. Such a pathetic-sounding name, *Paul*. Poor Paul, I think it suits him. His e-mail address is on his little author Web site, but then I thought no, you should be the one to tell him. Wasn't that considerate of me?" I turn to face him, my anger only slightly outweighing my fear. "You need to tell Paul the truth and ask him to leave. Then I'll move in and we can start again."

"Start again? You're fucked up, do you know that? You drugged me, you must have, none of this makes sense. I wouldn't do that."

His face twists into something sour. "You were begging for it," Edward says, standing right in front of me now. "Begging me to fill up every one of your dirty little holes."

I have to get out of here, I have to find Paul.

I rush for the door but Edward gets there before me, slamming it shut with one hand and slapping me hard across the face with the other.

He hits me again and I fall to the floor.

"Why must you always spoil everything? I've forgiven you for what you did to me years ago but I won't let you make a fool of me again."

I remember the letters that Claire said she wrote about him when we were students. I try to explain but he hits me again, knocking the wind and the words right out of me. I stop hearing what he is saying as his hands tighten around my throat. He lifts me off the floor and it's almost impossible to breathe. I hit him with my fists and try to kick him but it's as though he doesn't feel the blows; like a fly trying to hurt a horse, I'm just an irritation.

I have to do something, anything, he's going to kill me. . . .

"I'm pregnant," I manage to say. The two little words dance in the air between us. He wasn't the person I had imagined telling first. I don't think he hears me, I don't think he wants to. I can't think, can't breathe. The very edges of my vision start to turn black, the darkness slowly spreading like ink spilling on blotting paper.

I hear the back door open.

Edward hears it too and drops me to the floor. I stay perfectly still, scared of what is going to happen next. He steps back and I think he's going to kick me in the stomach. I wrap my arms around my belly and close my eyes, but there's no need. Edward calmly walks out through the front door, quietly closing it behind him. I hear Paul fill the kettle in the kitchen and I know that I am safe, for now. He can't see me like this. I stand up on shaky legs, double lock the front door, grab my phone from the coffee table, and hurry upstairs, locking myself in the bathroom. Within moments Paul has followed me up.

"Is that you?" he asks.

"Yes," I manage, struggling to remember how I normally sound and trying to mimic that.

"How was Claire?"

Lunch with Claire seems so long ago now that I'm confused at first as to why he is asking.

"She's good. I'm just going to have a quick bath, is that okay?" I lean against the door. I so badly want to open it and let him hold me. I want to tell him how sorry I am for everything and how much I love him. I wish I could tell him the truth but he'd never forgive the real me. I look down at the phone in my hand and see the frozen image of my naked body on the screen. I feel sick. I delete it and another takes its place.

"I put the Christmas decorations up," he says.

"I saw that, looks really nice. I'm glad you got a tree."

"I found something else in the attic, when I got the decorations down." I hold my hand up to the wood. Imagining his hand on the other side, wishing I could hold it.

"Not another wasp nest?"

"Not this time. I found a box of old notebooks."

I'm quite sure I stop breathing.

"They look like diaries."

We are all just ghosts of the people we hoped that we were and counterfeit replicas of the people we wanted to be.

"I hope you didn't read them," I say, wishing I could see his eyes, to know what he's thinking and whether his next response is the truth.

"Of course not. Well, at least not when I realized what they were. I was intrigued by the 1992 in big letters on the front of one of them though. How old were you then? Ten?"

"Eleven," I reply. "You should never read another person's diary," I add, sinking to the floor, closing my eyes, and leaning my head against the wall. "They're private."

# Before

*Christmas Eve 1992*

Dear Diary,

I have never been awake this late before. It's 1 A.M. and when the sun comes up it will be Christmas Eve. Taylor came to stay at our house last night and she's still here, asleep up in my bedroom. Mum and Dad said she could stay one last time before we move. I threatened to cut my hair even shorter if they said no. We're moving out on the 27th of December so that Dad can start his new job the next day. I'll have to start at another new school in a whole new country in January, they don't even know which one yet, that's how little they care about me. Mum says Taylor can come and visit us in Wales once we're settled in. Mum says things will be different this time. Mum is a LIAR.

Taylor didn't say much during dinner and hardly ate any pizza. It was Mum's fault because she got us a Hawaiian, which meant Taylor had to pick off all the little bits of pineapple before she could eat it. Taylor's mum would never have got that wrong, she knows what we both like to eat. We've really got no money left at all now, not even any coins in Nana's rainy-day jar. Dad was at the pub. He has a friend there called Tab who pays for all his drinks and I heard Dad say there was no need to pay him back before we leave. Mum was cross about it for some reason, so she put the pizza on Dad's credit card which is strictly for emergencies only and said not to tell. It was like we ate an emergency pizza.

Mum went to bed early, she said she was exhausted. If she's so tired all the time, I don't know why she has to take sleeping pills every night, but I was glad she left us alone. Taylor and I watched a film. I'd seen it before so I watched Taylor watching the big TV. I turned all the lights off, like her parents do on movie nights, and her face was all lit up from the glow of the screen, like she was an angel. She didn't laugh at some of the funny bits, even though I did, she just gave me a sad look and then stared back at the screen. I held her hand because I wanted to and she let me. I squeezed it three times and after a little while she squeezed it three times back. She still wouldn't look at me though.

When the film was finished we went up to my room. We talked for a while, but not for as long as we normally do, mainly because Taylor kept talking about things that had happened that I wasn't a part of. She's been hanging out with a girl called Nicola, they do ballet classes together at the church hall. I don't do ballet classes, we can't afford them. Apparently Nicola is really funny and tells jokes all the time. Taylor says I'm still her best friend, I checked to make sure. I don't know why she needs other friends, I don't have any and I'm fine.

Taylor told me she's really looking forward to Christmas Day. Her whole family will be at her house and Taylor says her mum has bought the biggest turkey she's ever seen, as big as an ostrich, which is very big. Her nana, who she calls Grandma, is going to stay with them and it made me feel sad about my nana, so I didn't speak for a while, just listened. I'm good at listening, people say all sorts if you just let them. That's when she said she didn't want me to go to Wales and it made me so happy that the thought of me leaving was what made her so sad. I promised her then that I wouldn't be going anywhere and I meant it. I keep my promises.

Dad came home drunk and made a lot of noise when he came up the stairs. I was embarrassed but also a bit glad. He sleeps very deeply when he's been to the pub, and Mum's sleeping tablets work so well it's almost impossible to wake her. Taylor is asleep upstairs too. They all are.

I'm not allowed matches. They are on the same list as scissors, but I have a whole box of them. I've had them for a while now. I took them from school the day we learned about Bunsen burners. I learned a lot that day. I lit one match before I came downstairs. A little bit of me wanted Taylor to wake up, so that we could do this together, but she didn't move so I let her carry on sleeping. I liked the smell of the match burning so much, I let it burn the ends of my fingers. I wanted the flame to extinguish itself.

I've packed my school rucksack with all the important stuff.

The three most important things I'm taking with me are:

1. My favorite books (including *Matilda, Alice in Wonderland,* and *The Lion, the Witch and the Wardrobe*).
2. My diaries.
3. My best friend Taylor. I'll never leave her behind, because we're like two peas in a pod.

# Then

*Christmas Eve 2016*

I lie in the bath wishing that the water was hot enough to burn my body, but I don't want to hurt the child trying to grow inside me. I imagine how this scene might look in a few weeks' time, a skin-colored hill protruding from the bathwater, a new land, waiting to be claimed. I rest my right hand on my stomach, gently, as though it might hurt me back, as though it isn't a part of me. I don't feel anything. Maybe it is just too soon.

When the water is colder than I can bear, I step out and dry myself. The steam has already run away and I'm shocked when I see my own reflection in the bathroom mirror—red fingerprints are clearly visible around my white neck. The bruises I have on the inside are less recent, but just as easy to see if you know how to look.

I open the bathroom door and hear that Paul is downstairs. Then I smell the fire and it almost makes me gag. I tread carefully over a carpet of lies, trying not to disturb them. Once I'm in the bedroom I pull on a polo-neck jumper and some comfy jogging bottoms before rushing downstairs to the front room.

"There you are," says Paul. "Drink?"

"Is it safe?"

"The drink?"

"The fire. Doesn't it need to be swept before we use it?"

"It's fine. I thought it would be cozy, given it's Christmas Eve."

The room is lit by the Christmas tree and the flames. He's trying to do a nice thing, but he's got it so wrong. I don't need to say anything; he reads the thoughts on my face.

"Shit, I'm sorry, it probably makes you think of . . . I'm sorry, I'm an idiot."

"No, it's fine, it'll just take a bit of getting used to, that's all."

He takes the bottle of red that Edward had opened and tops up the wineglasses. I don't want to touch them or drink it but I make myself play along. There is so much to say and yet I'm struggling to find any words willing to come out.

"Here's to you and the new book, congratulations," I manage, clinking my glass with his.

"Here's to us," he says, and kisses me on the cheek. I take a tiny sip and watch as he swallows half his glass. We sit in silence for a while, just staring at the flames. Funny how the same thing can have a different meaning for different people. I wish he knew about the baby. He'll think it's some kind of miracle. I suppose in a way it is. I can't tell him tonight now; too much has happened today. I want to create a memory that isn't torn before it's made. I reach for Paul's hand at the same time he reaches for his laptop.

"So, Laura e-mailed her initial thoughts for the tour. It's going to be amazing. New York; London, obviously; Paris; Berlin. Thank God it's just the two of us, we'd never be able to go if we were tied down."

My fantasy future pops like a child's bubble in the wind, cautiously floating along one minute, then obliterated the next. My words retreat and I offer a smile instead. Paul closes the laptop and puts it on the table, taking another sip of his drink. I stare at the flames dancing in the fireplace. They look wild and disobedient and make me want to run from the room.

"So do you still keep a diary now?" he asks.

"What? No."

He reaches down the side of the sofa, a mischievous smile creeping across his face.

"Maybe we should read a little bit, just for fun?"

I see the diary in his hands, the familiar swirl of "1992" on its cover, and I turn cold despite the heat.

"You said you'd put them back."

He mistakes my tone for playful; he thinks this is a game.

"Just one entry, go on."

"I said no." My voice is louder than I meant it to be and I realize I'm standing. His face changes and he holds the diary out for me to take. I snatch it like a child and hold it to my chest before sitting back down. Paul is staring straight at me but I can't look away from the fire, I'm scared of what might happen if I do.

"Why did you keep them if they upset you so much?" he asks.

I've spoiled the evening now and I hate myself for it. I ruin everything. My face feels hot and the flames look bigger to me somehow, as though it's only a matter of time before they reach out and burn what I've got left.

"I didn't. I found them in the attic at Mum and Dad's when I was clearing the house out last year." Paul puts his empty glass down on the coffee table, next to the one I've barely touched. I close my eyes so I can't see the flames, but I can still hear their screams.

"I thought we didn't have any secrets?" he says.

"We don't. They're not my secrets. The diaries belong to Claire."

# Now

My sister wasn't always my sister; she used to be my best friend. She always called me Taylor back then—almost everyone called me by my surname because that's what I preferred. Amber always sounded like second best to me, like a traffic light. Red, Amber, Green. Red for stop, green for go, Amber meant very little at all, it was insignificant, just like me. I was convinced my name was the reason the kids at school didn't like me. They didn't call me Amber, they called me other names instead. It drove my parents mad at first. They tried to convince me that Amber was a precious stone, but I knew I wasn't precious. I wouldn't respond to anything other than Taylor for weeks, so in the end they called me that too. Things only changed when I got married. Taylor got rubbed out, replaced by Reynolds. They started calling me Amber again after that and it felt like I was someone new.

I remember my mum getting off the phone and telling me I'd been invited to stay at Claire's house one last time before she moved. I didn't want to go, I was cross that she was leaving, but Mum said I should, said it was the right thing to do. She was wrong. It was the biggest mistake I've ever made and I've been paying for it ever since.

Claire's mum got us a pizza for our dinner that night; she wasn't much of a cook. I can still remember Claire screaming at her that I didn't like pineapple. She was terrifying when she got like that, out of control. I never spoke to my parents the way she did and always found it odd how they just let her get away with so much. Her dad wasn't around very often; he liked to gamble away what little money they had and was always losing jobs as well as bets. Her mum had a bit of a drinking problem and always seemed so sad and tired, as though life had defeated her. She gave up on Claire as well as life in the end and it made me realize that people who do nothing are just as dangerous as those who do.

Claire wasn't popular at school back then. She was an angry child, angry at the world and almost everyone in it. They'd moved a lot and she got herself into trouble at nearly all of the schools she attended. She was very clever. Too clever. It was like she was weary of most people as soon as she met them, as though she could instantly see who and what they were and was perpetually disappointed. She preferred reading stories to real life, so that some of her best friends were in the pages of books. I was her only real friend. She got jealous if I even spoke about anyone else, so I learned not to.

I still think about what happened every day. I wonder if it was all my fault, whether I could have done something to prevent it. She was just a little girl, but so was I. Little girls are different from little boys: they're made of sugar and spice and scar for life. I've still got my scars. Just because they're on the inside doesn't mean they're not there.

I heard her get up and creep around the room that night. I had my back to her but my eyes were open. I heard her light a match and I smelt it burn. I thought she must be lighting a candle or something—the electricity sometimes went off at her house, her parents always struggled to pay the bills. Then she went out into the hall. I waited a while, but when she didn't come back, I got up to see where she had gone. It was always cold in their house, so Mum had packed my new pink dressing gown. I wrapped it tightly around myself and tied a knot.

I crept out onto the landing, tiptoed past Claire's mum's room, and stood at the top of the stairs. All the doors were closed except the door to the bathroom and I could see that it was empty. I heard a noise downstairs and made my way down the first couple of steps, trying to be as quiet as possible. That's when I saw her—it was such a strange sight. I crouched down and watched through the banisters as she walked around the kitchen.

Claire was wearing her school backpack over her pajamas and I watched as she stood perfectly still in front of the old white oven. She turned one of the knobs and just stood there, staring at the cooker as though she was waiting for something to happen, then she turned another. I stayed where I was for a while, like I was frozen. Then she turned her head really slowly in my direction and I thought she could see me there on the stairs. It was like she was looking straight at me, her eyes flashing in the darkness, like a cat's. I remember having an urge to scream then. If only I had. She looked away and turned back to the cooker, twisting another knob.

I stood up as quietly as I could and crept back upstairs. I didn't really understand what was happening but I knew that it was bad and wrong. I tried the handle of her mum's room. It was locked. I should have knocked on the door, or done something, anything, but I went back to Claire's room and got into bed, still wearing my dressing gown. I think I just hoped it was all a bad dream.

It soon started to smell of gas even up in the bedroom, like an invisible cloud was spreading itself around the house, filling up every space, every dark corner. I pulled the duvet up over my head, hoping that would be enough to save me, then someone pulled it away. I opened my eyes and saw Claire, still wearing her backpack, standing over me. She shook me as though I was asleep, even though I was wide awake, then she smiled down at me. I'll always remember what she said then.

*I'm always going to look after you, Amber Taylor, take my hand.*

I always did what Claire told me; I still do. She stopped in the bedroom doorway as though she had seen a ghost. It was dark and at first I couldn't see what she was staring at. Then she bent down to pick up her nana's cast-iron doorstop and put it in her bag. It was shaped like a robin, a tiny statue of a bird that would never be able to fly away. She led me out onto the landing, then stopped again and turned to face me, putting her finger to her lips.

*Shh.*

She held my hand tight in hers and pulled me down the stairs, the smell of gas getting thicker in my nostrils with every step. At the bottom of the stairs she turned right, away from the kitchen and toward the front room. She sat me down in an armchair and bent down next to the fireplace. Her mum always had a little fire built and ready to go but they only lit it on Sundays. It was just a little pile of newspaper and sticks, sometimes with an old candle thrown on top. Claire lit a match, setting light to the small pile of kindling. Then she threw the box of matches on top of the pile, took my hand, and led me out the front door, which she closed behind us. I didn't have any slippers and I remember the cold gravel biting my feet as she dragged me down the drive. She held on to my hand so tightly, as though I might run away if she let me go. Then she told me not to cry. I hadn't realized that I was.

We went to sit on the wall of a house on the opposite side of the street. I could feel the cold of the stone even through my dressing gown. We sat on that little wall for what felt like a very long time. She didn't say a word, just held my hand too tight and stared up at the house, smiling. I was scared to look at her for too long, so I mostly just stared at my little bare feet, turning blue in the cold. Even when she started singing, I didn't look up.

*Twinkle twinkle little star,*
*How I wonder what you are.*
*Up above the world so high,*
*Like a fire in the sky.*

Claire loved nursery rhymes. She said they reminded her of her nana, but she was always getting the words wrong. Claire is the kind of person who sees what she wants to instead of what's actually there.

The house didn't explode, exactly. It was like it just slowly burst at the back. There was a bang, not as loud as you hear in the films, but like the silence was pulled out from under the bricks. The front of the house looked exactly the same at first, but I could soon see the flames dancing behind the windows. We heard the sirens way before we saw the fire engine. She was silent then. The smile slid off her face and tears ran down her cheeks. She cried for her parents for hours then, like a tap that couldn't be turned off. I've cried for them ever since.

The smoke became a part of me that night, so that no matter how many times I washed my hair or scrubbed my skin, I could still smell it. It twisted itself around my DNA and it changed me. She said she killed them for me. She said she thought it was what I wanted, so that we could stay together, so that she could keep me safe. I've spent my life since wondering what it takes for a person to do something like that. She said they didn't love her; I don't know if that's true. There are different kinds of love—one word could never accurately describe them all. Some are easier to feel than others, some are more dangerous. People say there's nothing like a mother's love—take that away and you'll find there is nothing like a daughter's hate.

The sound of an ambulance outside startles me and shakes the memories from my head. I stare at a tile on the hospital ceiling that doesn't quite match the rest and it takes a good few seconds before I realize that my eyes are open. It doesn't feel like a dream, it feels real. My eyelids seem to have just decided to roll up by themselves. The room is dark, and I can't move my head, but I can see, I'm sure of it. I blink, then I blink again. Each time my eyes close I'm scared they won't open again, but they do. Slowly, my eyes start to adjust to the dark and I can see my room. The window is right where it is supposed to be, but smaller than I had imagined. I can see a table next to the bed. There are some get-well cards, not many. Just beyond my useless, broken body stretched out in front of me, I can see the door. I hear someone outside and see the handle start to turn. Instinct tells me to close my eyes and I plunge myself back into the darkness, back to my world of being seen but not heard.

# Now

There are people right outside. I can't make out who they are so I keep my eyes closed. I start to interpret the words, just distilled fragments of sound straining through the tiny gap between the wood and the wall. The door opens a fraction more and the quick-spoken sentences refine themselves just enough to clarify that they're not the voices I want to hear.

"No, I'm sure. You head off, get a couple of hours' sleep. No need for us all to have a shit New Year. I'll see you in the morning."

It's Edward.

I keep my eyes shut and try to stay calm. He closes the door and I hear the lock turn. He leaves the lights off and walks slowly toward the bed.

"Well, hello there, Mrs. Reynolds, and how are we this evening? No change, I see. Well, that's a terrible shame." He walks over toward the window and I hear the sound of curtains being closed. I can picture my surroundings far more clearly now I've seen them. It's less like being in a dream and more like trying to see through a blindfold.

"It's New Year. Did you know that? I had such high hopes for the start of 2017. Thought I'd be spending it with this girl I used to know, but she Fucked. Things. Up. So I volunteered to do an extra night shift, actually volunteered so that I could be with her anyway. And now it's just the two of us, the way it always should have been."

I hear him doing something next to the bed, but I can't tell what.

"I've been thinking about your husband a lot over the last few days and I have to say, he isn't at all what I was expecting. The police still think he did this to you, by the way, but after everything I've been telling them, that's hardly a surprise. I'm amazed they still let him into the hospital. I told them I was one of the doctors here and they believed me. But then you believed me too, didn't you."

He stands right next to the bed and starts to stroke the top of my head. I involuntarily hold my breath. He tucks my hair behind my ears and I can hear my heartbeat banging loudly inside them, trying to raise the alarm.

"He's not an unattractive man, *poor Paul*, your husband, but he doesn't take care of himself, he looks a mess, frankly. Is that why you came back to me? Did you want a real man again instead of a skinny little runt?"

He traces the side of my face with his finger, caressing my cheek and then resting his hand across my mouth.

"It's fine if you don't want to answer, I understand. Besides, I learned the hard way that everything that comes out of this mouth is a lie."

He leans down, so that he is speaking directly into my right ear.

"You need to stop telling lies, Amber. They'll catch up with you."

I can't breathe and it gets to the stage where I think I'm going to push him away but then I remember that I can't. He removes his hand from my face.

"He does seem to love you, I'll give him that. But that was never enough for you, was it?"

I try to stay calm, control my breathing, bring myself back to center. I wonder if he might kiss me again and I feel sick at the thought of his tongue inside my mouth.

"Was he not fucking you right? Was that it? I remember how you like a good fuck, don't you, Amber? Must be difficult, come to think of it, lying there all this time with nobody taking care of your needs. I'm prepared to take some responsibility for that, as one of the staff at this medical establishment dedicated to making you as comfortable as we possibly can."

His hand strokes my right thigh and then slips under the covers. His fingers find their way between my legs and he pushes my thighs apart with ease. I scream inside my head as his fingers force their way inside me.

"How does that feel? Any better?" he says. "Do speak up, I can't hear you."

His fingers thrust harder. "I'll take your silence as a no. What a shame. But then it's hard to make people better when you're not really a doctor. And it's hard to be a doctor when some silly little bitch sabotages your career by sending bullshit letters."

His whispers have grown up into shouted words. Surely someone must be able to hear him. *Why don't they come? Why does nobody save me?*

"You broke my heart, destroyed my career, and thought you'd get away with it, didn't you."

I feel a spray of saliva as he spits his words out at me.

"I'm a fucking night porter because of you, but that's okay. I've got the keys to the whole hospital. I can lock any door and open any medical cupboard. And I know stuff. I haven't forgotten my training. I know how to keep you here and nobody suspects a thing."

He's breathing faster. I have to remind myself not to move, not to make a sound.

"Anything to say for yourself? No?" He's panting like a dog. "I still forgave you, watched you, waited for you to realize what a mistake you'd made and put things right. I still thought we might have a chance. But women like you never learn, that's why I have to teach you a lesson, do you see?" He stops what he's doing and for a moment I think it's over, but it isn't. "I saw you here at the hospital two years ago, when your bitch of a sister gave birth. You walked right past me. Twice. As though I was nobody, as though I was nothing to you. I followed you home that day. I've loved you for almost twenty years and you didn't even remember me. Well, perhaps you'll remember me now."

I hear him unfasten his belt. I hear a zip. He turns on a light above the bed, then roughly pulls the sheet down and my gown up.

"Look at all that filthy hair," he says, and repeatedly flicks his finger between my legs. "You used to wax when we were students, used to make an effort. Look at the state of you now. I'm doing you a favor, really. You better be grateful."

The bed shudders as he climbs on top, his skin touching my skin, his weight pinning me down, his breath on my face. He pushes himself inside me and I try to shut myself down. It's as though this is no longer happening to me, I'm just being forced to watch with my eyes closed. The top of the hospital bed thuds against the wall, a metronome of revulsion beating steady inside my head. I know I can't fight him. He's too strong, I'd lose.

"On a scale of one to ten, how is the pain now?"

He's hurting me and he's getting off on it. I have to keep still and silent. He'll kill me if not, I'm sure of that now. To live, I have to pretend like I'm already dead.

He climbs off me as soon as he is finished. Everything is quiet for a while and I think that he will leave, but he stays standing over me. I can hear his rushed breathing. I can smell him. It sounds like he is doing something to my drip. Without warning he plunges his fingers inside of me once more, then he pulls them out and rubs them on my face, inside my mouth, long fat digits pushing themselves between my lips, rubbing my teeth, my gums, my tongue.

"Can you taste that? That's you and me, that's what we taste like. It wasn't as good as I hoped, but then looking back it always was a bit like fucking a corpse."

I hear him fasten his belt. He pulls the sheet back over my body.

"Good-bye, Amber. Sleep well."

He turns off the light, then leaves.

It feels like I've reached a full stop and there is nothing after it. I'm scared I won't be able to open my eyes again, I'm scared of what I'll see if I do. I can't feel anything anymore, so I start to count. After one thousand, two hundred seconds I try to believe that I am safe. Twenty minutes have stuck together to form a wall between me and him. It isn't enough, but when I open my eyes I can at least see that his physical presence has gone. It's only now I realize that my fingers have been moving. I have been using them to count. I can move my hands. It's still dark and my eyes are adjusting. For now, all I can see beyond the edges of my bed is cloudy gray pain. If I can move my hands, I wonder what else I can do. Slowly, as though I might break it, I lift my right arm. It feels heavy, hard to balance, like an overloaded tray. I see a thin tube attached to the back of my hand and pull it out, crying in pain. I need to get help and I need to hurry, but everything seems to be very slow, very difficult.

I still can't move the rest of my body. I look around at what I can see from my position on the bed until my eyes find a red cord. It looks like the sort of thing you should pull if you need help, and I do need help. I launch my right arm and it shakily maneuvers itself into position, banging the drip on the way. I stop and stare at the half-empty bag of clear liquid gently swaying on the stand. I'm sure it contains the drugs he's been pumping inside me. I yank it free and manage to throw it in the side cabinet, hoping someone will find it and know what to do. Something is definitely wrong—my eyes want to close and they're becoming quite insistent. I reach up again for the red cord, and this time my fingers wrap around it and I pull. I see a red light come on above the bed and I let my arm fall. My hands grip onto the sheets so tight that my nails dig into my palms. Sleep is pulling me under. I let my eyes close and feel myself fold into black.

I think I might be dying but I'm so tired of living that maybe it's okay. I allow my mind to power down. Far above me, beyond the cold, black waves, I hear voices, but the words won't unravel themselves. Two of them swim down from the surface to find me.

"She's crashing."

*I crashed.*

# Then

*Christmas Day 2016*

Christmas is a time for tolerating the family you didn't choose.

"That's a lovely scarf," says Claire as she ushers us through the hallway. Paul and I follow her inside. There's not a hint of tension after our row at the Christmas market yesterday, but this is what my sister and I do best. Acting is something we've always had in common. Still, I doubt she'd be able to remain this calm if she knew that Paul had read her childhood diaries. She doesn't even know that I've read them. It's a strange sensation, reading your own history through another person's eyes. Your version of the truth becomes a little bent out of shape when it is no longer your own.

We step into the new open-plan kitchen and dining room. There are toys everywhere, but apart from that, the place is spotless. They've had a lot of work done since Mum and Dad died. The house is hardly recognizable—impressive, since I lived here from the day I was born. Claire has redecorated the whole place, papering over the cracks in our family. I still tell myself that it made sense for my parents to leave the house to Claire and David. They needed it more than we did and his garage is right next door; it's how they met.

"David is just upstairs changing the twins, he'll be down soon. Drink?" Claire's long blond hair is pulled back off her flawless face and she looks radiant. It wasn't always blond, of course, but the peroxide has been expertly applied for so many years now that you'd never know. Her black dress looks new and hugs her body. I feel like a frump in comparison; I hadn't realized we were dressing up. I'm the eldest but she looks considerably younger than me given we were born on the same day just a few hours apart.

"Not for me, thank you," I say.

"Don't be daft, it's Christmas!" says Claire. "I was going to open some bubbles to get us started. . . ."

"That sounds nice," says Paul.

"Okay then, just the one," I reply, looking over at the larder. My height every year of my life until I was a teenager used to be marked on the back of the wooden door. Claire had it painted over.

We sit down on the corner sofas and I feel like an accessory in a photo from one of Claire's home decorating magazines. The kitchen looks like it's never been cooked in, and yet something smells amazing. My sister, the undomestic goddess. David comes marching in with a child beneath each arm. He's too tall and always walks a little bent over, as though permanently worried he might bump his head. His hairline is rapidly retreating and the ten-year age gap between him and Claire is really starting to show.

When we were sixteen he fixed Dad's car and took Claire's virginity as well as his payment. I was shocked and a little disgusted at the time. She thought I was jealous, but I wasn't. The idea of him doing things to her repulsed me. I remember when she first started sneaking out to see him. I often went with her, then I'd wait on my own and try not to listen while they did whatever they were doing. One night like that, Claire and I stayed drinking in the park just the two of us. It was long after David had gone off to the pub we were too young to get into. When the bottles of cider he had given us were empty, we staggered out from the shelter of the trees. It was so late that the iron gates at the park entrance were already closed, with a padlock and thick chain.

We weren't worried, our teenage bodies could easily climb our way up and over, but Claire said she wanted to rest first and lay down on the concrete path. I lay down next to her and she held my hand. She gently squeezed it three times and I squeezed hers three times back. We lay there in the moonlight, drunkenly laughing at everything and nothing and then she stopped and turned to face me, supporting her head on her elbow. She whispered as though the trees and the grass might overhear us. I didn't ask what the two of them had been doing while I was waiting, but she told me anyway. She said it felt nice. I remember feeling sick, a little bit confused, and a lot betrayed somehow.

I thought she was making a huge mistake. A marriage, two children, and almost twenty years together suggest that maybe I was wrong. She's never been intimate with any other man. Never been interested. When Claire chooses to love you, it's forever.

"You're here," he booms. David has a tendency to speak louder than is necessary. "Make yourselves useful and entertain these two, will you?" He gives us a child each and walks over to the fridge, grabbing a handful of Claire's yoga-sculpted bottom as he walks past. She doesn't seem to mind or notice. I've got Katie; Paul has James.

The twins seem so alien to me, despite being family. Paul is naturally good with children; perhaps that's why he's always wanted his own. He makes the right sounds, gives off a good vibe. It's more of an effort for me and I don't always get it right. I try talking to Katie in a soft voice, asking her if she thinks Father Christmas has been to visit. Claire has gone completely overboard with presents and decorations this year—she says it's all for the twins, as though they'll even remember. Katie reaches for my scarf and tugs at it. I maneuver the material out from her tiny clenched fist. I need it to stay where it is, to cover the hand-shaped bruises on my neck. She isn't happy about it and starts to cry. Nothing I do works, so Paul offers to swap. He gives me James and as soon as Katie is in his arms she stops screaming. She stares at me, as though she's suspicious, as though she knows more than she possibly can. I make sure my scarf is still in place.

Paul is going to make a great dad. I'll tell him tonight. It will be my Christmas present to him this year. There isn't anything else I can give him that he doesn't already have. I'm glad I haven't told him already, he wouldn't have been able to keep it from Claire and I don't want her to know yet. I'll tell him as soon as we get home, when it's just the two of us.

The afternoon drags as the four of us eat our way through too much food, plugging the gaps with polite conversation and stories we've bored each other with too many times before. I imagine this scenario being replicated in thousands of homes all over the country. I spend the hours playing multiple roles: the caring sister, the doting wife, the adoring aunt, and take tiny sips of my wine so that I never need a refill. When Claire heads to the kitchen, I snatch the opportunity I've been waiting for, offering to help her. Paul shoots me an evil glance. He doesn't like being left alone with David, says they have nothing in common. They don't.

"Something has happened," I whisper as soon as we're alone in the kitchen.

"What?" asks Claire with her back to me.

"Something that shouldn't have."

"What are you talking about?" she says, stacking the plates in the dishwasher. My bravery retreats.

"Nothing. It doesn't matter. I'll deal with it myself."

She finishes what she is doing and turns to face me.

"Amber, are you okay?"

This is my chance. If I tell her about Edward, I know she'll help me. I study her face. I want to tell someone how afraid I am but the words won't come. This isn't the right time and I remember that I'm afraid of her too. She might make me go to the police. She might tell Paul. She might do something worse.

"Yes, I'm okay." It's her turn to analyze me now; she knows that I'm not. I need to give her something more. "I'm just tired, need some rest, that's all."

"I think you're tired too. You keep getting yourself all worked up over nothing."

The rest of the day goes by in a blur. The twins eat, sleep, play, cry, repeat. The adults wish they could do the same. Mum and Dad always made us wait until the afternoon to do presents and we seem to be continuing their rather miserable tradition. We watch as the twins half open beautifully wrapped gifts, predictably more interested in the wrapping than the contents. Then we exchange adult-sized presents, neatly wrapped with crisp gift receipts tucked inside. I open one from Paul and it takes me a while to register its relevance. I thank him and try to move on to something else.

"Hang on, what is it?" asks Claire. She likes us to take turns, for everyone to watch what everyone else gets.

"It's a diary," I say.

"A diary? Who are you, Anne Frank?" laughs David. I can see that Paul looks embarrassed.

"I thought she might like it because—"

Before he can finish his sentence, I interrupt him. "I love it, thank you," I say, and kiss him on the cheek.

"I used to write a diary," says Claire. "Always found it very therapeutic. I've read that it's good for anxiety, to write it all down. You should try it, Amber."

When we've all had our maximum fill of playing happy families I help David put the twins to bed. I read them a story that I've read them before and marvel at how easily they fall asleep. As I leave their bedroom I notice the robin-shaped lump of cast iron propping open the door. It was Claire's nana's. She still keeps it even now, the only old thing in a house that has been made new. I come downstairs to find Paul and Claire talking quietly in the kitchen. As soon as they see me they stop and it's a second too long before Paul smiles in my direction.

# Then

Paul and I walk home in silence. He walks quickly, so that I have to hurry to keep up with him. A fine mist of drizzle permeates the cold air but I don't mind, I'm just pleased to be outside, to have left Claire's home. That's all that house is now, hers. There is nothing left of mine within its walls; not even the memories are my own. It's a life I should have left behind by now, but something has always stopped me from moving on. Fear of the unknown is always greater than fear of the familiar.

The streets are empty. I like the quiet stillness of it all. Peace on suburban earth. Everyone is locked inside with relatives they don't have to see for the rest of the year. Stuffing turkey down their throats, watching nonsense on the television, unwrapping gifts they neither want or need. Drinking too much. Saying too much. Thinking too little.

The drizzle evolves into rain as we pass the petrol station. It's closed now; everything is closed. I've only ever been inside the place twice. The first time was a few weeks ago, to ask a question. No harm in that, people ask questions all the time. The cashier studied my face a little harder when I had finished speaking, but he soon concluded that I wasn't about to rob the place; I didn't look the type. He told me that the CCTV was kept for a week and then automatically deleted. I thanked him, then waited a moment in case he had wondered why I wanted to know. He didn't, so I left. He forgot about me before I even walked out the door.

The second time was a little more recent.

Madeline wasn't terribly grateful after I drove her home from work when she was sick the other day. After I helped her inside, she thrust her credit card at me and told me to fill her car up at the petrol station round the corner. She wasn't happy about the tank being almost empty and informed me that she wouldn't have time before work the following day. She assumed I'd be upset about her demands, so I arranged my face to fit her expectations but secretly I was rather pleased with myself. It meant that the mouthful of petrol I'd endured in the staff parking lot when I siphoned her tank earlier that morning had not been in vain. The taste of diesel lasted for hours, despite spitting it out straight away. I'd learned that trick at school, helping to clean out the class fish tank.

"You might have the others fooled with your Florence Nightingale act, but not me," she muttered before hauling herself up the stairs, one step at a time. She stopped halfway and turned her head to look down at me, a triumphant smile spreading itself across her clammy, round face. Madeline always had a real way with words, but I heard the ones she chose that afternoon long after they were spoken.

"I see straight through you, Amber. Never forget it. Work-shy and clueless, just like the rest of your generation. It's why you'll never amount to anything." With that, she turned to continue her ascent up the stairs I had once known and sat on. The house looked completely different since the fire twenty-five years ago, of course it did, but the new stairs were still in the same place and if I turned my head to the right, I could almost still picture Claire turning on the gas. She should have inherited this house after her birth parents died, she was sure it was what her nana would have wanted, but her godmother, Madeline Frost, saw to it that she never got a penny.

I thought about what Madeline had said to me as I filled up the car and again as I bought the petrol cans and filled them up too, before putting them inside the trunk. I thought about what Madeline had said as I paid using her credit card, and I heard her words repeat themselves inside my head as I cleaned the steering wheel and everything else I had touched with a cotton cloth.

As Paul and I walk together but alone past the road where Madeline lives, I turn to get a quick glimpse of her house. I realize for the first time that it looks just like any other. There could be a family inside, pulling crackers, playing games, creating memories with and of one another. There could be children, grandchildren, pets, noise, and laughter. There could be, but I know that there isn't. There is only one person inside, I'm sure of it. One sad, lonely, miserable mess of a person. A person who is only loved by strangers who believe in the version of her they hear on the radio. A person who will not be missed.

# Before

*Thursday, January 7, 1993*

Dear Diary,

It was the funeral today. It was strange because there weren't many people there, not like the funerals you see on TV. My aunt Madeline was invited, but she didn't come. She's the only family I have left but I don't even know what she looks like. Doesn't matter. I have a new family now. I cried when I saw the coffins because I know that's what you're supposed to do, but I don't miss Mum and Dad. I'm glad they're not here anymore; things are much better without them. I've been living with Taylor's family since the fire and it's great. It's as though my life before was all a big mistake, like I should have been born into *this* family. The only thing that makes me cry real tears is that I can't ever go back to Nana's house. I can't sit in her favorite chair or sleep in her bed. All I had left of her was there. They said Aunt Madeline owns it now, what's left of it.

I've got lots of new clothes and books and I even have my own bedroom at Taylor's house. I started off sharing her room, but she kept waking me up in the middle of the night. She has dreams about the fire all the time and wakes up screaming. It's really annoying. Sometimes she just can't sleep at all. I sing her the song that Nana used to sing me when I couldn't sleep. *The wheels on the bus go round and round.* I'm not sure it helps.

Taylor has been acting really strange in lots of ways since that night. I don't know why—she wasn't injured and nobody she cared about died. She said she'd tell on me, but she won't. I told her what would happen if she did. She keeps doing weird stuff though, like just standing in front of the oven and staring at it. And she's started picking the skin off her lips. Sometimes she picks them so hard that they bleed. It's disgusting. Taylor's mum said that different people deal with things in different ways and just to give her time. She took her to talk to someone at the hospital about how she is feeling, she thinks that might help. I'm not convinced.

I've had to talk to lots of people too since the fire. I had to talk to doctors at the hospital and then the police and twice a week I have to talk to a woman called Beth. Beth is a social worker, which means she tries to help people. She has big, sad eyes that forget to blink and a hairy dog called Gypsy. I've never met her dog, but her clothes are always covered in its hair and when we talk she pulls the hairs off and drops them on the floor. She talks very slowly and quietly as though I might not understand and she always wants to know whether I'm okay without actually just asking me if I'm okay.

It was Beth who told me about Aunt Madeline. I think my aunt might be poorly because she couldn't come to the funeral and she can't write her own letters. A solicitor writes them for her and then Beth reads bits of them out. Sometimes her big eyes keep reading but her mouth stops speaking and I wonder what words she doesn't want me to hear. I didn't really know what it meant when she said that Aunt Madeline was my godmother. Her eyes looked away and explained to the floor that it normally meant someone who would look after you if your parents couldn't anymore. I didn't say anything. I didn't want to be looked after by anyone except Taylor's mum. Then Beth said that Aunt Madeline loved me very much, but that she didn't think she could take care of me. Beth carried on wearing her extra-sad face, but I was feeling very relieved, until she said that I might have to live in a home for children until a foster place became available. When Granddad went to live in a home that wasn't his, he died. I don't want to die. I didn't like my aunt Madeline very much for not wanting to look after me then. She doesn't care whether I live or die but I don't know who she is, so my crossness grows inside my tummy instead of finding a way out and it hurts.

Beth left me alone in the room and told me to play with some toys. I didn't want to, I'm not a child, but she said I should, then left. I knew she was watching me through the mirror, I've seen the films where they do that, so I got up and walked over to the toy box. There was a doll inside, and it looked expensive, not like the plastic stuff. I sat her on my lap and told her how sad I was about my mum and dad and how grateful I was that Taylor's parents had been so kind to me. Then I said a little prayer. I

224 | **Alice Feeney**

even said "Amen" at the end because I thought Beth would be the sort of person who would like that. She did. She came back in and said I could go. She even said I could take the doll with me. *For being so brave.* I decided I'd give it to Taylor. Tell her the doll was watching her, even when I wasn't. I liked that idea a lot, it made me smile and that made Beth smile because she thought she had made me happy.

I'm not stupid, I knew what I had to do. I started crying in my room that night, just loud enough for Taylor's mum to hear me. She opened the door without knocking, but I didn't mind because it's a different door in a different house and she is a different mum. She tucked me back into bed properly, the way Nana used to, and then she sat with me and stroked my hair for a while. She was wearing a white robe and she had taken her makeup off, but she still looked beautiful and smelt of that pink shower gel she uses. When I grow up I want to be just like her. I told her I was scared of going to live with strangers and cried a bit more. She told me I mustn't worry and kissed me on the forehead before leaving the room and turning out the light. I heard them talking for hours after that, not shouting like my mum and dad used to, just talking quietly in the same bedroom as each other, like a proper married couple. The next day I saw the fostering paperwork on the dining room table, so things really have worked out for the best.

# Now

*Monday, January 2, 2017*

I'm still alive.

That's the first thought to voice itself inside my head. I don't know how, but I'm alive and I'm back—I'm just not sure where I've been. It takes me a moment to decide whether or not I'm happy to be here and what this all means. Edward tried to kill me, I'm sure of that, but I'm still alive. I suppose it must be hard to kill something that's already dead.

Given my strong dislike for hospitals, I've spent a considerable amount of time in this one. Paul and I came here when we were trying for a baby, it's where my sister gave birth and where my grandmother died. She didn't die of cancer, like Claire's nana, she died of old age disguised as pneumonia when we were thirty. Her death took its time and a toll on our fragmented family. We were temporarily united by overstretched grief and despair. But it flicked a switch on inside Claire that could not be turned off. The anger she had felt about her own nana's death as a child returned. The recalled rage she had suppressed for so long had grown over time. The hate still needed somewhere to go. Claire still needed someone to blame. That's when she traced Madeline. Imagine our surprise when she discovered who her godmother really was and where she still lived. Destroying Madeline became Claire's obsession, which in turn became mine. She became volatile again, mistrusting of everyone around her. The change in her mood increased the need for my routines, to be sure that everything was as safe as it could be when Claire was upset about something.

They call it OCD. It's not a big deal, but it's got worse as I've got older. I had to visit this very same hospital once a week when I was a teenager. I used to meet a short man who liked to talk too much and listen too little. He always wore the same shoes, gray leather with purple laces. I spent a lot of hours staring at them. After four months of weekly visits, he told me that I had obsessive thoughts and demonstrated compulsive activities to process an inexplicable level of anxiety. I told him he had halitosis. I stopped seeing him not long after that. My parents gave up trying to make me better and instead focused all their attention on Claire, the pretty, grade-A replacement daughter they had saved, forgetting all about the faulty original that they couldn't fix—me.

I try to pull myself from the past back to the present, not really wanting to be in either place. That's when I hear her crying. It takes me a while to translate the tears and to pinpoint where and when I am.

"I'm so sorry, Amber, for all of it," says Claire's voice from somewhere in the distance. The words seem to repeat themselves on the surface while I float down below. The sound of her voice pulls me up from where I've been and it feels like I've woken up from a very deep sleep. Something is different. The light and the shade have shifted. It feels unsettling, like someone has rearranged the furniture in my mind without even asking.

"You tried to tell me about him, didn't you? But I didn't listen. I'm so sorry," says Claire. She sounds closer now, as though I could reach out and touch her. It takes me a while to understand what she is saying, but the casting process finally settles on Edward for the role of "him."

I drift away. The words are too much to process in one go.

The mention of Edward's name seems to make the edges of the space I'm in darken. Something happened, something bad. Something worse than what I can remember. Whatever it was, Claire knows about it, so maybe I'll be okay now. She's always stopped people from hurting me in the past.

"Is there any change?" I hear Paul's voice.

"No, not yet. Have they got him?" asks Claire.

"No. They've been to his flat but he's not there."

I try to focus and sift their words through the reality filter I've been building inside my head, but it doesn't always work. I wish I could wipe some of the sad and bad memories that start to surface, but it's like I've been switched on and I can suddenly remember all of it. Even the parts I wish I couldn't.

I remember Edward in my room.

I remember what he did to me.

I don't understand how they know.

Then I remember that Paul said he had set up a camera in my room. He must have watched what happened. The idea of it makes me feel sick.

It still feels like I'm underwater, but the murky liquid is becoming clearer and I'm getting closer to the surface all the time. And then there's more.

I can remember the night of the accident. I can remember it all.

I know what happened now. It wasn't me driving on Christmas Day and it wasn't an accident at all. I've been away. I don't know how long for, but I'm back now and I remember everything.

# Then

You okay?" I ask as Paul flops down on the sofa, picking up the TV remote.

"What? Yes, fine."

"Drink?"

"Whisky, please."

I pause for a moment. Paul hasn't drunk whisky for a long time now. At one time it was all he drank, but the amber liquid changed him and his dependence on it changed us. It became a part of him. An ugly part. He thought it helped him to write and would stay up in the shed all night, just him, his laptop, and a bottle. A nightly literary threesome and a disappointing cliché. We became independent states with liquid borders and I was angry, lonely, scared. He did write, but they were the wrong kind of words; they didn't belong together. When we couldn't have a baby, things got worse. It was his drug of choice to heal the hurt and he poured it inside himself in its purest form. Neat. But the result was never tidy. It was like having a front-row seat for a slow suicide. When I couldn't watch anymore, I threatened to leave. He said he'd stop, but he didn't. He just poisoned himself in private. I left for ten days. He stopped then. That was over a year ago and I'm never going back to that.

"I don't think we have any, darling. . . ."

"Mum got me some, it's in the cupboard," he replies without looking up. He keeps changing the TV channel, unable to find what he's looking for.

I walk out to the kitchen and open the fridge. I ignore his request and take out the bottle of Champagne I've chilled deliberately. I'm going to tell him about the baby. His mood will change once he knows, and this will become a Christmas that we'll never forget. I've already had more than I should, but one tiny glass won't make any difference.

"Makes you glad we don't have kids, doesn't it?" says Paul from the lounge.

"What?"

"The chaos of it all. The whole day taken up with them, can't have a single conversation without an interruption of some kind or another."

"It wasn't that bad, was it?" I say, coming back into the front room.

A tear escapes my left eye, I can't stop it.

"No, the kids are fine. It's just Claire putting me in a bad mood. I'm sick of her dictating how we should live our lives. She's always interfering and you never call her on it. . . . What's this for?" he asks, pointing at the Champagne.

"I thought we could celebrate."

"We already celebrated my book deal. Are you crying?"

"I'm fine."

"If it's about Claire saying she doesn't want you to come to America with me, then I don't care what she says. She can cope without you for a few weeks, I'm sure."

"You told Claire about the book? When?"

"It just slipped out when you were upstairs reading the twins a bedtime story."

I understand now why she looked at me that way before we left. It was a warning. Paul carries on, oblivious to what he's done.

"Why shouldn't we tell people, anyway? And you're right, we should be celebrating." He takes the bottle from the table and opens it.

"What exactly did you tell her?" I ask, hearing my voice shake.

"Please can we stop talking about your sister, her dull husband, and the terrible twins?"

"What did you tell her, Paul? It's important."

"Why are you getting all bat shit? She was acting nuts too."

"Because she's upset about the idea of me going away, I knew she would be. I told you not to tell her yet."

"It wasn't that, it was her stupid diaries. She asked me why I bought you one and I told her because I'd found hers in the loft and then she went from nought to psycho in less than a few seconds."

It's all getting very loud inside my head.

"I told you not to tell Claire about the diaries and I told you not to read them."

"I didn't read them, not really. Just one line about you two being peas in a pod. I quoted it back at her, thought it was funny. She didn't seem to think so."

*Two peas in a pod.*

"She'll kill you."

He laughs. He doesn't understand that I'm not joking. She won't let anyone take me away from her, she never has. She's done terrible things to people over the years—friends, colleagues, lovers, none of them good enough for me, in her estimation. She thought I needed saving from every single one. I thought once the twins were born, once she had a family of her own, things might change, but they didn't, she held on more tightly than ever before. I think she was even a little bit pleased when I couldn't get pregnant, worried that my love for a child would somehow diminish my love for her. It was different with Paul, the celebrity author. She decided he was good for me and she was delighted when he was happy to live less than a mile away. It was like a test—he passed because he didn't try to take me away from her. But now he's failed.

I feel sick. I know what she's capable of. I walk out of the room, find my phone, and dial Claire's number.

Nothing.

I try again but it still goes straight to voicemail.

"He hasn't read them. Don't do it, you don't have to," I say as quietly as I can.

"Have you all lost your minds?" says Paul, appearing in the hallway behind me. "We're talking about a kid's diaries. Maybe I should have read them," he says.

"If she calls you or turns up here, tell her I already burned them. Don't open the door and don't let her in. Where are your car keys?"

"What are you talking about?"

I run over to the sideboard, opening up the drawers crammed full of odds and ends.

"Whatever happens, you are not to trust her, do you understand?" I find the spare set of keys, grab my handbag, without even checking what's inside, and run to the front door.

"Amber, wait . . ." He's too late, I'm already down the path, trying to make out the buttons on the car key through the dark and rain. I'm not wearing a coat and I'm already soaking wet. Paul follows me outside, still in his new Christmas slippers. He holds his phone up to his ear.

"It's me, your sister is really upset. I think it's got something to do with you, can you call me so we can try to sort this—" I spin around and knock the phone out of his hand. It smashes on the driveway. He stares at it, his mouth open, then looks up at me.

"What the fuck?"

"Stay away from Claire!"

"Can you hear yourself? You're acting fucking crazy! You can't drive. You must be over the limit—"

"I'm fine!"

A light comes on next door and I see our neighbor has come outside. I hadn't realized we were shouting. I turn to get in the car, and drop the key. My hands are shaking as I bend down to find it, feeling around in the dark. When my fingers find their prize, Paul tries to stop me from getting in the driver's seat. I push him back, get inside, and slam the door, trapping his hand in the metal. He screams in agony, yanks it back, and I slam the door again. I put the key in the ignition and drive away.

# Now

I'm going to go home for a bit, check that David hasn't killed the twins or vice versa," says Claire.

"Sure," Paul replies.

"Shit, I'm so sorry, I didn't mean to even mention the twins, let alone . . ."

"It's fine."

"You sure I can't give you a lift?"

"No. I'm not leaving her again. Not this time."

I hear the door open.

"Claire?"

"Yes?"

"This isn't your fault."

He's being kind to her, but he's wrong. This is Claire's fault. Everything that is wrong with my life is Claire's fault. I hear her leave and I'm glad.

Paul's hand holds mine. It feels strong and warm and safe.

"I'm so sorry," he whispers. "I just keep letting you down. I should have been here."

I imagine Paul watching what Edward did to me in this room. I picture him sitting at home, so far away, and seeing a stranger slip his hand beneath my sheet. I've been imprisoned inside a nightmare but Paul has been trapped outside, forced to watch me live it. He has been wanting to get in just as much as I wanted to get out.

"I love you so much," he says, and kisses me on the forehead.

He's been through his own personal hell while I've been sleeping in mine. I wish that I could tell him how sorry I am for putting him through all of this and that I love him too. I say the words over and over in my head until they sound fat and real.

"I love you."

"Oh my God," says Paul, and lets go of my hand. I instinctively want to see what the matter is so I try to open my eyes. The bright light overwhelms me at first and the pain of it shoots through to the back of my skull.

"Paul." I hear a voice and realize it is my own.

"I'm right here," he says, and I can see him. He's crying and now I'm crying. He's kissing me and I can see him. This is real. My eyes really are open. I'm awake.

# Then

I pull into Claire's driveway and can see her standing on the porch. She's been expecting me. I get out and march through the rain toward her, without even closing the car door. My dress is soaking wet and clings to my legs. It's as though the material is trying to hold me back, trying to stop me from going in there.

"Hello, Amber," she says. Arms folded. Features relaxed. Body perfectly still.

"We need to talk."

"I think you need to calm down."

"He hasn't seen anything, he doesn't know anything."

"I don't know what you're talking about."

"If you hurt him, if anything happens to him . . ."

She steps forward. "What? What will you do?"

I want to hit her. I want to hurt her so badly but I can't. I still love her more than I hate her. We can't have this conversation out here. You never know who might be listening.

"Can I come in, please?"

She stares at me for a while, as though assessing the risk. Her arms unfold themselves before her eyes decide. She nods and steps inside the hall, leaving just enough room for me to follow.

"You're wet, take your shoes off."

I quietly close the door behind us and do as I'm told. I stand barefoot on her new cream carpet and worry about what happens next. We're somewhere we've never been before. I wonder where David is, whether he can hear us.

"David is upstairs. He passed out not long after you and your husband left," she says, reading my mind. My husband, not "Paul" anymore. She's already disassociating herself from the person she has identified as a problem. Her eyes are dark, cold. I can see that she's already gone to that place inside herself that scares me so much.

"I want them back," she says. I don't need to ask what.

"I've burned them."

"I don't believe you."

"He didn't read them."

"Why do you even have them?"

"They were here. In the attic. I found them after Mum and Dad died. They'd kept everything of yours. There was nothing of mine."

"So you stole them?"

"No. I just wanted something. They left you everything. It was as though I didn't even exist anymore."

"You shouldn't have taken them and you shouldn't have let Paul read them. Or did you want something to happen to him?"

"No! He didn't read them. Stay away from him!"

"You need to calm down."

"You need to back the fuck off." I push her. I didn't mean to. She stumbles backwards, that flash of something I remember in her eyes. She steps forward again, her face in mine. I feel her breath.

"He read them and now the situation needs to be dealt with," she says calmly.

"He doesn't know."

"He read them."

"No, he didn't." I plead with her, already knowing her ears are closed to the sound of truth.

"*Two. Peas. In. A. Pod.* That's what he said to me. He read them." She spits the words at me and with each one, the pain in my stomach increases, so much so that I think she must have stabbed me. That's when I see the blood. I look at both of her hands, but they're empty, there's no knife. She's looking down too now at the single line of red running down the inside of my right leg. My hands reach down to my belly and the pain bends me in half.

"Oh God," I manage to whisper. And then my knees are folding and I'm sinking lower and lower into the pain.

"What's happening?" Claire asks.

"Oh God, no."

"Are you pregnant?" She looks down at me, a mix of awe and disgust on her face. She doesn't wait for my answer. "How could you not tell me something like that? We used to tell each other everything." I can see her mind working, overwhelmed with this new piece of information. Plotting a new course.

"I'm sorry," I manage to say, because she thinks I should be. Her face doesn't change.

"It's just a tiny bleed. You'll be okay. Give me the car keys."

I shake my head. "Call Paul."

"Just give me the keys. The hospital is fifteen minutes from here, it's quicker than calling for an ambulance. We'll call him on the way."

I do what she says, like I always have.

# Now

Tuesday, January 3, 2017

Are you hungry?" asks Paul. I've been sleeping, the kind of sleep you can wake up from. I sit up in the hospital bed and let him adjust the pillows behind me. The door is open and I can see a trolley just outside.

"She needs to take it slow, just a little at a time," Northern Nurse says to Paul, giving him a tray of food. I recognize her voice. She doesn't look the same in real life as she did in my head. She's younger, slimmer, less tired looking. I never pictured her smiling, but she does, all the time. Some people appear happy on the outside and you only know they're broken inside if you listen as well as look.

Paul takes the tray and puts it down in front of me. There's chicken, with mash and green beans. A carton of juice and what looks like strawberry jelly. I'm so hungry but now that I can see what's on offer, I'm less eager to eat it. Paul picks up the cutlery and loads some mashed potato onto a fork.

"I can do it," I say.

"Sorry."

I take the fork from him.

"Thank you."

I eat most of it. I chew and swallow small pieces at a time. My throat still hurts from the tube. It didn't look like much, but right now it feels like I might have eaten the best meal of my life. The chicken was over-cooked and the potatoes were lumpy, but just to be able to chew and swallow and taste again made every mouthful exquisite. Because it means that I'm alive.

"Can you remember any more?" Paul asks. I shake my head and look away.

"Not really."

He looks relieved. He talks about the future as though we have one and it makes me feel real again. I can't imagine how it must have felt, seeing what Paul saw, watching a man do that to me. But it doesn't seem to have changed things for him, not yet at least. My thoughts start to flatten out, his words ironing out the creases until the folds in my thinking are smooth. He persists over any remaining lines until the imperfect is made neat and tidy, as though brand-new, unused and unspoiled.

Paul's phone buzzes on the bedside table. He reaches over, reads it, then stares at me.

"What?" I ask.

"You've got a visitor."

I feel myself start to fade.

"Who?"

"Claire." He waits awhile for me to say something, but I don't. "Is that okay? You don't have to see her if you don't want to. You don't have to see anyone. But whatever happened between the two of you, I know she's very sorry."

"It's fine."

"Okay. She's in the parking lot, so she'll be a few minutes. I'll tell her to come up." I look away while he texts my sister. Paul doesn't know that I remember what happened that night. I haven't decided what to do yet, how much of it I should pretend not to know.

"Can I get you anything else?" Paul asks.

"I'd love a glass of wine," I reply. He laughs; it's a great sound.

"I'm sure you would, but I think it might still be a tiny bit too soon for grape juice. One day at a time."

He takes the tray and leaves it on the floor just outside, as though this is a hotel room and we've been ordering room service. I'd like to go somewhere when this is over. Run away from real life for just a little while. Any place where you can feel the sun by day and see the stars at night. The door is open but she knocks on it anyway.

"Hi," she says, waiting to be invited before coming any closer.

"Come in," says Paul.

"How are you?" she asks, looking between the two of us, but meaning me.

"I'm okay," I say. Paul gets up from his chair.

"Right, well. I might just pop out for a bit, leave you two to catch up?" I nod to let him know I'm all right. Claire and I stare at each other, a silent conversation already taking place behind our eyes. She sits in the chair Paul has vacated and waits until she's sure he's far away enough from the room not to hear.

"I'm sorry," she says, eventually.

"What for?"

"All of it."

# Before

*Sunday, February 14, 1993*

Dear Diary,

Today is Valentine's Day. I didn't get any cards but I don't care about that. I have a family now, a proper one, and that's all I ever wanted. I've even got a new name. Claire Taylor. I think it sounds nice. I call Taylor's mum "Mum" and I call Taylor's dad "Dad" and I think they like it. I like it. Everyone likes it apart from Taylor. She sulked all morning today in her bedroom, playing with the doll I gave her like a little girl. She calls the doll Emily and sits and talks to her when she thinks nobody can hear.

After lunch I asked to go to my room and Mum said yes. I said I wanted to read my new book and she believed me. Because it is a Sunday, we had a roast dinner. We always have a roast on Sundays. Today we had chicken, a whole one, with roast potatoes and puddings from Yorkshire and lots of gravy. I ate all of mine, Taylor left most of hers. I would have eaten that too but I was already so full up I thought I might burst. I could hear Mum asking Taylor what was wrong as I climbed up the staircase. They're always asking her what is wrong and it makes me so cross. Nothing is wrong. She should be just as happy as I am and stop spoiling things.

I passed Taylor's bedroom on the way to my own and spotted Emily sitting on the bed, her glass eyes looking right at me. I remembered choosing her on one of the visits with the social worker. She was mine really and I could take her back if I wanted to. I had never seen a doll like her before, so real looking. She had shiny black hair, pink cheeks, and a pretty blue dress with matching shoes. She looked precious. Perfect. I didn't like her. I don't remember picking her up or taking her to my room. I only remember looking down and seeing the compass from my pencil case in my hand and Emily on my lap, with her eyes all scratched out.

I wasn't sure what to do after that, so I took Emily by the hand and went out into the front garden. I'm too old to play with dolls so I put Emily down. In the road. Her little feet tucked into the curb. I still felt very full from lunch so I sat down on the front lawn and pulled out little tufts of grass with my fingers. The sun was shining and the sky was blue but it was cold. I didn't mind though. I wanted to be outside, I wanted to see.

I got that feeling you get when you know that someone is watching you and turned back to look at the house. Taylor was there in the upstairs window of her bedroom looking down at us both. Her eyes moved from me to the doll and back again. She turned away and I wondered if she would cry. She is always crying lately.

The first car didn't touch Emily at all and I felt cross about it—cars don't drive down our road all that often. Taylor was there in the garden in time to see the second car though, so that was good. It didn't miss. Its front left tire went over the doll's face, her hair getting caught up in the wheel. I watched as she went round and under, round and under. The back left tire went over her then too, but it left her where it found her, lying flat on the tarmac. Taylor stood next to me, still staring at the doll in the distance. Her face didn't change, her body didn't move, she just stood there. I carried on pulling out blades of grass, rolling them up between my fingers. I started humming a tune without even meaning to.

*The wheels on the bus go round and round, all day long.*

"Did you tell anyone?" I asked.

She didn't ask what about, just shook her head and looked down. "Good," I told her. "Bad things happen when you tell tales on people." She looked at me then, and her face was sort of blank, not happy but not sad either. I tapped the patch of grass next to where I was sitting and eventually she came and sat down next to me. She wasn't wearing a coat and I knew she must be cold so I reached out to hold her hand and she let me. I squeezed it three times and she squeezed it three times back. I knew then that we were going to be all right, that nothing had changed, not really. She'd got herself a bit lost, but I'd found her again. We might be sisters now, but we'll always be peas in a pod.

# Then

*Christmas Day 2016—*
*Night*

Claire puts her head under my arm, taking most of my weight, then leads me back out to the car. I let her—I'm not sure I can stand on my own anyway. I'm still barefoot as we stumble down the driveway, wet gravel slicing at my toes. She lowers me into the passenger seat and I notice she's wearing red leather gloves I've never seen before. I'm sitting sideways and I can hear someone crying inside the car. It takes a few seconds to realize that it's me. She gets in behind the wheel, fastens her seat belt, and closes the door.

"Where are the diaries, Amber?"

"I told you, I burned them."

"You're lying."

"For God's sake, just get me to the hospital."

She's never driven Paul's MG before but reverses out of the driveway as though it's her own car. One red glove on the steering wheel, the other resting on the gearstick at all times, like a racing driver; someone in control. I close my eyes and place my own hands over my belly, as though I'm trying to hold her inside of me. I'm sure it's a girl.

Claire and I don't speak as she steers us out of her road. The only voices I can hear are on the radio, but even they're not real, it's all prerecorded. Occasionally I open my eyes to look out of the windows, to make sure she's going the right way, but all I can see is black. I have to press one hand against the dashboard to hold myself steady as we turn a corner.

"I thought you couldn't get pregnant," she says, changing into second gear. I think we're on the main road now. It won't be long.

"Neither did I."

*Third gear.*

"Does Paul know?"

"No."

*Fourth gear.*

"Why didn't you tell me?"

"You always said we didn't need anyone else."

*Fifth.*

I open my eyes and realize that the cramping has stopped. I don't know what that means.

"The pain has gone," I say, and try to sit up a little. "I think I might be okay." A trickle of relief floods through me. I look over at Claire but her face hasn't changed, as though she didn't hear me. "You bled once when you were pregnant with the twins, didn't you?" I ask.

"You should still get yourself checked out at the hospital. Better safe than sorry."

"You're right. But you can slow down a bit now." She doesn't respond, just stares straight ahead. "Claire, I said you should slow down, I think I'm okay." My hands move instinctively back to my stomach.

"You should have told me," she says, so quietly I'm not sure I would have heard the words at all if I hadn't seen her lips move. Her face has twisted into something ugly. "We used to tell each other everything. If you just did what I told you and stopped telling lies none of this would be happening. You've only yourself to blame if it's dead."

"It's not dead," I say. Tears burst the banks of my eyelids and roll down my cheeks. I'm sure of it too, I swear I can feel my unborn child's heartbeat as well as my own. Claire nods. She believes me that the baby is still alive. I close my eyes and grip the side of my chair a little harder. I just need to hold on. It can't be much farther. We're going so fast now, we must nearly be there.

"Amber."

Claire puts her gloved hand on mine. It's cold and I open my eyes to see her staring at me instead of at the road. She smiles and the instant terror numbs me.

"I love you," she says before turning back to the road with both hands on the steering wheel.

I hear the brakes screech, and then everything slows down. My body lifts from the chair and I'm flying. I crash through the windshield hands first, as though diving through a pool of glass. A thousand tiny pieces rip through every part of my body. It doesn't hurt; all the pain is gone. I fly high into the night sky. I can see the stars, so close I can almost touch them, but then my head smashes into the tarmac followed by a shoulder, then my chest, tearing pieces of my skin as I skid to an abrupt halt. Everything is still. I'm not flying anymore.

The pain returns, except now it's everywhere and so much worse than before. I'm broken inside and out and I'm afraid. I don't cry, I can't, but I feel the blood run down my face like red tears. I hear a car door slam and the faint sound of the radio—a Christmas song is still playing. The agony increases until it turns everything black. And then I can't feel the pain anymore, I can't feel anything, I can only sleep.

# Now

You left me there."

"I'd been drinking, I shouldn't have been behind the wheel. I was scared."

"*You* were scared? Did you even call for help?"

She looks away. "I thought you were dead."

"You *hoped* I was dead."

"That's not true, don't ever say that, I love you."

"You need me, you don't love me. The two things are different."

"Do you know what would have happened if they found out I was driving? I have two young children who need me."

"I was pregnant. And now I'm not."

"I know. I'm so sorry. I would never deliberately do anything to hurt you, you know that."

"Have you told Paul?"

"Told him what?"

"That you were driving?"

"No. Have you?"

"Do you think he would have let you in here if I had?"

The anger hisses out of her then.

"It was an accident, Amber. I was trying to help you. I was trying to get you to the hospital, don't you remember?"

"I remember you fastening your own seat belt, driving really fast, then slamming the brakes. I remember me flying through the air."

"I had to stop."

"No, you didn't."

"We were driving along, you were crying in pain, and then you said something about a little girl in a pink dressing gown. I thought there was a child in the street. You screamed at me to stop."

She empties her words into my ears and eventually they find me. I don't know what's real anymore. I don't know which version of events to believe. My sister's or my own. The room attempts to nurse my wounds in the suspended quiet, but Claire tears out the stitches.

"There was no child when I got out of the car, I never saw her. Either you imagined her or she ran away," she says.

*Both.*

I turn away, I can't look at her anymore. It took a lot of love to hate her the way I do.

"I shouldn't have left you there. But you should have told me about the baby. And you should have told me about him. This is what happens when we lie to each other."

"I didn't lie."

"You didn't tell me the truth either. I've looked him up, Edward Clarke. He was thrown out of medical school not long after you broke up with him."

"Because of the letters you wrote."

"Maybe. Either way I was right—I knew there was something wrong with him. He took odd jobs at different hospitals until he got this one. I think he chose this hospital to be close to you. Do you understand? I think he's been following you for years and I don't think this is over. Tell me where he lives."

"I don't remember."

"Yes, you do. Tell me. I won't let him hurt you again. I won't let anyone hurt you again."

"I'd like to sleep now," I say, and close my eyes.

"I brought this for you," she says, and I hear her put something down on the bedside table. I open my eyes long enough to look at it, but I don't look at her. "I thought it might remind you who we were, who we could be again," she says. I don't answer. The gold bracelet looks so much smaller than I remember. I'm amazed it ever fitted around my wrist. It's the one she stole from me when we were children. My date of birth carved into the gold. Her date of birth too. Terrible twins. It still has the safety pin I used to mend it when she broke it. So fragile. I'm amazed she still has it. I want to touch it, but I don't. I close my eyes and turn my back on her. I long for the silence to return and swallow me down into the darkness, I don't want to hear any more. I get my wish. The door closes and I am left alone. The bracelet is gone and so is my sister.

# After

I stand at the end of our bed, watching his face as he sleeps. Paul's eyes move beneath his closed eyelids and his mouth has fallen slightly open. He's aged over the last couple of months; the lines have carved themselves deeper, the circles beneath his eyes a shade darker than before. I'm watching over a fully grown man and yet all I can see is a picture of vulnerability. I stand in the glorious silence that only the night can deliver and carefully consider whether I have made the right choice. I decide that I have. I won't let my past dictate our future.

I've been home for just over a month now. After so long in the quiet darkness, it felt like sensory overload when I first left the hospital. The world seemed so fast, so loud, and so real. Perhaps it was always that way and I just never really noticed before. It took a while to adjust, to process it all. I've been to the site of the accident—a trauma counselor at the hospital thought it would be a good idea. There was a bunch of dead flowers by the tree. Someone kind must have thought that I died that night. I think a version of me did.

I am trying to move on. I have forgiven Claire now too; so much so that we offered to look after the twins while David and Claire had a romantic Valentine's celebration yesterday. I thought they deserved some quality time alone together. I even prepared a special meal for them.

It was nice having the twins here. They had an afternoon nap in our spare bedroom. It was the first time they slept here and I kept checking on them to make sure they were okay. I stood in the doorway and stared at their pink cheeks, wild tufts of hair, both dreaming away like two peas in a pod. I'd stuck some luminous stars on the ceiling, which they seemed to love. I kept turning the light on and off to show them that stars can't shine without darkness. They cried less than normal today—Paul was so good at knowing how to keep them happy. Speaking to them in the right tone, always making everything better. The house is silent again now. I check the time: 03:02.

Even a few weeks later, there are still some side effects from the coma. I experience horribly disturbing nightmares and I have trouble sleeping since I woke up. I creep downstairs and Digby comes to meet me. We have a puppy now, a black Labrador. It was Paul's idea. I walk through to the kitchen, glancing at the clock before beginning my routine:

03:07

I start with the back door and repeatedly turn the handle until I'm sure it is locked.

Up, down. Up, down. Up, down.

Next, I stand in front of the large range oven with my arms bent at the elbows. My fingers form the familiar shape: the index and middle finger finding the thumb on each hand. I whisper quietly to myself, while visually checking that everything is switched off, my fingernails clicking together. I do it again. I do it a third time.

Digby is watching me from the kitchen doorway, his head tilted to one side. I go to leave, lingering briefly, wondering if I should check everything one last time before I do. I look at the clock: 03:15. There isn't time. I put on my coat, grab my bag, and check the contents. Phone. Wallet. Keys. As well as a few other bits and pieces. I check twice more before attaching Digby's lead to his collar, then make myself leave the house, checking the front door is locked three times before marching down the moonlit garden path.

I find walking helps, and the puppy appreciates it whether it's night or day. Just a couple of blocks and some fresh air and I can normally get back to sleep. Nothing else seems to work. I walk along the main road. Not a single light shines from any of the houses, as though everyone else has gone and I'm the only person left in the world.

I carry on through the sleeping streets under a black blanket of night sky covered in stars, like sequins. They're the same stars I looked up at over twenty years ago, but I am forever changed. There's no moon, so I am completely cloaked in darkness as I turn into Claire's road. I stare up at the house, taking it in as though looking at it properly for the first time. It should have been mine; I was born here. I tie Digby's lead to a lamppost, take out my key, and head inside.

I check on Claire and David first. They look so peaceful, lying completely still, facing away from each other.

*The wheels on the bus go round and round.*

I think that's supposed to mean something, them lying like that. Something about their relationship, but I can't remember and it doesn't matter now anyway.

*Round and round.*

I check David's pulse. There isn't one; he's already cold. I move around to the other side of the bed to check on Claire. Her pulse is weak but she has one. I guess he ate more of the meal I made them. The bag of drugs from the hospital seems to have worked. I had my doubts, but then if a hospital porter can figure this stuff out, with the help of the Internet it really shouldn't be beyond someone like me.

*Round and round.*

I walk to the children's bedroom before coming back to Claire.

*The wheels on the bus go round and round.*

The sound of the twins crying shatters the silence. I lean down closer to the bed, hoping she can hear them.

*All day long.*

I whisper in her ear, "Two peas in a pod."

Her eyes open and I jump back from the bed. She looks toward the sound of her children screaming down the hall. I relax when I realize she can't move anything other than her eyes. They're wide and wild as she stares in my direction with a look I've never seen in them before. Fear. I hold the petrol can up so that it's within Claire's field of vision. She looks at it, then back to me. I study my sister's face one last time, then take her hand in mine, squeezing it three times before letting her go.

"I never was fond of gas," I say, before leaving the room.

# After

*Wednesday, February 15, 2017—*
*04:00*

I take a different route home, a slight detour, with Digby in tow. It's cold and I walk a little faster when I hear the fire engines. I think about Edward, perhaps because of the sound of sirens; the police never did catch him. I remember the afternoon when Detective Handley came to the house to tell me what they had found. He sat down on our sofa with such gentle consideration, as though not wishing to disturb the air in the room or dent the cushions. He refused my offer of tea with a polite shake of his head, then paused for a long time, visibly searching for the right words and deliberating the order in which they should be spoken. His skin turned a whiter shade of pale as he began to describe the traces of blood and burned skin that had been found inside the sunbed at Edward's flat. Claire didn't have an alibi for the night the neighbors said they heard a man screaming. Neither did I, but it didn't matter; nobody ever asked where either of us were. A possible accident, the detective thought, and suggested that something might have short-circuited. I remember nodding as he spoke. Something or someone most likely did. There was no body. No neat conclusion. Sometimes things have to get messy in order to be cleaned up.

My thoughts shift to Madeline as I turn a corner onto the main road. I think of her often since I woke up. I pass the petrol station where I bought the petrol over two months ago. The CCTV of that day will have been deleted now, but their records will show that it was paid for with a credit card belonging to Madeline Frost. She was always giving me her credit card to buy her lunches or pay for her dry cleaning, but I used it for a lot of other things too, including an extra set of her house keys when she asked me to get a spare cut for her new cleaner.

Taking a job that was clearly beneath me was useful for things like that, but the best part about it was knowing Madeline's schedule, because as her PA, I created it. I knew where she was every minute of the day, weeks in advance, and I knew when she didn't have an alibi.

The final blackmail note I delivered before the Christmas party had Claire's name on it, so there could be no misunderstandings about who was responsible. Madeline was toast after her epic fail on the lunchtime news, which went far better than planned and exceeded my expectations. The face of Crisis Child said so many awful things live on television that the small matter of her abandoning her orphaned goddaughter and stealing her inheritance seemed trivial in comparison. But I hadn't finished with Madeline yet. I'd always thought of blackmail as something ugly, but this was something else; this was beautiful. This was justice. People think that good and bad are opposites but they're wrong, they're just a mirror image of each other in broken glass.

I've rehearsed my lines for the police. I've written a letter from Madeline to Claire where she threatens to deal with her in the same way she dealt with her parents. I'm well practiced at writing letters from Madeline as her PA, so I'm confident the handwriting will be a perfect match. Claire never read it, of course, but when the time comes, I'll explain how she gave it to me for safekeeping, just in case the unthinkable ever happened. Everyone thought Madeline would lose the plot if she stopped working—that job was all she had. They'll all think they were right when the police find the empty petrol cans securely locked inside her shed. They'll find the pen used to write the letter to Claire on the oak desk in her front room. They'll find everything they need to.

I arrive back home, let myself in quietly, and take off my coat. 04:36. I'm slightly earlier than I expected, but I can't go back to sleep, not now. I feel dirty, contaminated, so I head upstairs to take a shower. I lock the bathroom door and turn to face myself in the mirror. I don't like what I see, so I close my eyes. I unzip the body of who I used to be and step outside of myself; a newborn Russian doll, a little smaller than I was before, wondering how many other versions of me are still hidden inside. I turn on the shower and step beneath it too quickly. The water is freezing cold but I don't flinch. I let the temperature rise slowly so that I almost don't feel the water burn my skin when it gets too hot. I don't know how long I stand like that, I don't remember. I don't remember drying myself or wrapping my robe around my body. I don't remember leaving the bathroom or coming back downstairs. I only remember being back in the lounge, looking in the big mirror above the fireplace and liking the look of the woman who stared back at me. I pick up Digby and sit with him on my lap, stroking his soft black fur in the dark. All that's left to do now is wait.

One of the twins starts crying. I pop Digby down on the carpet and rush up the stairs to comfort them. Earlier when I was trying to record the sound of them screaming they were all smiles, but we got there in the end. It's light in their room now. I pull the curtains back and look out at the new dawn spreading itself over the streets and houses below. Paul is still sleeping, so I take the twins downstairs and make them some breakfast. I sit them in their high chairs and worry about them being too cold in our old house. I have another idea and decide it's a good one; don't know why I didn't think of it before, really.

The flames dance in the fireplace, throwing their light and warmth around the room. The twins look on, transfixed, as though they've never seen a fire before and I realize that maybe they haven't. I pick up the diaries one at a time, looking through a few pages before I throw each one onto the flames. I pause briefly over the final one, run my index finger over the 1992 written on the front, then turn to the last few pages at the back. I can't read the words at first, they stick in my throat, but I make myself do it. Just one last time I let my eyes translate Claire's words from that night, the night that changed everything.

*Taylor told me to do it.*

I tear out the page and screw the paper into a ball before throwing it in the fire. After I have watched it burn to nothing, I throw on the last of Claire's diaries. The twins and I sit and watch until everything their mother wrote is nothing but smoke and ash.

# Later

*Spring 2017*

I've always delighted in the free fall between sleep and wakefulness. Those precious few semiconscious seconds before you open your eyes, when you catch yourself believing that your dreams might just be your reality. For now, for just a second longer, I'm enjoying the self-medicated delusion that permits me to imagine that I could be anyone, I could be anywhere, I could be loved.

I sense a shadow cast itself over my eyelids and they immediately flick open. The light is so bright that at first I don't remember where I am. For a moment I think I'm back in the hospital room, but then I hear the sound of the sea, calm waves gently lapping at the edge of the white sand in the distance. I hold my hand up to shelter my eyes from the sun. I find myself staring at the branches of lines etched into my palm and the fingerprints my skin has remembered for all these years. It knows who I am, my skin, no matter how uncomfortable it has been to wear.

I sit up when I hear the children, their infectious laughter dancing inside my ears until a smile spreads itself across my face. It doesn't matter that I didn't give birth to them, they are mine now and I know that water can be thicker than blood if you let it. I scold myself for falling asleep when I should have been watching them, but I relax a little once I've looked around the beach. Apart from a couple of palm trees, we have the place to ourselves. There is nobody else here. Nobody to be afraid of. I try to relax. I lean back in the chair and knit my hands together, resting them in my lap. When I look down, it's my mother's hands that I see. I look back over at my niece and nephew and decide that I will always love these children the same, no matter what they do, no matter how they change, no matter who or what they grow into.

The hot sun warms my skin and lights our new life. Our own little corner of paradise for a couple of weeks, a stopover before Paul needs to be in America. I turn back toward the hotel, wondering where he is. We booked a room on the ground floor, right on the beach, so that we could just step out into the sun during the day and sit beneath the stars at night. It's enormous, more of a suite than a room really, and we hardly ever see anyone. There aren't many other guests due to it being rainy season, not that it's rained once since we arrived.

The shutters are all open and I can see the shape of Paul inside, sitting on the bed. He's on the phone. Again. He hasn't adjusted to our new life as quickly as I hoped he might, but he adores the children, loves them as though they are his own. I have finally given him the family he wanted and nobody can take that away from us now. I glance over at the children once more. They're fine. I peel myself up and off the sun lounger to check on Paul. I keep reminding myself that he needs watching over too.

Paul hangs up the phone on the bedside table as soon as I step inside the room. He doesn't look up, and I feel like I have interrupted something.

"Who was that?" I ask.

"No one," he says, still avoiding eye contact. The bed is buried by a patchwork of white A4 paper, covered in black type and red ink. The never-ending edit has taken over again.

"Well, it must have been someone." I struggle to hide the irritation in my voice. This is supposed to be a holiday. A chance to spend time together as a family, not hide away in here staring at words and speaking to his agent. I look back out at the children, they're fine, so I turn back to Paul. He's looking at me now, the corners of his mouth turned upward.

"It was supposed to be a surprise," he says, standing up and coming over to kiss me. "Your shoulders are red, do you need some more cream on?"

"What was?"

"I've ordered a little something from room service." I still don't believe him.

"What? Why? It's only a couple of hours until dinner."

"That's true, but we normally have Champagne on our anniversary."

"It's not our anniversary. . . ."

"I didn't say wedding." He smiles. I know the anniversary he means and I smile too.

"I thought you were speaking to your agent again."

"Not guilty this time," he says, holding up his hands. "But you have just reminded me of something. I might Skype her, just for a quick chat before the drinks come, then I'm all yours." I roll my eyes. "Just five minutes, surely you can forgive me that?"

"Fine, five minutes," I say, and kiss him on the cheek.

I want to freshen up but I look out and check on the twins first. They've become my latest routine, something I must check three times. They're exactly as I left them, building castles of sand, squashing them, and starting again. They are so content in each other's company. I wonder if that is unusual. I wonder if they will always be that way.

"Look at this," says Paul. He's already moved to the small desk in the corner of the room, his laptop open in front of him. I notice that the label is sticking up from the neck of his T-shirt. I walk over and reach to tuck it in, then change my mind. I'm not sure why. I peer at the screen over his shoulder instead. "The dog sitter sent it, looks like Digby is having a nice holiday too." I smile at the photo. The dog is panting but it looks like he's smiling at the camera.

"I know you miss him; we'll see him soon enough," I say. Paul loves that dog, hates leaving him behind. We all have to have something or someone to love, otherwise the love inside us has nowhere to go. "Will you keep one eye on them while I have a quick shower?" I say, looking back out at the twins.

"Of course."

On my way to the bathroom I notice that Paul has left the TV on again. It's on silent but a familiar image catches my eye and I stop, unable to look away. I see a news correspondent I used to know standing outside a courthouse, TV crews and more reporters jostling for space on the pavement around her. The picture changes to the image of a police van driving through a gate to get inside the building. Then I see the shots of Claire's house, the house we grew up in, blackened and burnt. I read the words scrolling at the bottom of the screen. A string of capital letters silently screaming at me.

MADELINE FROST'S MURDER TRIAL BEGINS.

Even with the mute button switched on, the TV is far too loud. I don't know why he insists on having it on in the background all the time. It's like an obsession. I switch it off and turn back to say something to Paul, but he's already started the Skype call. The sound of it dialing up that has become so familiar stops and he starts speaking at his laptop before I get a chance to say anything. I leave him to it and step into the bathroom. I catch sight of my reflection in the mirror. I look good. I look like the me I am supposed to be, living the life I was supposed to live. The life that was stolen from me.

I close the door and turn on the shower. I'll be quick. Just want to get the sand and cream off my body, wash my hair, and change into something else. I take off my bikini and step inside, letting the jets of cool water slap my face. I hear the knock on the hotel room door and curse their timing.

"Come in," says Paul. I can hear that he is still on the call to London, but I'm relieved he is dealing with it. Five minutes on my own has become a rare indulgence that I no longer take for granted. "That's great, thank you, just leave it over there," he says. His words are muffled by the shower, but he sounds distracted, borderline rude, and I hope he's remembered to give them a tip.

I dress myself quickly, rushing a brush through my tangled hair and slapping some after-sun on my face and shoulders. Paul is already sitting on the decking just outside the room, facing out to a turquoise sea. He's brought the children a little nearer to us so that they are sitting on a blanket in the shade and I love him for loving them the way I hoped he would.

"Here you are, thought you might have drowned," he says as I step outside to join them. "Drink, madam?" he asks, taking a bottle of Champagne from a silver bucket on a tray on the table.

"Lovely, yes please." I sit down next to him, feeling the heat from the wooden chair through my skirt. Katie turns as she hears me and smiles.

"Mummy," she says, then carries on playing. She's never called me that before and it makes me feel so happy. I was their godmother after all—is it so wrong to want to be more than that? Paul uses the nail on his thumb to cut into the gold foil around the neck of the bottle. He tears it off before his fingers twist the metal holding the cork in place, then he removes it expertly. No pop, no fuss, no mess. He fills our glasses and I realize I am happy. Things are so much better between us now. Back to how they used to be. This is all I ever wanted. I am in paradise with my family and this is what happiness feels like. I'm not sure I have ever truly known it before.

He puts the bottle back on the round tray and I spot something next to it that catches the light.

"What's that?" I say, looking down at the sliver of gold on silver.

"What's what?" he asks, following my gaze. I smile, thinking this is another surprise, a gift, a game.

It isn't.

For a moment the words won't form.

"Did you see who delivered this to our room?"

"I was still on Skype, they just came in and left it on the side. Why? What's wrong?"

I don't answer. I'm transfixed by the thin bracelet on the tray, small enough for a child's wrist. It's held together with an old, slightly rusty safety pin and my date of birth is engraved on the gold.

My name is Amber Taylor Reynolds. There are three things you should know about me:

1. *I was in a coma.*
2. *My sister died in a tragic accident.*
3. *Sometimes I lie.*

# Acknowledgments

There are many people I would like to thank for bringing this book to life.

Firstly, I would like to thank my amazing agent, Jonny Geller, for taking a chance on me. I would also like to thank Catherine Cho, Kate Cooper, and all the lovely people at Curtis Brown. Kari Stuart at ICM is a legend and I am forever thankful to her too.

I feel incredibly lucky that *Sometimes I Lie* found a home at Flatiron/Macmillan in the U.S. and HQ/HarperCollins in the UK. I have two wonderful editors whom I will always be indebted to—Amy Einhorn in the U.S., who is a whirlwind and a magician of words, and Sally Williamson in the UK, who believed in this book so passionately and has the most wonderful laugh.

Next, I'd like to say a word or two about the best teacher I ever had—Richard Skinner. He taught me too many things to list here, but above all, he taught me to believe in myself enough to keep going. I am forever in your debt.

Thank you to the staff at Milton Keynes University Hospital for allowing me into your world and answering my many, many questions. And thank you to Wayne Moulds for your advice and help with research.

Thank you to my parents for encouraging me to read and love books from a young age—you cannot be a writer if you are not a reader. Heartfelt thanks to the rest of my family and friends for your ongoing love and support. Special thanks to Charlotte Essex, my oldest writing friend, for pushing my bottom up a cliff in Bolivia many years ago and continuing to push me to do things I'm afraid of ever since. Thanks to Jasmine Williams for believing in me and to my dear friends Anna MacDonald and Alex Vanotti for making me laugh, keeping me calm, and always being there when I need you.

Lastly, I'd like to thank my husband, Daniel. A fellow writer who knows just how long this journey has been. There is nobody I would rather have made it with. My first reader, my best friend, my everything, I wouldn't be here without you. Thanks for putting up with me and for loving me back.

Recommend

*Sometimes I Lie*

**for your next book club!**


Reading Group Guide available at
www.readinggroupgold.com